Praise for *Come Out, Come Out, Whatever You Are*

"…mystery-loving readers will keep turning the pages to uncover the characters' secrets and learn the truth…"

—*Kirkus Reviews*

"…will appeal to readers seeking dark YA fiction with a handful of thrills and chills . . ."

—*School Library Journal*

"…the drama and reality show aspects truly made this an exceptional read!"

—*Read and Review It*

T0284062

Praise for *Good Girls Die First*

★ "Undeniably creepy from the start… With a macabre escape and a surprising amount of heart, this will leave readers feeling oddly optimistic and perhaps a little kinder to themselves…"
—*The Bulletin of the Center for Children's Books*, STARRED Review

"Foxfield's focus on social niches and escalating suspense will appeal to fans of Karen McManus."
—*Publishers Weekly*

"This gothic-inspired thriller with nods to Agatha Christie and Daphne du Maurier will keep readers on the edge of their seats and turning pages as quickly as they can. It is immersing, puzzling, and unpredictable, with a surprise ending that's sure to have teens talking."
—*School Library Journal*

"…The most gripping thriller of the year; hugely entertaining, high-octane, and read-in-a-single-sitting."
—*ReadingZone*

Also by Kathryn Foxfield

Come Out, Come Out, Whatever You Are
Good Girls Die First

TAG, YOU'RE DEAD

KATHRYN FOXFIELD

sourcebooks
fire

Published by Sourcebooks Fire, an imprint of Sourcebooks
P.O. Box 4410, Naperville, Illinois 60567–4410
(630) 961-3900
sourcebooks.com

Originally published as *Tag, You're Dead* in 2022 in the UK by Scholastic.

Cataloging-in-Publication Data is on file with the Library of Congress.

Printed and bound in the United States of America.
VP 10 9 8 7 6 5 4 3 2 1

For everyone who wishes they were braver.

GAME ON

Disgraced teenage millionaire Anton Frazer stages a comeback, but continues to be haunted by ghosts of his own making. Eleventh-grader Emma Sano reports for *St. Bernadette's School Press* on the controversial reboot of the *Shadow City* tech genius–turned–social media personality.

Anton Frazer, as well known for his public pranks as he is his hugely popular iOS/Android cross-platform game *Shadow City*, is back.

After nine months in hiding, following an accidental death at his home, he brought Central London to a standstill last night to announce his latest stunt—a livestreamed game of tag.

Teasers appeared online last week in the form of a countdown and GPS coordinates. Thousands of Anton fans descended upon Shaftesbury Avenue, where Frazer took over the Piccadilly Circus electronic billboards with an unauthorized broadcast.

According to his announcement, he plans to stage a citywide game of tag in one month's time. He revealed that one hundred competitors will be chosen to compete for a prize that includes £100,000 and the opportunity to join his team as he relaunches his online presence.

But police have already slammed Frazer's plans, decrying them as "dangerous, illegal, and utterly irresponsible."

Frazer has previously been criticized for the disruption caused by his stunts, which have included camping overnight in a furniture superstore and releasing seventeen male peacocks into the London Underground.

According to an insider, Frazer hopes that his game of tag will move the conversation on from the events of last year, when eighteen-year-old Rose Tavistock drowned during a party at Frazer's now-abandoned London mansion.

Tavistock was one of Frazer's cocreators. She is widely credited with helping him make the leap from game designer to one of the world's most popular social media personalities. Her death came at a time when Frazer and his team were under scrutiny following rumors of infighting and a toxic work environment.

Tavistock's death was ruled to be a drug-related accident. Frazer's admission of drug use at his home caused him to lose most of his lucrative sponsorship deals and led to him shutting down his social media accounts.

This latest stunt appears to mark the end of Frazer's

self-imposed exile. Judging by the online response to his announcement, his fans are ready to move on from the Tavistock era. Not everyone is ready to forgive and forget though.

"I don't understand why anyone still pays him any attention," one of Frazer's past employees told *St. Bernadette's School Press*. "Does no one care that a girl died on his watch?"

Anton Frazer responded to a request for comment with a photo of his tongue.

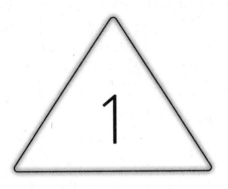

GRAYSON

By the end of tonight, Anton Frazer will be dead. But first, I have to convince the world that I'm his biggest fan.

"Do these sunglasses make me look *too* handsome?" I say. "I don't want to steal the limelight."

Lenny glances at me, a licorice bootlace hanging from her mouth and dark braids dangling over her face. She goes back to her magazine, ignoring the street vendor's glare. "You look like a dorky Harry Styles."

I replace the sunglasses on the rotating display and pick another pair. "You know how to make a boy feel special. What about these?"

I crane my head to see my reflection in the little mirror. The red frames stand out against my pale freckled skin. I swish my hair to one side. Chestnut waves skim the collar of a bedazzled leather jacket that belonged to my ex Rose. It sits heavy on my shoulders.

Rose would have told me to get the damn glasses. Hell, she would have strolled off without paying for them, and no one would have said a thing. Rose was stop-and-stare beautiful. She was a lot of other things too. But nearly a year after her death, it's her face that most people remember. The beautiful dead girl found in a teenage megastar's pool, as if that's all that matters.

"I'll have these," I say, handing a ten-pound note to the street vendor.

Lenny pointedly tucks the magazine into the rack. Anton Frazer's grinning face watches me from the cover. "Anton Makes His Move," reads the headline. Ever since he announced his stunt, the bastard is everywhere. There are no consequences for him. He gets to wipe his reputation clean and relaunch his empire, but I'm stuck with my police warning, school suspension, and no future.

Sirens approach. An ambulance noisily weaves through the bumper-to-bumper Oxford Street traffic, forcing black cabs and cyclists to mount the sidewalk. It's all background noise, drowned out by a shit ton of dark thoughts that I don't want to think.

"Why am I here again?" Lenny says. "I have schoolwork to finish."

"I don't function well on my own," I mutter, still glaring at Anton's picture. It's true. Other people get me out of my head. Pretty sure I'd get lost in there if I spent too much time alone.

"Do I look like a plug?" Lenny says.

"Huh?" I glance up at the sharpness of her tone. Her warm-brown skin is flushed, arms folded.

"To fill the holes in your life?"

I don't know if she's teasing, serious, or both. So I escape to a public bench, dispersing a million dirty pigeons that were loitering on the cracked sidewalk. I take my phone out and pretend I'm reading a very important message. Lenny sits next to me, a few inches of air and a million miles between us. I brace myself, but the usual complaints about what a terrible friend I am don't come.

"I get it, it's a big day for you," she says gently. "You nervous?"

"Shitting myself." I glance up at her. Lenny doesn't wear makeup, and usually her skin is shiny and flawless. Today, thanks to her late nights studying, there's a sallow tone to her face and shadows under her eyes. She looks how I feel.

"You'll be OK." She pats my knee with not much affection.

"You're not going to try to talk me out of it?" I ask.

"Entering Anton's game of tag to avenge your ex? I guess it's your choice."

Except it doesn't feel like a choice. This is all I have left. "It's not fair that he gets to carry on like nothing happened," I say. "Rose's death was his fault."

"Do you think he killed her?"

My stomach flips. She's never asked me that before. I'm hit by a vision of Rose floating dead in his pool. The water's pink and her skin's grayish white. I push it away. "The police said it was an accident. But that doesn't mean Anton wasn't responsible. He dragged her into his fucked-up world. If it weren't for him, she'd still be alive."

"I suppose she would." She fixes me with a questioning stare. "Would you still be together?"

I can't answer that one. Rose was always too good for me, I know that. She burned so bright that when I blink she's there, seared into my memories. There was this magnetic pull surrounding her that drew people in, but it was me she chose. For a life-changing, magical ten months, she was mine. And then she applied for a job with Anton Frazer.

I hadn't heard of him back then. Few people outside the gaming world had. He was seventeen and already a multimillionaire thanks to a combination of tournaments, online play-alongs, and designing his own Minecraft and Roblox content. But he was about to release *Shadow City* as an immersive hyperreality experience. And when he did, everyone would know his name.

Shadow City is a bit like *Pokémon GO*, only without the cuteness. The game claims it can use subtle fluctuations in light and shadow to detect the presence of ghosts. Through your phone's screen, it reveals these supposed ghosts overlaid on the real world as creepy shadow things. When one comes at you, you have ten seconds to exorcise it. Or in my case, you switch the game off.

It's too scary for me. I don't believe the *Shadow City* ghosts are real, but ghosts definitely exist. What if the game lets them sneak into our world, like a Ouija board? Rose used to laugh at me for being such a coward. She never understood my problem with the game. But then Rose wasn't scared of anything except boredom.

She started collaborating with Anton six months before she died, one of the team helping him stage his famous stunts—ridiculous things like jumping out at people dressed as ghosts, firing money out of a cannon, and floating a Lego house down the Thames, all captured on TikTok and YouTube. Anton called his cocreators the Accomplices and moved them into his house.

I didn't like the sound of any of this. Rose told me I didn't get it. That I had the soul of an old person when it came to online stuff. Turns out I was right to be uneasy.

Within weeks, Rose was ignoring my calls. The few occasions she found time to see me, it was like I didn't know her anymore. I'd watch the videos she was making with Anton, and my imagination ran away with me. We had this huge argument where she called me a jealous bore and I called her a pathetic fame chaser, and that was it. I didn't speak to her again. Five months later, she was dead.

"I wish I could let her go," I say, more to myself than to Lenny.

"Me too. She's always there." She takes a deep breath. "I've got to get going."

"Len, I know that this must be weird for you."

She laughs and flicks her hair over her shoulder. "Weird is your taste in T-shirts. Our entire friendship revolving around a ghost is something else."

"It's not all about her. You and me, we're—"

She silences me with a raised hand. "I don't know how this is going to pan out tonight. Just remember that I'm rooting for you."

She walks away, and being the asshole I am, I let her leave.

Sighing, I watch the blank screen of my phone. I applied for the game weeks ago but didn't find out I'd been chosen until this morning when I received an anonymous message telling me to come to Oxford Street at 11:00 a.m. It's now 11:30, and no one's contacted me with further instructions. Maybe they've spotted that I didn't come alone and decided not to risk it. Ever since it was announced, the police have been trying to shut Anton's game down.

I eye the road in both directions. Oxford Street is heaving with people and traffic. Cyclists yell at tourists who cross the road without looking. Taxi drivers hold down their horns. I see no sign of anyone who might work for Anton. I see Anton, though, peering up at me from the front pages of the free newspapers discarded next to overflowing trash cans.

I pick one up and dust it off. In the officially released photos, Anton's purple-streaked hair is styled into its usual exaggerated quiff, and his skin is clear and healthy, like he has shares in a skin-care brand. He's the epitome of boy-next-door good looks, with his perpetual smile and strong jaw. His secret, though, has always been the slightest hint of geekiness. Enough to make him seem smart and original, but not so much that people think he's a loser.

It's a carefully constructed image, and it's bullshit like everything else his PR machine puts out. It infuriates me that he rode out the storm surrounding Rose's death with such ease. Men like him always get away with it. He's white, straight, and rich. The rules do not apply.

My phone buzzes. I hesitate, then answer. It's a woman's voice, heavily distorted.

"Are you alone?" she says.

"Quite possibly forever," I reply sadly.

"Turn right and keep walking."

The line goes dead. I get to my feet and peer around the corner. To the right there's a thoroughfare lined with racks of rental bikes and scaffolding-surrounded buildings. I walk down the street, then stop. The city's noise dims almost immediately, replaced by an eerie hum.

I turn on the spot, even looking up at the rooftops to see if I'm being watched. I really wish I hadn't let Lenny leave now. It's broad daylight, but this is creepy as hell. *Teenage boy murdered yards from expensive shoe shop*, the newspaper will read. I'll be the page two to Anton's headline. When Rose died, the articles were all about him. The famous man and the beautiful dead girl in *his* pool.

Suddenly, I hear the roar of an engine. I leap aside as a big black van hurtles toward me. It bounces off the curb with a clunk of metal against concrete. It screeches to a halt, the front wheel well scraping noisily against a large black concrete post. The door opens and bashes into a bike rack. I stumble backward. *Shit shit shit.*

The driver swings her body out and jumps down. "Oh my god," she says, crouching to examine the damage. "What is wrong with me?"

I place a hand on my heart to stop it from trying to escape my rib cage *Alien* style. As my visions of being murdered in an alley recede, I realize who the girl is: Beatrix Frazer, Anton's younger sister and one of his Accomplices. She's the nice one. The cute smiley one who blended into the background while Rose took center stage.

"OK, OK. Maybe it will rub off." She scrubs at the scratches on the van with the sleeve of her chunky knit cardigan. A big flake of paint comes loose, making her shriek.

"Um, I think you're making it worse?" I offer.

She sweeps her two long braids behind her shoulders. One of them is a shiny brown; the other is bleached blond. "Do you know about cars?"

I laugh nervously. "Do I look like I know about cars?"

She stands and gives me a huge fake smile, Anton-style. She double points at me. "What you *do* look like is a winner. Are you a winner?"

"I mean, people don't tend to use that *exact* word," I say. "Um, are you all right?"

Her smile drops. "No, I'm not actually. My brother has me driving up and down the city dropping off equipment to *thirty* people, and there's this whole script I'm supposed to say, but I've only managed four contestants so far, and one of them was sick when they met me. Also, I passed my driving test last week so this is"—she pauses to take a deep breath—"a lot. It's a lot."

"Tell me about it," I say.

She shoves a backpack at me. "This is for you."

I hold her gaze a little too long. Her eyes are ridiculous. Like, this golden hazel color that has to be contacts, with long dark eyelashes and black eyeliner that makes them even more striking. Her face is rounded and young looking, and she dresses like a skater-granny. But her eyes are amazing.

I remind myself that I'm here to destroy her brother. It doesn't matter that his sister seems really sweet. I'll take her down too if I have to.

"*You* all right?" she says, scrunching up her face.

I pull myself together and remember that I'm supposed to be acting like a massive Anton fan. "Yeah. You look like your brother," I say quickly.

Her expression darkens. "I will forever be Anton's sister," she says cryptically.

I clear my throat. "I'm being weird. Sorry. I'm just excited."

She eyes me suspiciously, then waves her foot at me, hopping to keep her balance. "You see that?"

She's wearing slightly grubby red Converse shoes with baggy jeans over the top. I'm not sure what I'm supposed to see.

"That's sick on my shoe. Literal vomit," she says. "So unless you're going to puke like the last contestant I met, you're doing fine."

I laugh. She's nice. To distract myself, I open the backpack. Inside, there's some kind of bracelet like the electronic tags criminals wear on their ankles and a pair of chunky glasses in a plastic case that reminds me of Snow White's coffin. They're ugly things, with thick lenses and bulky arms. Beatrix reaches to take the glasses and puts them on. They look good on her.

"I'm supposed to tell you that there's nothing like this on the market yet," she says. "Anton owns shares in the company that makes them, so we're getting to take them for a test run."

"What's so special about them?"

"Augmented reality smart glasses. You know how *Shadow City* works?"

I wince. "You look through your phone, and the world becomes a literal hellscape with ghosts jumping out at you?"

She laughs. "You're scared of *Shadow City*? Oh my god, it's so tame. Well, I hate to tell you this, but we've hooked these glasses up to our *Shadow City* servers, so it will feel like you're actually *in* the game."

That sounds horrifying. Terrifying. Awful in every way. "Can I vomit on your shoes now?"

"Shush, I'll forget my lines. The glasses have a built-in camera. We're going to livestream everything you see and say during the game."

"We'll be playing *Shadow City*?" I ask.

"Not exactly. It's a special modified version of the game that we've put together for you lovely contestants." She returns the glasses to the bag. "They'll activate at five p.m., along with the wristband, ready for the game to start at five thirty."

I take out the bracelet and try it on. It's a wide plastic thing that clips around my wrist.

"This is where the action happens." She takes my hand and gently turns the bracelet the right way up. Her fingers are warm, and the frayed sleeves of her cardigan tickle my skin. "The wristband will also send your GPS location to Anton HQ, precise to less than a yard. You see this light? It will change color depending on whether you're a Chaser or a Runner. But Anton's going to explain that to you."

Her fingers linger on my palm. I remind myself again that Beatrix is Anton's sister. She was one of the people who took Rose from me.

"Do you miss Rose?" I say quietly.

Her whole demeanor changes, and it's like the temperature of the entire city drops. "Yeah. Of course. She was a sister to me."

I force myself to meet her eyes. "Only...I guess the prize is kind of her job. The winner gets to be her replacement. Gets to be an Accomplice."

"No. That's not going to happen. Rose's death...changed things. The Accomplices are gone, no matter what Anton wants and—" She stops talking. "Look, the game will be lots of fun, but keep your expectations in check."

"I'll get to meet Anton though?" Because that's the reason I'm doing this. To ruin his game and humiliate him to death. Or failing that, cause him some lasting psychological damage.

She looks at me sadly, then gives me a small smile. "Yes, you'll get to meet my famous, wonderful brother, don't worry." She nods at the van. "I have equipment to deliver to another twenty-five people. So I'll see you around."

"Yeah, I'll see you," I manage to say. "Good luck with the driving."

She's already slamming the van door. She reverses and manages to perform a three-point turn without hitting anything.

My phone buzzes. It's a link to a prerecorded video. I click it, and Anton's face pops up on my screen. "Hey, *Accomplice*," he says, drawing out the words like they're made of molasses. "I'm back!"

There he is. This is the boy Rose ditched me for, leaving me with nothing but regret and this cheap leather jacket that no longer fit with her image.

He leans forward so that his face takes up most of the shot. "Did you miss me?"

The sharp edge to his tone and his unblinking leer are unsettling. But then he pulls it back with a grin and slumps into his chair.

"This game's going to change *everything*," he continues, "and you're part of it. We had over a hundred thousand applications, which is… Well, that's a big number, right? I've whittled you down to the top one hundred. People who made me laugh in your application videos or impressed me with your commitment to the cause or were plain easy on the eye."

He pretends to slap his own cheek and grins crookedly.

"Kidding, kidding, this is a serious operation. Let's talk rules. The game's a lot like tag. Everyone will take turns being a Chaser and a Runner."

A game of tag, I can manage. Although I doubt it will be that simple.

Anton continues. "When it's your turn to be a Chaser, you will need to locate the Runners and tag them out of the competition. You can tag someone by getting close enough that your bracelet registers theirs. Stay within five yards of a Runner for longer than ten seconds, and the Runner is tagged."

My brain struggles to take in the information. He starts talking about special challenges and bonuses, but my attention drifts to memories of Rose. Her smile, her laugh, the way her hand felt in mine. The thought of her kissing Anton Frazer. His plump lips smeared red with her lipstick.

"Got all that?" Anton says.

My attention snaps back to him. Nope. I got nothing.

"Finally, let's talk what happens if you're the winner of my little game. Oh my god, these prizes are excellent. I can't wait for one of you to win. Not only will you receive one hundred thousand pounds, but you'll get the opportunity to audition to be my new Accomplice."

My stomach clenches. I guess Rose really was disposable when there are thousands of others lining up to take her place.

"Oh yes, I nearly forgot the best part. You win a BFF hangout sesh with me. No cameras, no audience, just you and me." He waggles his eyebrows. "I know what you ladies out there are thinking, and yes, I am single. Who knows what might happen?"

My swirling thoughts coalesce to a single point. I know exactly what will happen.

"I've got everything you need in life," Anton says, with a hopeful half smile. "Money, fame, and maybe even love. Tell me, which one are you here for?"

He begins to laugh. I pause the video on a close-up of his face. His mouth's open in frozen laughter, but it could be a scream.

"You missed one," I say quietly. "Revenge."

CHARLOTTE

Anton's been crying.

"What are you doing here?" I peer up and down the gray street. Everywhere is sheets of cold rain and puddles that reflect the empty sky. There's no sign of his entourage or the cameras that follow his every move. He's just a boy. Standing in the rain. Here, with me.

"I can't do it. The game. I don't want to do it," he says.

I gasp. "But you've been planning this for months. There are a hundred people taking part."

He turns away. His hands make fists in his wet hair. Then he spins around again. His dreamy blue eyes are wild. "None of it matters. Only you, Lola. It's always been you, ever since that night at the party."

"What?" I whisper, and the world stops spinning beneath us.

He steps toward me and trails his fingers down my bare arms.

"I love you. And I don't want to love you because it scares me so, so much. But I can't help it. I…I…"

He doesn't finish because that's the moment when we melt into each other. His mouth grazes mine, and I don't care that he's pulled me outside with him into the pouring rain. I laugh against his lips and kiss him harder. Wow, I'm literally kissing Anton.

And then the DLR train sways from side to side, and I smack myself in the face, shattering the fantasy. I'm back in a subway car that smells of kebab meat and body odor. The woman sitting opposite me gawks in my direction with her mouth hanging open. I realize too late that I've been kissing my own hand. I wipe my face on my sleeve and busy myself typing the scene into my phone. She's still staring, but I try to ignore her.

My story—"Anton Meets His Match"—has been a lukewarm hit with the Anton community on GossApp. It's my best yet, I think because I've put so much of myself into it. My hopes, my dreams, my heart. Writing it hasn't felt like make-believe; it's felt like writing the truth. And now all that's left to post is the final scene.

I read what I wrote. My stomach drops in disappointment and shame. I hold down the delete button until it's gone. My endings always suck when I try to write a happily ever after. But my readers haven't been exactly complimentary about my attempts at excitement and danger either.

Anton wouldn't say that, loser.

What, no boning?

How old are you 12?

I gaze out the window at the city as it rushes past. We're heading toward West India Quay, and the Canary Wharf skyscrapers stand proudly in the distance. Towering cranes crisscross against an almost colorless sky, bringing to mind immense dueling monsters. Just looking at them gives me vertigo. A plot idea hits me.

I imagine that Anton's hanging one-handed from a crane, swinging from the huge hook as the wind tears through his amethyst hair. His other hand is holding mine, the one thing between me and a hundred-story fall. Our fingers are slipping apart, and his grip on the hook is failing. He can't hold on much longer.

"Let me go," I say, my pounding heart slowing as I realize what I must do. "If you don't let me go, then we'll both die."

"Lola, no. I don't want to live without you." He sobs.

I smile bravely. "But you must. Live for both of us, Anton. Love for both of us."

"I can't let you go," he whispers. "I can't say goodbye, not when I just found you."

"But, my darling, I'll always be with you. Always." I start to slip my fingers free of his and wink at him before I plummet to my death. "Stay sexy," I say, letting go.

Urgh, no. This is trash. As if he'd *drop* me. Also, I've never been able to wink. I notice the woman opposite is staring again. I suspect I was whispering the words to my story out loud.

"I'm a writer," I tell her, like that explains everything.

The woman hides behind her newspaper. I sigh again, then scroll up through my story to read it from the beginning. I've been posting a new installment every day in the run-up to Anton's game. There are over a dozen comments already. Most people are desperate to find out what's going to happen at the end. If only I knew.

I return to staring out the window. My reflection stares back at me. I'm wearing my favorite neon-orange Anton hoodie, with his face on the front. Unfortunately, my hair's ruining what's otherwise a perfect outfit. I'm pretty sure my hairdresser hates me. It's the only explanation for why she cut 80 percent of my hair into massive bangs, making me look like I'm wearing a mousy-blond Lego girl wig.

My vanity is brought to an abrupt halt by a buzzing sensation on my wrist. I check out my bracelet. It's lit up white, which is weird because I didn't think the tech was supposed to come on till later—I'm heading to my starting position two hours early, just in case. I guess HQ is testing the system. The glasses aren't doing anything yet though. I've been wearing them ever since they were given to me by some assistant called Caro, who I only vaguely recognized.

The woman opposite is peeking at me from behind her newspaper again. She lowers the paper and folds it carefully in her lap. "Are you taking part in that big game of chase tonight?" she asks, gesturing to my bracelet. "The one organized by that famous boy on the Internet."

I nod and smile, my mind already returning to my story. Dangling from a crane was too much. An explosion perhaps, or an escaped lion…

"What do your parents think?" The woman persists, shuffling forward in her seat. "My daughter wanted to take part, but I told her it was far too dangerous. You never know what kind of men might be out at night."

I shrug. Truth is, I haven't told my mom. Even if I had, she probably wouldn't have cared. Once upon a time, we were so close. But that was during the Before, when Dad was still around. That makes it sound as if he died, but the reality is far less dramatic. No, he just decided that he didn't much like family life anymore, so he left.

When I was a little kid, I had this unshakable belief that parents would always love their children. That they always *wanted* their children. Turns out it's not true. Dad hasn't tried to contact me in years, except for a birthday card sent a month late, written in neat handwriting that wasn't his own.

And my mom? Well, she didn't check out as literally as Dad did, but ever since we moved in with Roger two years ago, it's very clear that I'm a guest in her life. I sleep in horrible Matthew's old room, with his gaming posters on the walls and his childhood *Minecraft* comforter on the bed. Matthew's my stepbrother-to-be. I hate him.

"Someone does know where you are, don't they?" the woman says gently.

I flash her my best A-student smile. "Of course," I lie. "Actually, my dad's driving down to keep an eye on me. He's really overprotective."

"Oh, that's good." She sits back in her seat. "It's for the best with that much money involved."

The prize certainly is a lot of money, but I'm planning to refuse it. I don't want Anton thinking my intentions are anything less than honorable. The idea of profiting from him feels cheap. I wrote this little scene in one of my fanfics in which my character, Lola, turns Anton's prize down, and Anton's so touched that he cries. Thinking about it, he cries in a lot of my stories. I hope he isn't offended by that.

My eyes widen. I've never stopped to think that Anton might actually read my writing. Heat floods to my cheeks as I remember that one story in which Anton is transformed into a guinea pig and Lola spends hours brushing his fur. That one was...weird. But then I remember how I've always used a pen name. There's no way anyone will find out that AntonsGirlXOXO is me. Which is a very good thing, since it's not only fiction that I've posted.

My bracelet buzzes again, and the lights flash. I hope it's not broken.

The train pulls into the next station, and we sit there forever. There's some commotion on the platform, but I can't see anything. Finally, the doors beep and begin to close with a hiss. Someone throws themselves through the gap at the last minute. He swears and brushes himself down, his light brown skin beaded with sweat.

I jump out of my seat, and my glasses nearly slip off my head. "Matthew!"

He points at me while trying to catch his breath. There's a big damp patch down the front of his gray T-shirt. I don't even want to think about what might be happening inside the tight leather pants he's wearing. Urgh, now I'm thinking about it.

"What are you doing here? How did you find me?" I say.

"Caro texted me—she said you looked familiar when she dropped off the tech package. I followed the signal from the GPS tracking bracelet, and here you are. Entering under a fake name? Fuck, Charlotte."

"Please don't swear at me. And Sanderson isn't a fake name; it's my mom's maiden name, although I don't see how it's any of your beeswax." I sit down and straighten my glasses.

Horrible Matthew? Roger's eighteen-year-old son? My future stepbrother? Yeah, he's one of Anton's two surviving Accomplices. Once upon a time, he lived with us. He gave up his room for me and slept on the sofa. He invited me to parties with his famous friends. Then, just as I got used to having a brother, he left.

Now Matthew lives in Anton's house and dates Anton's sister. Every month or two, he comes home to torment me with his arrogance and his overpowering aftershave and the fact he's living the life that I want to be living.

Look at him, the slimy little dude-bro. Predictable good looks?

Check. Well-rehearsed wink? Of course. Expensive clothes that he wears once? Obviously. *Oh no, my T-shirt's accidentally a child's size and now everyone can see the outline of my six-pack.* Barf.

He slides into the seat next to me, knocking knees with the woman opposite. "Charlotte, this isn't a game!" he hisses.

"Err, that's exactly what it is. A livestreamed *game* of tag. Which I intend to win."

"Win? You?"

"Yes, me! I'm going to win that date with Anton, and then we—"

"Wait, what? Anton's not about to *date* you, Charlotte. Fuck's sake. You really think he'd be interested in you?"

The woman opposite gasps softly. Someone else whispers to their friend. The entire car is now listening in on our conversation, turning in their seats. I can taste their pity. *Look at that poor deluded girl, with her pudgy pink cheeks and child's haircut.*

"You think that because I'm not perfect, amazing Beatrix, I'm not worthy of love? Shame on you, Matthew," I say, keeping my voice as quiet as I can.

"Love?" He slowly shakes his head. "Anton's not going to fall in love with you."

"He would have already if you weren't always getting between us. Anton and I had a connection, and you've kept us apart. You could've passed on my messages, but no! You deliberately ruined my life."

"I was protecting you. You think you know Anton because you used to watch his show. But none of that shit was real. You don't know what you're getting yourself into."

"You're wrong. Anton and I are perfect for each other, and I'm not letting you spoil my one chance. Now leave me alone." I turn my head and refuse to look at him.

"Charlotte. Charlotte! You're being ridiculous. I'm not the bad guy here."

"Says the boy who interferes with other people's relationships and cheats on his own girlfriend."

He throws both arms up in disbelief, smacking the nosy woman's newspaper out of her hands, into her face. "I've never cheated on Beatrix. Jesus, Charlotte, what's wrong with you?"

I scoff at him. "So your sordid reputation is make-believe? All those influencer types filming videos about how you dated them?"

"That was before I got together with Beatrix, and you know it."

"Really? And what about those photos outside that hotel? Why were you running around in your underwear, Matthew?"

He goes very still. "That wasn't... You don't know what you're talking about."

"Cheat," I shout at him. "Cheaty, cheaty, cheat-cheat."

Abruptly, he storms off with his jaw clenched so tight I worry his teeth will shatter. As the train pulls into the next station, he hammers on the Open Doors button even though they always open by themselves and steps out onto the platform. I wave to him through the glass. He mouths something unrepeatable.

"I always thought he was such a nice boy," the woman opposite muses.

"Yeah, everyone thinks that. But he's not." I've known exactly who the real Matthew is since he left me behind without a backward glance. He's a user and a pretender. I wish I could make everyone else see him for what he is too. I scroll to the top of the Anton message board on GossApp. Typing quickly, I write a new post without really thinking about what I'm saying.

What's this I hear? Matthew is sneaking around behind the lovely Beatrix's back again, getting up to no good? Perhaps it's time for Anton to wake up to what kind of person is living in his home and dating his sister—AntonsGirlXOXO

As soon as I hit Send, I wonder if it's too much. Too bitter and jealous. I push the thoughts aside and remind myself why I'm here and how much is at stake. Nobody—especially not my horrible stepbrother—is going to stand in my way.

ERIN

Call me plastic, I don't care. Call me a princess or a bitch or a slut. Type it into a DM. Shout it in the street. Strap it to the leg of a carrier pigeon if that's your weird, twisted thing. It doesn't matter. You and I both know you're just jealous.

Either you want me or you want to be me.

I swing my flame-red hair over one shoulder and laugh for the camera, making sure they get my best angles: slightly to the side, chin angled down, eyes flicking up. These smart glasses aren't easy to work with. They're big and blocky, and my false lashes keep scratching against the lenses. But the rules state that I can't take them off once the game begins, even for a moment.

I have twenty minutes until everything kicks off. There's always time for a photo shoot though. My starting position is outside the aquarium, which means swarms of tourists. Look at them all, in their poorly fitting chino shorts and backpacks, watching me pose against the backdrop of the Thames. I try to act like I'm the only one here, gazing serenely across the water.

Then the makeup artist we hired leans too close, and I'm hit by a waft of the meat pasty he had for lunch. My stomach lurches and I stumble back. My mother, Amber, rushes in to catch me, but I've already righted myself. I swat the powder brush aside.

"Give me some space," I snap. "This isn't a fucking date."

The man rolls his eyes and mutters, "As if," under his breath. He strokes his brush, comforting it.

"Erin, darling," Amber says, laughing nervously. "Let's take a moment."

She shoos our entourage away and tries to raise a perfectly stenciled eyebrow at me, except she had her Botox topped up last week, and everything is smooth and shiny. It's impossible to tell if she's furious or worried or holding in a fart.

"You're lucky we're not being filmed right now," Amber whispers. "This is our chance to nudge our subscribers past four million. We need people to *like* you, remember?"

I curl my lip but don't bother arguing. She plays this fame game better than me, but then she's been doing it far longer. She started her parenting, lifestyle, and fashion blog—*Amber Loves*—when she was seventeen and had just had me. For a while it was huge, but she lost a lot of subscribers when I hit my tweens and stopped being quite so cute.

Fast-forward to two years ago when I turned fifteen. Amber set up a YouTube vlog and brought me on board again, this time wearing her clothes and her makeup. Chasing her dreams. Her second chance.

And for a while it worked.

Amber and Erin Love grew in popularity to the point that magazines wrote articles about us, illustrated with dozens of fashion shots in which Amber and I could have been sisters. Glossy red hair, laughing smiles, the kind of figures that come from spending hours in the gym and a strict paleo-vegan diet.

Then our subscriber numbers plateaued. Amber's always pinning the blame on me for being "unlikeable." She says I'm arrogant and cold, and there's only so much I can get away with based on looks. She's right, I suppose—about the first part.

The problem is, Amber wants more. She *needs* more if she's going to continue to afford her lifestyle. She spends thousands a month trying to wind back the clock and look seventeen again. Sometimes I catch her observing me with disgust, like it's my fault that I'm young and she's not. And then she'll book another procedure.

She sighs. "If I could enter myself…"

"The cutoff's twenty-one and you're thirty-four," I say before I can stop myself.

"Yes, I'm aware of how old I am," she snarls. "Quit being such a brat."

I feel my whole face coloring. I hate that my mother can hurt me with her bad opinion. When I was a kid, I'd do anything to make her happy, but it was never enough. I wish I could stop caring what she thinks of me. I try to keep my emotions locked tightly away when it comes to her, but still they bleed through the cracks.

"Anton's a friend of mine," Amber continues, glancing nervously at the photographer. "You'd better not embarrass me."

Anton's not her friend. They collaborated a number of times, a year ago, before Rose died. He used to invite us to his parties, but he was never really interested in hanging out with a woman fifteen years his senior or with me, a surly sixteen-year-old.

That's where this game comes in. According to her, tonight is our ticket to fame and fortune. The prize money will pay for the butt implants she's been eyeing, and winning would also boost our audience. After all, Anton has a cool hundred million subscribers to our four million. But she needs *me* to win.

I need me to win.

She takes a slow breath. "Eyes on the prize, Erin."

I nod. "I know. I've got it under control."

"I'm trusting you with this. Now let me look at you." She fusses with my extensions, scrunching the long curls and letting them fall again. Her swollen lips are pursed, like my hair has personally insulted her by not being bouncy enough. But three hours in the stylist's chair was never going to be a match for the damp London air.

"He should have used more hairspray. You'll be flat by midnight," she says.

"Urgh, limp hair is the worst," an overly confident voice says.

We both look up with a start. Striding over is Matthew, his dark faux-hawk and cheesy grin making him look like he's in an old-school boy band. I have to admit that he's fairly hot, even if he does try a bit too hard. I mean, the personalized motorcycle leathers? The low-necked T-shirt that shows off a flash of waxed chest? The shark's tooth necklace? Call me a hypocrite, but I've never been a fan of boys who care too much about their appearance.

He's recording me with an action cam mounted on a flashlight-sized stabilizer. That explains his friendliness. We met dozens of times during our channels' collaborations, pre–Rose's death. He always used to ignore me when there was no camera around, which is surprising given his reputation. Perhaps dating Beatrix really has changed him.

"I'm checking in on some of our top contestants before the game starts," he says. "Are you ready, Erin?"

I instantly switch on the charm. "The real question is, are you ready for *me*?"

He holds out the camera to get us both in the shot and laughs along with me, as good-natured as he is in Anton's videos. We both know the parts we're supposed to play, the lines we have to say. I sometimes wonder if, like me, Matthew ever feels as if he's made of hollow plastic, waiting for someone else to fill him with their own fantasies. Or maybe he's bought into the lies and believes it's real.

"The people at home will want to know if you've remembered to pack your thermos and a spare pair of underwear," he says.

I smile even wider, making my cheeks ache. "I'm always pre-pared, Matthew."

He briefly looks me over. Today, I'm wearing skintight, wet-look leggings and an off-the-shoulder T-shirt. It's not the most obvious outfit for playing a game of tag, but sportswear isn't on-brand for the *Amber and Erin Love* channel.

"I don't want to know where you've got them stashed," he says with his famous wink.

"Cheeky." I laugh, adjusting my T-shirt.

He clears his throat and looks away, his gaze briefly settling on Amber as he does. His whole demeanor darkens. I've always had the feeling that he doesn't like her, but he used to hide it better than this. He claps his hands, upbeat again. "All right, everything's a go in ten minutes. Your glasses will give you a countdown, and Anton will introduce the game. You good on your starting coordinates?"

"Of course," I say, gesturing over my shoulder to a white cross on the chewing gum–stained sidewalk. A unique set of coordinates was texted to me earlier today. All the contestants are spread across several square miles, the sleeper cells of an invasion. "I'm ready to go."

Matthew narrows his eyes at my shoes. "You know, I almost wore those exact same six-inch spike heels today. Could have been embarrassing. Also, can you actually run in those things?"

"Faster than you," I say. "Want to have a race?"

"My ego couldn't take it if I lost." He lowers the camera and turns off the smile. "Got to go, Erin. I'll be in big trouble if I'm late."

"With Beatrix?" Amber pipes up.

He frowns. "With Anton. OK, I'll be seeing you later, Erin."

"Bye, Matthew," Amber says.

He ignores her and jogs off toward Westminster Bridge, taking the steps two at a time. There's a Segway parked at the top. Pushing the handlebars forward, he rolls off at a blistering five miles an hour. The motorbike gear is serious overkill.

Amber glares after him, then checks her watch. "I need to get to the hotel. I'll follow your progress online." I think she's going to leave, but she hesitates. When she speaks again, her voice is uncharacteristically quiet. "We need this, Erin. You can't let us down."

"I won't."

She watches me closely, but if she wants to say anything else, she doesn't. She clicks her fingers at the photographer, makeup artist, and hairdresser, then sashays away, already scrolling through the photos from our pregame shoot. She'll have them uploaded onto our socials in no time.

Then she's gone, and I'm on my own, if you ignore the endless stream of aquarium visitors kicked out at closing time. A countdown appears on my smart glasses. Ten minutes to go.

Time to get my head in the game. I stretch out my shoulders and make sure I've memorized the routes I can take from my starting position. My big advantage—other than the fact that I'm as fit as most professional athletes—is that I'm not here to play. I'm here to win. It's a competitive streak that's served me well in life, even if it doesn't earn me many friends.

I'm interrupted by something flickering in my field of vision. A half-transparent screen swipes open on my lenses, and a video call from Anton appears. I can see through him, like he's overlaid on the real world. I've tried smart glasses before, and they always make me feel motion sick. These new models are no better.

I focus on Anton and try to block out the world behind him. He's in his well-lit office, lounging in his race car bucket seat and grinning into the camera. On the wall, there are framed images from *Shadow City*, ghostly monsters lunging with their claws outstretched.

He's dressed in one of his own branded rainbow hoodies, and he's whitened his teeth. He could almost be the fresh-faced teenager who first started up his channel all those years ago. There's the faintest sign of dark circles under his eyes, masked with concealer though.

"Accomplices!" Anton yells, spreading his arms wide.

I wince. The glasses have built-in speakers. It sounds like Anton is shouting right into my brain.

"Welcome to my game! Sucks to be home alone while you're having all the fun, but someone has to take the helm at Anton HQ." He turns the camera. One wall of his office is set up with dozens of screens, like a closed-circuit TV operations room. On them are the one hundred feeds from our smart glasses. "I'll be watching everything. Like God, only hotter."

His ego clearly hasn't mellowed with time. He winks at the camera like it was a joke. I don't think it was though.

"Oh, and if you want to be all-seeing like me, you can check out your competition's feeds too. Flick your eyes down and to the left, and your smart glasses will open the menu. It's like magic. These smart glasses are the greatest. And in a few months, they'll go on sale. Hint, hint."

I ignore the advertising spiel and try out the menu. Several icons appear superimposed over the real world. I scroll between them with a flick of my gaze and open them with a blink. It's clever, I have to give him that. Like having your cell phone projected in front of your eyes.

"You've also got a map where you'll be able to see the locations of the opposition. Now, here's the best part. I can change the accuracy of your position shown on the map—anything from a precise location to a fifty-yard radius—meaning my favorites will have an advantage and be harder to catch."

He's not telling me anything that his prerecorded video didn't explain earlier, but I listen carefully all the same.

"Any minute now, the wristband lights will come on, and you'll find out if you're starting the game as a Chaser or a Runner. Remember, Chasers are blue, and they can tag out a red Runner by getting within five yards of them for longer than ten seconds. How long you stay a Chaser or Runner is up to me. So get ready to fight for your prize."

Fight, I can do. I'm no spoiled princess who's scared of breaking a nail, even if that's what you'd believe from watching my channel. I'll break whatever it takes, break whoever it takes.

Anton sits forward in his chair and stops smiling. "Now, being serious for a minute. There have been some health and safety concerns raised about my game. I wanted to reassure everyone that this is totally under control. I have people out there keeping an eye on things, and if anyone gets in trouble, someone will be right there to help. OK? OK."

I snort. Wouldn't want any more negative publicity, would you Anton? One dead girl is enough.

"One final thing." He claps his hands. "My Accomplices Matthew and Beatrix have been busy organizing a few special surprises. You'll be able to earn advantages by competing in a little treasure hunt of challenges that I've set up. The first location is the place where we created my second stunt. You do know where my second stunt was filmed, right?"

Like I pay attention to that sort of thing. So it's lucky that, for the past year, I've been dating someone who happens to now be working behind the scenes on Anton's game. Jesse isn't the kind of boy people expect me to be dating. He's quiet and skinny, with unruly hair that never lies flat. He doesn't care about his clothes and has never been inside a gym. But that's why I like him. It's refreshing to be with someone for whom those things don't matter. There's enough vanity in my world.

Jesse's my boy on the inside. He's going to help me win this competition.

"Get ready to play, Accomplices," Anton says.

The video call ends, and the projected screen closes. The map in the corner of my vision updates. I bring it up with a glance. My closest competitor is a hundred yards away. Depending on whether my bracelet goes blue for Chaser or red for Runner, I will either be running toward or away from Gray26.

This is it. This is my chance. See, I'm not playing to win for my mother's ambitions. I'm playing for me and Jesse. The money would be enough for us to start a new life. Jesse could pay to record his demo album and go on tour; I wouldn't have to pose for a photo ever again.

All those hours in the gym, pretending to care about my thigh gap and my bicep definition. All those climbing lessons, and Pilates and spin classes. All that wasted time pandering to my mother's obsession with my looks. Protein shakes, chin-ups, hours being primped and plucked. All of it has led up to this moment.

I'm done being made of hollow plastic, ready for my mother to fill me with her dreams and her ambitions. This game is my way out. My future.

And losing is not an option.

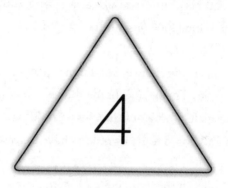

GRAYSON

Five minutes and counting.

I should be thinking about the game. Instead, I'm worrying about Lenny. I've texted her close to a dozen times since she left. I even sent her photos of the smart glasses, which I know she must be salivating over. No reply. Lenny is permanently attached to her phone—she must have seen my messages.

The only explanation is that she's deliberately ghosting me. Lenny isn't the sulking type. She's either fully in or she's completely out. Like, when I ask her about old friends and relationships, she'll brush it off as the past. Walk away and never look back.

Three minutes.

I pace next to a gaudy carousel by the river, unsure of which way to go. I don't want to lose Lenny. But I also can't stop thinking about how much I want to kick Anton in the 'nads, livestreamed for all to see. Is revenge worth the price of losing my best mate?

I check my phone again. Nothing.

One minute.

I need to focus. The closest spot on the map is Erin19. I have to be ready to run or chase. I'm not ready. I'm panicking.

Thirty seconds.

I feel like I'm going to puke. And the glasses-cam will catch it all. Awesome. I take a deep, slow breath. *Calm the hell down, Grayson.* Only I can't. I'm not analytical and logical like Lenny. I'm not fiery and confident like Rose. I need someone to keep me from spinning out of control, and now I have no one.

I *know* that this vendetta will change nothing. So why am I not walking away?

Ten seconds.

What is wrong with me? I still don't have a plan! My brain is a colander, and my thoughts are water, trickling everywhere.

Three, two, one...

Game on flashes in front of my eyes.

The light on my wrist turns red. But I can't remember if that means I'm a Runner or a Chaser. So I just stand there.

Go, go, go! the smart glasses say.

The map superimposed over my field of vision activates. The spots start to move. Erin19 is heading my way, extremely fast. She's blue and I'm red. Red is for Runner. I need to be running.

OK. I can do this. One foot in front of the other. I speed up to a jog, earning me ogles from a group of preppy student types drinking at a pop-up gin bar. One of them, already drunk and red-faced despite the hour, stumbles in front of me, and I nearly trip. I glance over my shoulder, but there's no sign of Erin19 yet.

There's a flicker in the corner of my vision. I think it's a person watching me, but they step out of sight almost immediately. When I look, there's no one there. I tell myself it's the glasses glitching, but a heavy feeling of dread settles in my belly.

"Steady on," a lad in a wrinkled shirt says, nudging his mate. "Check that out."

That's when I spot her. A beautiful redheaded girl is sprinting along the embankment like an athlete, although she's dressed more like she's heading to a club. Shiny black leggings, an off-the-shoulder band T-shirt, and lace-up ankle boots with huge sharp heels. The rock chick look for people who don't actually listen to rock music.

Erin19.

I gawk at her as she runs at me with her hair a billowing storm. A pre-Raphaelite goddess with her flawless skin and bone structure that could cut you to pieces. She reaches the group of drinkers and shoves people aside like they're bowling pins. A plastic glass explodes its contents. A slow-motion eruption of mint leaves and cucumber slices goes flying into the air.

Bloody hell.

I snap out of my daze and run. Erin19 is right behind me. My wristband buzzes, and a countdown starts on my screen. Ten seconds, and I'll be tagged out. Unless I can get more than five yards away from this girl and stay that way.

I speed up. The countdown stops. I race beneath a rusty railway bridge where builders are constructing a shipping-container taco bar. I risk another look over my shoulder. She's still chasing me, and her porcelain skin is barely flushed. This girl's the goddam Terminator.

I emerge onto the South Bank. I weave through the trees, past

TAG, YOU'RE DEAD · 39

the outdoor diners. I can hardly breathe. There's a graffiti-covered skate park tucked away under the Royal Festival Hall. I vault over the metal fence and slalom between skaters. I think I can get out the other side, but it's a dead end. Shit.

I spin around. Erin19 has caught up. She slows to a walk on the other side of the fence. I can see her eyeing every direction I could take, figuring out my possible trajectories and our intercept points. I try to do the same, but my hamster-wheel brain won't engage.

I walk backward into a dirty puddle. Erin19 ducks beneath the fence and carefully descends the steps. The skaters have noticed something's going on and most have stopped moving. They watch me and Erin19, some of them recording us on their phones.

"You're good," I gasp. "We've only been playing for a few minutes."

"It's nothing personal," she says, eyeing me like I'm prey.

"It feels kind of personal." I flick my hair out of my eyes and look for a way to escape. *Think, think, think*, I tell myself.

"Why aren't you running?" Erin says. "You're choking, aren't you? Five minutes in and you can't hack it."

"Shush, Ms. Motivator. I'm still trying to come up with a game plan." My vision flickers again. A figure, just out of sight, watching me.

"You can't stay here forever. Your GPS location has to move, or you're disqualified."

"I listened to the rules too, you know." I didn't listen to the rules. "I need to win this thing, all right? So can't we…you know?"

She laughs cruelly in reply. It was a long shot, I suppose. All right. A plan. I have a plan.

"Anton?" I say, craning my head to peer around her. "No way."

And she falls for it!

The moment she turns to glance over her shoulder, I run. I vault the fence and push my way through our audience. My tracker countdown briefly activates, but then I'm running with everything I have. Which isn't much.

People cheer and jeer. "Run, run, run," a group of girls chants, whistling at me and applauding.

I do run, but so does Erin19. And she's much faster than I am. I can hear her heels clicking as she gets closer. I glance back. She's nearly within five yards of me.

"Did you train for this?" I gasp.

"I work out for four hours a day," she calls out, and I don't think she's joking.

I head along the river, past the ugly brutalism of the National Theatre, toward an arty little wharf where I was hoping I could lose her. I'm not sure how long I can keep on going though. I have to hope that my bracelet turns blue soon and I'm no longer a Runner. It's the only way I'm going to escape.

A group of people gets in my way, and Erin19 gains on me enough to activate my countdown again.

Ten, nine…

I pull away. She catches up again.

Ten, nine, eight…

I shove my way past a group of women with buggies chatting by the river. I bounce off a tree. My heart's an overinflated balloon. Erin19 manages to catch hold of my leather jacket.

Ten, nine…

I yank myself free and quicken my pace.

"I've got you," she says, and the monster isn't even out of breath.

"You haven't tagged me yet."

"I will."

Ten, nine, eight…

I change direction and use a large group of kids with matching red backpacks and baseball caps to put a few extra yards between me and Erin19. But she goes straight through them, ignoring their shouts of surprise.

Ten, nine, eight…

I stretch my body away from her. My muscles scream from the effort.

Seven, six, five…

She really does have me.

Four, three…

Then there's a cry and a thud. The countdown stops. I skid to a halt. When I look back, Erin19 is sprawled facedown on the cobbles. She pushes herself up onto her hands and knees and stares at me open-mouthed.

"You OK?" I say.

She slowly heaves herself upright with a wince. She doesn't come at me. We stand there, watching each other from a safe distance. She looks seriously angry. A stereotypical mean girl, all pretty and polished and raging when she doesn't get her way. Girls like her are terrifying.

"You know, I couldn't run in those shoes either," I say.

She makes a disgusted face. "I can run fine, you asshole. *They* tripped me up."

I look in the direction she's pointing. There's a dark-clothed jogger heading away from our position. Perhaps they bumped into her. They didn't even stop to make sure she wasn't hurt. This city is brutal.

"Friend of yours?" Erin19 says.

I laugh. "You really think I planned this? I don't plan anything."

Before she can reply, my wristband buzzes. The color has changed from red to blue. Runner to Chaser. *Reverse, reverse, reverse,* my glasses flash.

Erin19 is no longer a Chaser. She's the one who needs to run now. She doesn't. She studies me closely. It's like she's challenging me to make a move. I'm way too scared of her though.

"I'll see you around, Gray26," she finally says.

She jogs away and doesn't even bother checking to see if I'm chasing her. Rock-hard. I breathe out slowly and try to get my heart rate under control. People are staring, so I leave the river behind and turn onto a street where hundreds of soulless windows look down on me. I stop outside a posh hotel and sit on the edge of their ornamental flower bed, resting my head on my knees. I've been there a minute when I hear someone walk up behind me.

"Smooth," they say. "You've got the prize in the bag."

I look around. Lenny eyes me coldly, her braids escaping from beneath a hood pulled low over her face. She's dressed head to toe in black. There's even a mask covering her lower face, so only her dark brown eyes are visible.

"Don't look at me."

"What are you doing here?" I say, staring at my feet.

"Or talk. Come on."

Shielding her face with a hand, she gestures for me to follow her. We head toward Waterloo train station. Lenny keeps her back to me and stays mostly off to the side, so the cam on my glasses won't pick her up. I'm not sure where she's going; then she turns off into the brightly lit Leake Street tunnel.

Inside, the walls are covered in graffiti. There are several artists working away and visitors taking photos. Rose brought me here for a date once, and I was awed by the colors and the way she kissed me. The smell of paint solvent brings it all back.

I've gone a few yards when my signal cuts out. A five-minute timer appears on my lenses. "I'm out of range," I say. "What are you doing here?"

She pulls her face mask down so I can experience the full impact of her glare. "Other than saving your unprepared ass from being the first person tagged out?"

"You were the jogger who tripped Erin19? Thanks for that. Even if you have made me an enemy of the toughest girl in this competition."

"That girl was Erin Love. The famous influencer?" She digs in her bag and takes out a tiny earpiece and a box the size of a cell phone with a long cord. She loops the cord around my neck and tucks the box into my pocket.

"This will allow us to talk," she says, offering me the earpiece. "I can listen in on what you're up to and feed you instructions."

"We'll be spies!" I put the small earbud in and wiggle it for good measure. "Um, why?"

"Let's be realistic. You'll never survive without me." She hesitates. "I can't promise I'll be able to help you win, but I can help you stay in the competition longer than five minutes."

"You're going to *help* me?"

She shrugs. "It's helping myself too. Maybe after tonight I won't have to listen to you pining over Rose."

This is what she was doing all afternoon when I couldn't reach her. Preparing for the game because she knew I wouldn't. I'm hit by a sudden surge of affection and pull her into a hug. "After this is over, there'll be no more ghosts. I promise."

To my surprise, her expression darkens. She disentangles herself and steps away.

"Let's get through tonight first." She forces a smile. "Five minutes is almost up. You'd better go."

She's right. The timer on my glasses is nearly down to the last minute.

"Are you sure you're OK with this?" I ask.

"I'm not sure I have any choice." Her expression softens, and she gestures for me to go. "Run out the other end of the tunnel, and they'll believe you were cutting through."

The countdown on my glasses says thirty seconds, so run is what I do. I burst out into the fresh air with moments to go. The timer stops, and I pause to catch my breath. I want to look back to see if Lenny is there, but my camera would pick her up. I have to walk away.

I feel more alone than ever, but then Lenny's voice is in my ear. "Let's get you to that first challenge," she says. "You've got some butt to kick if you want to redeem yourself."

I smile to myself. With Lenny on my side, things are looking up. Then I turn a corner and am met with bright red words spray-painted on a concrete wall. They're dripping, like blood; each letter is two feet high and traced over twice.

The words read, I WAS MURDERED.

I can't help but think this message is meant for me.

CHARLOTTE

Half an hour into the game, and I'm already stuck up a tree. One with a spindly trunk and creaking branches that are threatening to snap at any moment.

The tree's growing inside the church ruins of St. Dunstan-in-the-East. It's totally the sort of place I'd go on a daydream date with Anton. Creepers grow out of huge Gothic windows. Benches are hidden in little alcoves. The roof is open to the elements, so I'm bathed in dappled sunlight rustling through leaves.

Anton and I would sit together, our fingers grazing as we snuck our hands closer and closer. There'd be a string quartet playing in the background. He'd pull me toward him, and I'd close my eyes, lips parting. I haven't had the chance to plot out any more of the fantasy though.

The problem is the two boys flanking the base of my tree. They're working together and have chased me up here. Now they're jumping at me like badly dressed Labradors. Their handles are Sean23 and Spar97, but I've renamed them Blondie and Spike based on their hairstyles.

"Grab her leg and pull her down," Blondie says. He's not much older than me, with an explosion of bleached hair.

"I can't reach," Spike says. His brown hair is styled into sharp points.

My bracelet briefly activates with a buzz. I edge farther up the tree and stretch my arm high above my head so that it's out of range. Every time a breeze catches the tree, it bends enough that the bracelet buzzes.

A small crowd of people who were picnicking inside the ruins have gathered to watch us. Presumably they think we're acting out some kind of weird performance art since none of them are trying to help me. A girl being bullied by two boys? Someone should definitely be intervening!

"Come down already," Spike taunts. "You can't stay in one place for longer than five minutes."

This is true. And I've already been up the tree for two minutes. My one hope is the colors will switch again, like they have twice already.

"You're going to have to run," Blondie says. "And we'll chase you." He barks and his friend laughs.

"We'll give you a head start," Spike says, smirking. "Honest."

I glare at him. Bullies really get my goat. Especially bullies who dress in skintight red jeans. No one in red jeans has ever turned out to be a decent human—fact. Urgh, I feel such disgust just looking at him. He's a fungal crotch infection waiting to happen.

"You're laughing now, but when your mate turns on you, you'll be tagged out within seconds. You look slow," I say.

His smirk fades. "We're working together, so that won't happen."

"But you are slow, right?"

"Shut up." He fidgets in his stupid jeans. "Strategy is more important than speed."

Blondie snorts with laughter.

Spike rounds on him. "Seriously? We have a deal, right? You better stick to the deal."

"Sure," Blondie says. "Rock, Paper, Scissors once we're down to the final two."

"As if," I say.

"Shut up!" Spike snaps.

My bracelet buzzes with a thirty-second warning. Damn. I'm out of time. I briefly consider staying up in the tree and letting it time out. That way, neither of the horrible boys gets to claim the tag. But I'm not giving up on Anton that easily. Besides, my branch makes the decision for me and breaks.

Screaming slasher-movie-victim style, I grab at leaves and twigs in an attempt to stay in the tree, but it's no use. I'm going down, and Anton's not here to catch me. Which is why I stretch out my arms and legs like a flying squirrel and aim for Spike.

"What the...? Arghhh!" he cries.

All in all, he's a fairly soft landing. I don't have time to check whether he's OK. My bracelet has activated, and I need to run.

I scramble to my feet and shove my way through the gasping crowd. I trip over a spiky bush, barely keeping my balance. The archway leading outside is ahead, and I think I'm going to make it, but then Blondie grabs my hood, yanking me backward.

Anger surges inside me. I pull myself free, then grab both halves of his scarf and yank them tight, briefly choking him. I set off at a sprint, tripping and flailing as I race to get my bracelet out of range.

The countdown gets all the way to three, but then it stops. I'm safe, for a few seconds at least. I glance over my shoulder. I spot Blondie searching for me in the crowd, but Spike is missing.

"Gotcha," he says, appearing from around the side of the church, panting with exertion and favoring his left leg.

I fly toward one of the glassless windows and scramble up the rough stone. I squeeze through and drop onto the opposite side, landing in a flower bed. I'm on my feet in no time, running for the gates. But the boys are already right behind me.

I'm not proud to admit it, yet I can't help but scream as I run. I'm expending valuable energy and making myself look like a real idiot, but being chased is literally the worst thing. I skid out of the gate and around the corner, but I lose my footing and have to grab at the railings. Then my bracelet buzzes and, with a sinking feeling, I know I'm done for.

Except…the light's gone blue. Blue! I'm no longer a Runner; I'm a Chaser. I triumphantly face the boys.

"Ha!" I say. "Who's first?"

It takes a moment for the boys to understand; then they run back through the church garden. I go after Spike. He's as slow as I expected, especially now that he's limping.

"You shouldn't have worn skinny jeans," I say. "You've sacrificed speed for fashion."

"Help," Spike yells. "Mate, some help?"

Blondie doesn't come to Spike's aid. I grab him by the waistband. My fingers touch sweaty flesh, which is revolting. But I hold on tight as he struggles.

"This is what happens when you are a mean person," I say. "You think Anton wants a mean person working for him? No, he doesn't.

Which is why I'm making it my night's mission to protect him from people like you."

The timer buzzes faster and faster, and then his light goes out. I release him immediately and wipe my hand on my jeans.

"Psycho," he snarls and storms off red-faced.

"I'm not a psycho," I call after him, my tone sugary sweet. I smooth down my Anton hoodie. "I'm Anton's number one fan."

I'm also on the leaderboard. I jump up and down in delight as it refreshes, with me in tenth place. My excitement earns me some more odd glances, so I figure it's time to get moving. I compose myself and leave St. Dunstan's little oasis and return to the noisy city. Fantasy Anton strolls at my side.

"Nice one, Lola," he says, his fingers accidentally brushing against mine. "I knew you could do this."

"I'm actually surprising myself," I admit. "I guess anything's possible with a bit of motivation."

"I am very motivating," he says with a wink.

We stop on London Bridge and gaze down the river toward the magnificent Tower Bridge. The water sparkles where the sun hits its ripples, and all these boats bob along so peacefully. A light breeze catches my hair, and I'm filled with this feeling of pure joy that makes me want to laugh out loud.

"This city is so beautiful," I murmur.

"Yeah, totally," Anton says, and I can see that he's staring at me, not the river.

I shake my head. That isn't quite right, so I rewind a few seconds.

"This city is beautiful," I say.

"So beautiful," Anton says, his voice catching. He reaches out to brush a stray hair from my face. "So, so beautiful."

No—that's too soppy. I've ruined the fantasy now, and Anton's vanished.

"I'm going to find you," I tell the empty space. "I'll win this game, and then you'll finally see me."

With renewed determination, I set off for the Natural History Museum, where Anton's second stunt was filmed. Back when my mom last took me there, she was still trying to be a mom, and there was a giant diplodocus taking center stage in the atrium. By the time Anton staged his stunt, my mom had checked out and the dinosaur had been replaced by a whale. I shouldn't blame the whale, I know.

That stunt was the first time I saw Anton. We were visiting Roger at his house, a few weeks before Mom abruptly moved us in with him and his son. We sat squished together in the living room, with its garish daisy-print wallpaper and clashing curtains, chosen by Roger's first wife over a decade ago. Roger and Mom chatted and laughed, leaving me sitting awkwardly on the edge of the sofa beside Matthew.

He was a selfish ass even then. Slouched into his seat, he rested his feet on the coffee table and spread his legs so far apart I had to huddle into a ball to avoid being touched by his knee. He spent the whole time playing on his phone, chuckling to himself.

I was bored. So I peeked over his shoulder at the video he was watching. I kept a lid on my curiosity for a full ten minutes until I couldn't take it anymore.

"What is that?" I said.

He looked up, surprised that I'd dared to speak to him. "This? Oh, it's a stunt me and some friends filmed the other day. I'm uploading it once I've looked it over."

"A stunt? Bikes jumping through rings of fire?"

He laughed and shook his head. "Nah, nothing so daring. It's more of a prank or a practical joke. People make millions out of this sort of thing. We're going to be huge."

He shuffled closer to me and restarted the video. Anton and the Accomplices—Anton, Matthew, and Beatrix back then—were dressed in Halloween skeleton costumes. They were filming themselves as they ran around the museum, chasing each other and tripping over their own feet, unable to talk for laughing. A couple of security guards were trying to stop them, but the skeletons kept diving out of the way.

It doesn't sound that funny, except one of the boys caught my eye. He was at the center of everything at the museum. I'd never seen someone so animated. Someone so confident. So loud and hilarious. The boys I knew at school talked in grunts and mumbles, making jokes about their balls and farting on the bus. But he was different. Everything he said was clever and witty. When he took off his mask, he was beautiful, with glossy hair and sparkling eyes.

"This is really good," I said, taking the phone from Matthew's hand.

"Yeah?" he said. "Thanks. You know, you should come and meet Anton and the lads sometime. We're having a party in a few weeks. It's going to be legendary."

Of course, this was back when Matthew was still making an effort to be nice to me. Before he decided I was beneath him and unworthy of dating his friend.

"Anton," I repeated, unable to take my eyes off the beautiful boy. That was where it started. The moment I fell in love.

I stop walking. A flashing spot on my map has caught my

attention. There's another contestant—Emma98—nearby. We're both Chasers, so it's not like I'm in any danger—but it's weird that I can't see them anywhere. According to the map, they should be right here.

Suddenly, a hand clamps over my mouth and someone drags me down a concrete ramp into a poorly lit underground parking garage. I struggle, but they're too strong. My GPS signal fails, and I realize with horror that I have five minutes before I'm out of Anton's game. I bite down hard on their finger.

"Ouch," a girl's voice says. "I just wanted to talk to you without being recorded!"

Their grip loosens and I jump around, raising my fists into a fighting stance. The figure is hard to make out since it's so dark in here. Also, she's wearing a wide-brimmed hat and trench coat like she bought a comedy spy costume off the Internet. I lower my hands slightly and squint at her.

"What do you want?" I say.

"The truth," she says meaningfully. She takes a voice recorder out of her pocket and holds it in front of her. "I'm a reporter. Or I want to be one day. For now, I'm covering Anton's game from the inside for my school paper."

I cross my arms. "Does he know?"

"Not exactly. But he loves publicity, right?"

She has a point. "I'm listening."

"You're Charlotte, Matthew Bright's sister?"

Not the direction I thought this conversation would go in. "Stepsister-to-be. What about it?"

"My name's Emma Sano and—"

I gasp. "Wait, you're the girl who tried to sell that story about

Matthew's affair. You took it to the tabloids. He told me about you!"

"Did he also tell you how Anton's lawyers threatened me with all sorts of trouble that terrified my parents?" She shifts slightly, and I get to see the outline of her features. She looks even more like a teenager playing dress-up now, with her smooth, straight ponytail and metal braces. "I had to drop the whole thing. But it wasn't like I'd get much money for a story about Matthew anyway. I just wanted to get noticed."

"Well, I believed you. Why else would he have been pictured in his underwear leaving a hotel if he weren't cheating?"

"Exactly. But he's not why I wanted to talk to you. I'm more interested in Rose."

I step back from her, our brief camaraderie gone. "What about Rose?"

"I was at the party where she died. Or I was for a while at least. Matthew threw me out when he realized I was taking photos for an article on Anton and his team. Ever since then, I've wondered what really happened that night. I overheard some of them arguing and—"

"Wait, what sort of article?" I interrupt.

"All those rumors of fighting between the Accomplices? And the drug and alcohol use at Anton's parties? It was going to be a super cool exposé that I could have pitched to real magazines. Only then Rose died, and the parties stopped."

"No. I'm not interested. You're a parasite, and you need to leave poor Anton alone." I turn on my heel and march away. "Don't you think he's been through enough?"

"Don't you think Rose went through enough?"

I ignore her and hurry up the ramp into the open. My GPS signal returns, and I breathe a sigh of relief. There's no time to dwell on some wannabe journalist. I have a game to win. When tonight is over, I'm determined that no one will think of me as Matthew Bright's sister ever again. It's time that they saw me for who I really am.

ERIN

I am going to destroy him.

Gray26, pretending to be harmless and vulnerable, with his pretty-boy looks and skinny black jeans—when, all along, the scheming bastard had some girl waiting in the wings to help him cheat. The cheating is understandable. It's the fact that someone who looks like an emo hair model got one up on me that really pisses me off.

And the fact that I didn't see it coming.

The thought makes me squeeze my cardboard cup too hard, and a fountain of lukewarm black coffee erupts from the top. "God damn it!" I yell, hurling the cup at the wall and shaking liquid from my hand.

My map updates, and I spot another contestant sneaking toward me. I'm a Runner, so strictly speaking, I should be running. But

I'm too angry to put up with anyone trying to chase me. Instead, I march in their direction with my hands in tight little rage balls.

The girl halts when she sees me coming. "Oh my god, it's you. I can't believe this."

"Take a photo. It will last longer."

Her eyes widen like I've slapped her.

"Come on, then," I say. "I fucking dare you."

She opens her mouth like a fish. I roar at her—a guttural noise of pent-up frustration and fury—and she scampers. Coward. I lean against the wall and try to get my breathing under control. Amber will be furious that I'm not making more effort to be *likable*. But it's actually liberating to not give a shit.

My phone rings. I worry that it's Amber, but it's Jesse. At last. I was beginning to think he was ignoring me. Usually, he's the one texting me all the time. I sit on the edge of the sidewalk and answer. "I was wondering when you'd call."

"Yeah, I know, I know. Some of us have to work for a living," he teases. "And it's not like you need my help or anything."

He's right. I'm winning the competition by an easy margin. Of the thirty contestants tagged out so far, I've gotten six of them. Like I said, I'm done being a princess with lowered eyes and a pretty smile. I want to be the scary monster with teeth for once.

"Anton will start choosing favorites soon," he continues. "You're obviously up there, with Sean23 and Char02."

I recognize one of those handles. Sean23's been almost matching me for points the whole time. They're my only real competition. I scan the leaderboard and find Char02 in ninth, with two tags. "Why is the last one a problem?"

"I overheard Anton FaceTiming Matthew about her. She's

Matthew's little sister, so he wants her out of the contest. Obviously Anton is going to keep her."

"To piss M off?" I have to be careful what I say in case someone's listening in on my feed and realizes one of Anton's crew is helping me.

"Anton doesn't like being told what to do. And he thinks it's funny that she's entered."

"Poor boy." I laugh, thinking about how much Matthew must be quaking in that muscle tee of his.

Jesse goes quiet. He hates Matthew almost as much as he hates Anton.

"Are you there?" I say.

"I can't stand this. You running around all tarted up while Anton and Matthew play you like a pawn."

It upsets me when Jesse gets jealous. Don't get me wrong—it's flattering that he cares so much about me. But he acts as if I'm some naive kid who can't handle boys like Anton and Matthew. I'm no pawn. If they're the king and his knight, then I'm the opposing queen.

"They only think they're in charge," I say. "We're going to show them."

"Yeah. I can't wait to be out of this hellhole. You and me, babe. Just us." He moves the phone to his other hand with a rustle. "All right, so the first challenge. That's why I called. You need to be heading for the Natural History Museum."

I eye my map. It's a bit of a trek. Gray26 is heading there too. This could be my chance to take him down.

"I'm here now, setting up. If we bump into each other, you'd better pretend you don't find me irresistible, or I'll lose my job."

"I'll try to hold myself back."

"Hold yourself back from Matthew too. If he even looks at you the wrong way, I swear—"

"I can deal with him," I interrupt.

"Yeah. I know." He must step outside as his voice is partially obscured by traffic noise. "Win this thing, Erin. We need this."

"Love you," I say, but he's already gone. Usually, talking to Jesse makes me feel warm on the inside, but this conversation has left me uneasy—slightly grubby—and I don't know why. There's no time to dwell on it. I jump to my feet and break into a jog. I have thirty minutes to get to the challenge and two miles to run. I can do it in twenty-five, though, even in these shoes.

It's exhilarating pounding the pavement with the cool breeze against my face. Amber doesn't like it when I go out running—it's too sweaty and unattractive according to her. But it's one of the few times that I feel free and the only way I can meet up with Jesse. I plan my runs to coincide with the time he gets off work at a local guitar shop.

When I first met Jesse, he was a member of Anton's security team and a general drudge. Jesse hated taking orders from Anton and Matthew. He put up with the bullying and impossible demands because he's a grafter who rarely turns down a paycheck, plus he wanted to get into the music industry and Anton had contacts. Then Rose died and the operation shut down.

Nearly a year later, Matthew called Jesse to offer him his old job back. Jesse came to me right away and told me his plan—to trick Anton out of the prize money and then disappear. We let Amber think entering me was her idea. In reality, Jesse had everything mapped out long before she even heard of the game.

Before I know it, I've reached the tree-lined street on which the museum is located. The museum has just closed for the evening, and there are dozens of families with small kids milling about outside. I stop for a few moments to catch my breath and stretch my calves. When I walk on, my bracelet turns white and I lose my map, so I must have entered a geofenced area. That means there will be no Runners and Chasers for this challenge.

The red metal gates leading into the museum grounds stand slightly ajar. I walk up the path toward the building. It's huge, with intricate stone carvings and an impressive arched entranceway that reminds me of a cathedral. I pause. Materializing from the shadows, then disintegrating again are smoky specters with glowing red eyes. *Shadow City* ghosts. I was wondering when Anton's baby would rear its ugly head. The speaker in my smart glasses crackles close to my ear. "Erin, you made it just in time," Matthew says. "Your mission is to rescue Anton from the ghosts. He is somewhere inside the museum."

I raise an eyebrow. "He's in the museum? I thought he was in his home office."

"Shush," Matthew says. "Use your imagination."

I eye the deserted entrance. "You have permission for us to be here?"

Matthew chuckles. "Of course not. There are thirteen ghosts inside, each worth a different number of points if you can exorcise them. Once they've been found, Anton's location will be revealed. The first person to reach him will win the final points. At the end of the challenge, the person with the highest score wins a special prize. Anyone with zero is out of the game."

I hesitate outside the doors. "Wait. Out of the whole game?"

"Yup. Still want to play?"

"I'm not playing." I take one of the foam swords propped up outside. It's black and white checked, like a QR code, and when I lift it, my smart glasses turn it into a glowing axe. I spin it on my palm and step inside.

"Last one in." This time, Matthew's voice is real rather than coming through my speakers. I spot him standing inside the doors, slouching up against the wall with his quiff sagging over one eye. He's changed into a tight white T-shirt, paired with the biker pants. He's filming me with his action cam.

I angle my body to look my best on camera. "I like to make an entrance. Get myself noticed."

He smiles joylessly and puts the camera away, immediately dropping the friendly act. "You should watch out for the security guards. Maybe try *not* being noticed for once. You get caught and no one's going to rescue you."

"I can rescue myself," I say.

"I don't doubt that." He strolls outside and gently closes the door.

The atrium is vast and empty like a cave. It smells of the ghosts of café food and screaming children. Without visitors, it feels wrong. Somewhere I'm not supposed to be. The dusky space is lit up with glowing blue lights. They illuminate a huge skeleton suspended from the ceiling. A blue whale, I believe. Its jawbone is the size of a car.

At ground level, there are fewer lights, so everything is shadows and dark nooks. Arched tunnels lead out of the atrium into other wings of the museum or small side rooms housing more exhibits. Hurried footsteps make me duck behind a display case. A security guard comes jogging down the stairs and across the main hall.

"It's a bunch of kids with foam swords," he says into his radio. "No, I don't know how they got in."

He tries the front door and, finding it unlocked, swears under his breath. He throws the bolts.

"They were moving toward the Earth galleries. Head them off."

The radio crackles with a reply that I can't make out.

"They've put up cameras to record themselves? I'm going to kick their asses," the man barks. "No, hold off on the police for now. We'll be in deep shit for not securing the building."

I wait until he's gone, then slip out of my hiding place. I could let myself out. Escape into the night and live to play another challenge. But I'm not going to do that. Instead, I head to the left, in the opposite direction of the security guard. Thirteen ghosts, Matthew said. It's time to go hunting.

I venture down a long corridor, my feet echoing on the stone floor. Growing up, my mother never brought me anywhere like this. We were always too busy with modeling shoots or interviews or filming. A museum crammed full of noise and smelly bodies— ugh, I would have hated it. At least, that's what I tell myself.

Suddenly there's a terrible scream. It sounds like a murder. As quickly as it started, it ends. I walk on, this time turning slowly on the spot so that nothing can creep up on me. I weave through a room of dinosaurs—some skeletons, some fiberglass models. There's a suspended metal walkway overhead. I hear footsteps, but when I look up, they stop.

There's so little light I can't tell if there's someone up there, watching me from above. But I do spot a small camera attached to the wall. I'm presuming this is part of what Jesse was talking about when he said he was setting up for the challenge. I blow the camera a kiss and continue on my way.

The shadows shift, and a shape peels itself from the wall. I've played *Shadow City* on my phone a few times, but it's different through the smart glasses. The specter is human shaped but not. Its limbs are too long and its fingers trail almost to the ground as it moves. Where there should be features, there's nothing but two glowing red embers in a gray stretched-skin face.

I ready myself with the sword, but right then, a security guard appears in the doorway. His flashlight flicks its long beam from wall to wall. I quickly jump back and slip behind a model of a raptor. If I stay dead still, he might miss me. The man slowly paces toward my hiding place, and so does the ghost. It reaches its arms out, and its face tears open to reveal a gaping mouth breathing out wisps of smoke.

"Uh-oh, you're in trouble," Matthew's voice taunts in my ear.

The ghost drifts closer on legs made of smoke. If I move, the security guard will spot me, and I'll not only be out of the competition, but I'll probably be arrested. The guard approaches. If he comes much closer, then he'll see me. The ghost opens its mouth into a wide black hole that takes up most of its face. Its lips are ragged, split skin.

Then there's a shout from a neighboring gallery, and the security guard runs toward it. I quickly bring my axe up and slash it across the ghost's torso in an X shape, then strike it in the heart. It explodes into smoke.

"So close," Matthew says. Is it me, or does he sound disappointed? "Congratulations on making it on to the leaderboard with twenty-five points."

I open the menu on my smart glasses, and a leaderboard drops in front of the real world. I'm in fourth place, behind Char02—Matthew's sister. Gray26 is at the bottom, with zero points. I don't know how I feel about him flaking out of the contest thanks to his own ineptitude. It's not the revenge I was hoping for.

I exorcise two more ghosts, and soon, I'm top of the leaderboard. Sean23 is in second place. Gray26 is yet to score. With eleven of the thirteen ghosts found, it won't be long until Anton's location is revealed and someone scores big.

I walk through the deserted galleries. Every now and then, I hear a scream or running footsteps. I step into a long narrow room full of stuffed mammals. They're creepy in the near dark, with their shriveled black lips and glass eyes. I'm so busy staring at them that I nearly miss a familiar figure lurking in the narrow gap between a display case and the wall.

Shiny hair, sparkly leather jacket, jeans too short for his skinny legs, air of confusion. He seems to be having a conversation with a stuffed polar bear's butt.

"I'm trying," he whispers. "But this game terrifies me."

"Who are you talking to?" I say.

Gray26 jumps and thuds against the glass. His arms and legs do an impression of a panicked octopus as he falls out from behind the display case. "Whoa, where'd you come from? You scared the life out of me!"

"Keep your voice down," I hiss. "You'll get us arrested."

"Why'd you think I'm hiding in here?" he says, grinning. He removes something from his ear and tucks it hurriedly into his pocket.

I'm suddenly hit by a surge of unexpected fury. Here I am, giving this game everything, and he's *hiding*?

"I don't know what you think's so funny," I snap. "You'll be out for good if you don't score some points."

His face falls. "Maybe that would be for the best." He sighs.

"Then quit," I say. "Leave the competition for those of us with the balls for it."

I walk away with a swish of my hair. My long fingernails dig into the palms of my hands. I don't understand why I'm letting this dopey-ass boy get to me. He's not particularly hot or interesting or a threat to me. Maybe that's the problem. He's *nothing*, and still he got one over on me.

"Thanks for the pep talk," Gray26 shouts after me, laughter in his voice.

"Go blow a koala," I snap without looking back.

Outside the gallery, I lean against the checkerboard bricks to catch my breath. *Hold it together*, I tell myself. I'm winning this thing. Gray26 doesn't matter. He doesn't need me to send him out of the competition. He's doing that by himself.

Footsteps approach, and I figure Gray26's decided to continue our conversation. I quickly duck into an unfinished exhibition titled *Ghosts of the Past*. It's about technology that can save endangered and extinct species, or it will be once everything's been unpacked. At the moment, there's a maze of poster boards, crates that spill over with packing material, and a few animal specimens.

I hear something. I stand on tiptoe to look through a gap between empty display cases. The gallery is unlit and quiet, like a held breath. Suddenly, someone kicks my knee out and shoves me in the small of my back. I fall face-first into a crate, swallowed by reams of suffocating plastic.

A bang. No light. A series of heavy thuds thunder through the small box. A nail gun, I realize. I struggle to turn on to my back. I kick out, but the box's lid doesn't budge.

I'm trapped in this coffin-like crate, and there's no way out.

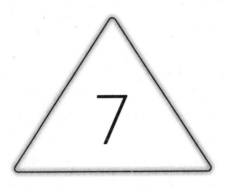

GRAYSON

"What do you mean, she has a point?" I cross my arms and glare at the taxidermy lion, with its accusing eyes and disapproving frown. "I have balls!"

But I am no predator. I'm tall and skinny and weak. If I were one of the animals in the cabinet, I'd be some kind of goat. A slow-running prey animal.

I came here for revenge, but I'm a coward. The little goat inside me keeps bleating that I'm making a fool of myself. I came here hoping to ruin Anton's game/life. I'm rapidly realizing that hatred is not the same thing as a well-thought-through plan. Now I don't know if I should go home or soldier on.

One thing is for sure: I can't stay here, hiding among these dead things. I need to do *something*.

The leaderboard updates as the last of the thirteen ghosts is exorcised by Sean23. A new flashing spot appears on my map, in the main atrium. The final points. The boss level. I sigh and force myself to move.

I'm on my way when I hear a hollow knocking sound, like pounding at the door. It's accompanied by a muffled cry. I stop. If Lenny were talking in my ear, she'd tell me to leave it. But I took the earpiece out when Erin19 got the jump on me. So I'm alone with my own poor decision-making abilities and endless capacity for self-sabotage. I follow the noise into a gallery closed off to the public.

The banging gets louder as I walk between the half erected displays. A familiar voice yells and swears from inside a wooden crate. I have no idea how she got herself trapped, but I allow myself a few seconds to enjoy the sounds of sweet, sweet karma before I look around for something I can use to pry the box open. I find a broom.

As soon as I've loosened a corner, Erin19 kicks the lid off the crate. She scrambles free, tangled in Bubble Wrap. "What did you do that for?" she yells, shoving my shoulders.

I duck aside. "Thanks for rescuing me, Grayson, I appreciate it, Grayson. Yikes."

She blocks my path, hands on her hips, eyes wild. "*You* trapped me in there!"

"No, I didn't," I say slowly. "Can you step aside? I have a game to lose."

"You've already lost," she snarls, marching away.

I don't have the energy to bite back. I follow her out of the gallery with an empty feeling in my chest. I should be happy to have the decision taken out of my hands. This way, I won't have to deal with the feelings Anton's game is dredging up. Except Rose will still be gone, and Anton will still not give a shit.

We reach the end of the corridor. Erin19 stops abruptly and I bump into her. There are about twenty people standing in the atrium wearing identical smart glasses. Most must be contestants, but I also spot Matthew and Beatrix among their number. Everyone is looking up at the ceiling.

"What are they doing?" I whisper to Erin.

She shrugs. We step out of the arched walkway, and I look up. Through my glasses, there's a strange disturbance in the air. It's like looking through shimmering water at a distant light. The light is getting closer.

"What the hell? This isn't part of the game," Matthew says.

It's weird seeing him in real life after watching him online for so long. He's a walking advertisement for masculinity, with his gym body and the way he takes up more space than he needs. Beatrix, small at his side, is his polar opposite, with her vintage clothes and quirky hair.

Whispers start up as the light grows brighter and brighter. I move to shield my eyes, but then I remember that what I'm seeing isn't real. It's projected on to the lenses of my glasses like the *Shadow City* ghosts.

At the center of the light, a figure materializes. It flickers like it's losing signal. I can't quite make it out. Finally it settles.

But it's not another one of Anton's computer-generated ghosts.

It's a girl, translucent and edged with smoke. And she can't be part of the game. Because Anton has spent the good part of a year distancing himself from this person. There's no way he'd conjure *her* into existence.

My legs go wobbly, and I have to support myself on the wall. It feels as if someone's cut my strings, and I can't remember how to stand or move or breathe. This isn't possible. It can't be real.

"Hello, losers," Rose says. "Do you want to play a game?"

The ghost has her red-lipped smirk. Her thick shiny curls and heavy brows. An oversize sweater so big that it skims her knees and covers her hands. I remember that sweater. It was her favorite.

But it can't really be her, can it?

Because Rose is dead.

"You'll love this game," Rose purrs, her voice breathy in my ear.

Only it's not quite her voice. It sounds like it's coming from a very long way away. It crackles and distorts, and so does her ghost. Her edges are indistinct. Any second now she'll disintegrate.

"I'm imagining this, right?" Beatrix says. "Insomnia and energy drinks have addled my brain."

Matthew snaps out of his open-mouthed inaction. "The feed's been hacked. Get through to Anton HQ. Now," he says, pointing at a shell-shocked crew member.

"Is she real?" Beatrix whispers. "She looks real."

"Of course she's not. Someone's gotten clever with a green screen and a face-swap filter."

I don't believe him though. The transparent projection is jerky and keeps flickering from 2D to 3D. Her face has an avatar-like quality, not quite real. But in my heart, it *feels* like it's her. I'm not sure if I should throw myself at her feet or run far, far away.

"Do you want to hear a secret?" Rose continues. "My death wasn't an accident. I was murdered."

The graffiti outside the tunnel. *I was murdered.* I slump to the floor. This can't be happening.

"That's a lie!" A blond girl with Anton's ugly face on her orange hoodie pushes through the other contestants to address the whole room. "Everyone knows she took drugs and then knocked herself out in the swimming pool."

She's right. I attended the inquest into Rose's death, or some of it. The room was stifling and packed with journalists. By the time they started talking about the details of how Rose died, I felt like I couldn't breathe. I had to run outside.

I read about it the next day. *Death by misadventure. Drugs and alcohol involved. Drowning. No suspicious circumstances.*

It didn't matter. I already knew who was responsible.

Rose flickers. "Do you want to find out who did it? Here's a promise for you all. By the end of tonight, everyone will know *exactly* who killed me. And to make it more exciting, I'm going to let you do the hard work and figure it out. Six suspects, six secrets. One murderer."

She clicks her fingers, and a giant spinning prize wheel appears next to her. It's like something from a game show. Each of the six segments is a different garish color and marked with a black silhouette and a question mark. There's an arrow at the top and a swirly red circle in the middle, like a piece of candy.

Six segments, six suspects. With a grin, she spins the wheel. It makes a rapid clicking noise as the arrow races past each suspect, the colors blurring into one. It doesn't show any sign of stopping; it just spins and spins.

"Oh my god, this is a total disaster! We need to get this shut down," Beatrix cries.

"You think they're not trying?" Matthew retorts. "Will *someone* get Anton on a call already?"

"We can't get through," a crew member replies. "She's locked us out of everything. Our phones, the smart cams, even *Shadow City*. I don't know how. It's like she's…"

"She's what?" Beatrix says, holding a hand to her mouth.

"Like she's not broadcasting from this world," the man replies.

"Don't be ridiculous," Matthew says.

"Do you want to see something cool?" Rose whispers, the wheel spinning and clicking. "I think you do."

A screen unrolls on my lenses, and a video plays.

———

It's Anton and the Accomplices. The four of them are standing in the street as a Lamborghini burns violently behind them. The noise of the flames is enough to make me sweat. I don't remember seeing this video. Perhaps it was never released.

"What the hell were you thinking?" Rose shouts, squaring up to Anton. She's wearing an expensive leather jacket over a summer dress, lips painted red, hair long and loose. She looks so *alive*.

"It was a prank." Anton laughs, holding up his hands in playful defense. He has tattoos down both arms that clash with his big nerdy spectacles. "I didn't know it would literally explode."

"You could have killed me, you narcissistic asshole!"

"Please don't argue." Beatrix intervenes, stepping between them. Two-tone hair, scruffy Converse. "No one's hurt, are they?"

"And here comes sweet little Beatrix, rushing in to protect her brother," Rose snarls. "Grow up, Beatrix. They don't deserve your loyalty."

"Why do you have to be such a bitch?" Matthew interjects.

"I give you a month, tops." Rose steps closer to Matthew. They're the same height, but Matthew's built much heavier than her. She jabs a finger against his sternum. "You'll cheat on her like you cheated on the others."

"Stop it," Beatrix shouts, on the verge of tears. "All of you, stop it."

Anton laughs. The flames crackle and roar, and he throws his head back, mouth open, tears in his eyes. With the fire lighting him up in reds and oranges, he's almost demonic.

Rose rounds on him, and I think she might hit him. Rose always did have a temper. Then the fight goes out of her, and somehow, it's even scarier. "I'm done. I'm just done."

Anton removes his glasses to wipe his eyes, still laughing. "What do you mean, *done*? Come on, Rose."

Rose's voice is level. "I mean I'm out. I'm not doing this anymore. I've had dozens of sponsorship offers. Collaborations. Public appearances. Fuck, Anton, *look* at me. I can make ten times the money that you pay me. And bonus, I won't have to put up with your bullshit anymore."

Anton's smile fades. He goes very still. Behind him, Beatrix and Matthew exchange worried looks.

"You're setting up your own rival channel? No, that's not happening," Anton says quietly.

"You don't get a choice in it," Rose says. "You don't own me."

"I made you!" he screams, all spittle with veins pulsating in his neck. "And I can end you just as easily."

Whoever's filming the argument laughs nervously. Anton notices the camera for the first time and storms toward it, his face contorted.

"Turn that off. Right now. Turn it—"

The video ends.

———————

Everyone in the hall is silent. That was a very different Anton from the one we usually see. No charm—just animalistic bloodlust.

Rose claps her hands. "Fun times, right?" She grins. "That was recorded a few weeks before I died. Makes you think, doesn't it?"

"Where did she get that video?" Beatrix whispers. "Has she hacked into Anton's computer? That's the only place there was a copy."

Matthew stands next to her, slowly shaking his head, arms hanging limply. The clicking on the prize wheel grows slower and slower. The arrow drags itself into the purple segment and stops. Rose peels the silhouette off the wheel, revealing a photo of Anton beneath.

"Give it up for our first suspect," she says. She is no longer smiling.

"Anton wouldn't," the blond girl in the orange hoodie whispers. "He's not a murderer."

"Tonight is under my control now. You're playing *my* game." Rose salutes us like Anton does in his videos. "Play on, *Accomplices*."

Then, just like that, she vanishes.

CHARLOTTE

There's a big moment of silence after Rose disappears. Everyone stares at the spot where the ghost was standing. It feels like the air's been sucked from the room.

"Was that part of the game?" a familiar voice asks. I groan. It's Blondie—a.k.a. Sean23.

"It's a stupid prank, that's all," Matthew says. "One of Anton's competitors trying to be funny."

"But how did they hack into *Shadow City*?" I say. "Anton has his own servers. They'd need to know his passwords."

No one says anything.

"The game's going to continue though, right?" I say, glaring at Matthew. He doesn't reply.

My lenses flicker, and a glowing cartoon Anton appears on the landing at the top of a wide flight of stone steps. The avatar turns slowly in the air like he's in suspended animation.

"The game's coming back online," Beatrix says, nervously sucking on one of her braids. "Please say Anton's back."

"I can't log in." Matthew is jabbing at a mini tablet with his big thick fingers.

"Have you tried restarting?" Beatrix makes a grab for the tablet, but he snatches it away.

"I do know how to use the program I designed," he snaps.

High heels tap toward us. "Is that avatar part of the original challenge?" a stuck-up voice says.

It's the influencer Erin Love, the one with the ridiculous mother-daughter lifestyle channel and the perfect everything. She used to come to Anton's parties, and I saw enough to confirm that she's bad news.

"I can't believe you're still thinking about the challenge," I mutter, even though that's what I'm thinking about too. "Obsessed, much?"

With a curl of her lip, Erin Love looks me up and down. Her eyes rest on my Anton hoodie. "Obsessed? You're one to talk."

I draw myself up to my full height. "Except, unlike you, I'm here for Anton, not the money and definitely not the fame."

"Good for you." She turns to Matthew and Beatrix. "You said the game's back online. Does that mean the final points are still in play?"

"Um, maybe? You'd have to ask Mr. *I Designed the Program* though," Beatrix says. She makes a face at Matthew, who is chewing his lip, too absorbed by his tablet to answer.

Erin Love's intentions crystallize in my mind. She's worried that she won't win the challenge. She's planning to go for the final points. I look at her the exact same moment that she looks at me. The smugness of her expression makes my teeth prickle. *What. A. Cow.*

There's no way I'm letting her get to Anton first.

We both move at the same time, racing toward the glowing avatar on the landing. According to the leaderboard, I'm in third place. Those final points will be more than enough for me to win the whole challenge. I push my legs to pump faster.

She's ahead as we reach the bottom of the stairs, but there's a boy standing in the way, and shoving him aside slows her down. I make a grab for her and get hold of a fistful of hair. She cries out in pain and surprise as her head whips back. She swings an elbow at me, but I duck out of the way.

Sucker. I scramble up the steps on my hands and knees. The avatar is so close. But then Erin yanks on my hood so hard that I slip down a few steps. I lose my balance and hit my chin on the cold stone, making me bite my tongue.

"Girl fight!" someone yells. Sean23, probably.

I wrap my arms around Erin's ankles and resort to the most anti-social weapon I have—my teeth. Erin screams as I clamp my jaws shut on a chunk of her unfeasibly toned calf muscle. It's like trying to chew a piece of vacuum-packed meat.

"What the hell is wrong with you?" Erin yells. "Get off!"

I can't answer as my mouth is full. I know it's a really horrid thing to do. I used to get in trouble at elementary school for getting angry or overexcited and biting my classmates. The other children used to call me Bitey Charlotte, to distinguish me from Nice Charlotte, and there were a few years when I didn't get invited to any birthday parties.

But desperate times call for desperate measures.

"Grow those goddamn balls," Erin spits. I don't understand for a second, but then I realize she's not speaking to me. She's addressing the boy at the bottom of the stairs. He has long hair and pouty lips, and he'd be handsome if it weren't for his annoyingly bewildered expression.

"Oh," he says. "Yeah! All right."

Are they working *together*? That is in no way fair.

The boy takes the steps two at a time, and I realize with horror that he's going for the avatar. There's nothing I can do but scream as he launches himself through the air, arms outstretched. Fireworks explode. Music plays. It's over. My heart sinks, and I limply release Erin Love's leg.

"You saved me, you saved me," Anton's voice cries. "We have a winner."

The leaderboard flashes and the names rearrange themselves. I end up in fourth place, which seriously sucks, especially as Erin Love still wins overall. The boy—his handle is Gray26—has jumped into second, and Sean23 is third. I leap to my feet. "That's not fair," I cry. "She cheated!"

I look across the atrium for support, but all I find is a sea of horrified faces. Everyone is staring at the three of us with open mouths. None of the other contestants have moved from where they were standing when Rose appeared. None of them even tried to win the points.

I self-consciously pat down my hair and straighten my glasses. "You all saw her pull me over," I say.

Matthew's eyes widen to match his gaping mouth. "You serious? You *bit* her."

"Oh, of course you're siding with *her*," I say. "And in front of your girlfriend too."

"Don't," Matthew snaps.

We're interrupted by the sound of canned applause. Something drops from overhead. It floats slowly to the ground, followed by another something, and another. Fifty pound notes. There are hundreds of them, falling from a net suspended from the ceiling.

"It's money!" someone shouts.

At this, the other contestants rush forward, grabbing handfuls of the notes. They were all quick to judge me for wanting to win the challenge, but now that there's money involved? The only contestants not moving are me, Erin Love, and Gray26. The three of us stand there, staring up at the high ceiling as the money falls.

One of the notes lands on my face. It sticks to my skin, cold and kind of moist. I peel it off, and to my horror, the plastic is clammy with what has to be blood. More money falls, and the other contestants start to notice. They back away with sticky hands and full pockets.

"Blood money," Erin Love says, raising an elegant eyebrow at Matthew. "Is *this* part of the game?"

"No," he says, his voice shaking. He turns on the spot, squinting into the dark alcoves. "Someone else set this up."

"Like who?" I say. "That nasty ghost?"

"It's not... Ghosts aren't real," Matthew says weakly.

"They totally are," Beatrix says. "Obviously not *this* one. I think. But the point stands, if you want to be strictly accurate..." She goes back to chewing her hair.

Erin picks up a larger bloody piece of paper. A word is scrawled across the front in smudged blood. *LIARS*, it says.

"It's the coroner's report on Rose's death," Erin explains.

"Does this mean Anton had something to do with it?" a contestant asks. "Did he pay someone to fake the coroner's report?"

"Of course not!" I cry, rounding on her. "He would never."

I look to Matthew for backup. His eyes are haunted and unblinking. "Anton had an alibi for that night. He couldn't have killed Rose," he says flatly.

Right then, two security guards skid around the corner. I'm kind of relieved, to be honest. We could do with some actual adults taking control of the situation. The guards stop when they see all the money and all the blood dripping down from the empty net hanging overhead. "What the…?" one of them says.

"Go, go, go," Matthew says, shoving me in front of him. "Everyone, run."

The security guards shout at us to stop but no one does. "Wait," I say, but Matthew keeps propelling me forward.

"Do you want Anton to get in trouble?" Beatrix says. "This could ruin him."

"What? Oh no!" I gasp.

"Just keep moving," Matthew says.

I stop trying to resist. We race down a passageway behind the stairs into an empty café. It's eerily open with lots of little round tables and a high ceiling. Our footsteps echo as we pass through. Behind me, there's more shouting. I don't check to see if anyone's been grabbed by the guards. Beatrix shoves open a fire door. There's a black van with a smashed front headlight parked on a narrow access road. Matthew yanks the sliding door, but it's locked. "The keys!" he shouts.

Beatrix pats her pockets. "I gave them to Jesse so I wouldn't lose them."

Matthew spins around. "What's he doing? Having a nice chat?"

I follow their line of sight to a familiar-looking man with sharp features dressed in baggy clothes. His sleeves and hands have blood on them like he's helped himself to some of the tainted money. He's talking to that cheating Gray26 outside the museum doors, a bloody hand gripping Gray26's arm to stop him from leaving. Gray26 looks terrified.

"Jesse! You have the van keys!" Matthew shouts to him.

Jesse breaks away from Gray26. He fumbles with the key fob to unlock the van. He heads for the driver's side but glances over his shoulder at the younger boy several times. As he passes me, I remember where I've seen him before. He was at the party where Rose died. He knows what I did.

"Everyone get in," Beatrix says. "Come on!"

I scramble inside the van. Gray26 climbs in too, banging his head on the roof. Karma. Beatrix squeezes into the back with us contestants, squashing me against the wall. We're not all going to fit. The van was already half-full of props for the game, and there are a dozen contestants left outside. Erin Love must realize this as she shoves her way to the front of the crowd.

"No more room. Bad luck." She climbs in and yanks the door closed. The ten or so contestants outside shout and hammer on the side of the van, but seconds later, we screech up the access lane.

The van turns out onto the main road as several police cars come careening past in the opposite direction. I say a little prayer, but they don't chase us. All the same, I don't start to relax until Jesse has driven us a mile away, into a busy, built-up part of the city.

We stop at traffic lights. It's getting hot in the van. Everyone's crammed in together, but no one's talking. We're sitting on the floor. Erin Love has ended up next to me, and her meticulously waved hair is tickling my face. On my other side, Gray26 is pretzeled up into a space much smaller than he is. He jiggles his leg, making the floor vibrate. The whole time, he's staring nervously at the back of Jesse's head.

Suddenly there's a loud slap. Erin Love has reached across me to slam her hand down onto Gray26's knee. She holds it for a second to make her point, then releases him without saying a thing. He keeps still after that.

In the front of the van, a phone buzzes. Matthew quickly answers. "Anton, mate," he says quietly. "We lost you for a while."

Everyone holds their breath to listen in.

"No, dude," Matthew says at last. "We can't hire an exorcist... I don't know what that was, but it wasn't real. Look, we need to consider if this game is worth..." He sighs and closes his eyes. "Yeah, I know. Your game, your rules."

"Let me talk to him," Beatrix says, wrestling Matthew's phone from his hand. "I know, I can't believe it either. Yes, some of them are here with us now." She eyes us contestants in turn. "Gray26, Erin19, and Char02...yeah, Matthew's Charlotte."

I flush with pride that Anton knows who I am.

"We'll drop them off in five," Beatrix continues. "Yeah, we cut the feeds right away. Most of the others were stopped by the security guards... Really? We leave them?"

Beatrix tosses the phone to Matthew. He holds it to his ear and listens but doesn't say a thing. Then he hangs up. "Well, he's in a panic back at HQ. But it looks like the game's still on," he says.

I lift my arms in a little cheer, but no one else joins in. The van pulls over and, one by one, we are dropped off. They've spaced us out so that when the game restarts, we're not right on top of each other. Matthew says it will be ten minutes tops. They just have to sort out a problem with the audio not coming back online.

"You'd better fix this," I say to him, as I step down onto the sidewalk. "All of it."

He presses his lips together in a tight line. Beatrix waves enthusiastically at me as she slams the van door closed. She drops the smile a second too early. I think the stressful situation is getting to her.

I look around. They've left me across the road from Paddington Station. The entrance to the concourse is a huge yawning mouth. The warm lighting inside makes me realize dusk is starting to fall. The people in this part of the city seem to sense this, and everyone is hurrying toward their trains like they don't want to be caught outside when the sun goes down.

I wander along the main road. It's all fast-food joints and restaurants, and electric buses that feel too big to be so quiet. I buy a bagel to keep myself nourished, then relive the events of the museum while I wait for my map and wristband to reactivate. This time, I imagine I'm not merely a dumbfounded observer.

"I've been waiting for you, Rose," I say, pulling off my hoodie and jeans to reveal a formfitting bodysuit. "Or should I say…Erin Love."

I punch the ghost through its chest, and the projection shatters. I'm not sure how that would work, actually. Maybe I'm holding an interference device in my hand and it cuts the signal… That part's not important.

"You can't stop me!" Erin pulls this huge gun from her boot and aims it at Anton, and it's not his avatar anymore, but the real him. She fires!

In slow motion, I throw myself toward Anton, shielding him with my own body—

My wrist buzzes, shocking me back to reality. It's a shame since I was enjoying the daydream, but I'll return to it later. The next second, everything else comes online. A video call instantly opens. It's Anton. I can't tell you how happy I am to see his face.

"Baby, I'm back," he says. "How's it going, Accomplices? I'm hoping you can hear me. I can see your feeds, but the audio is no longer working. Someone give me a thumbs-up in front of their glasses so I know you're getting this."

I do it right away.

"Amazing, that's perfect." He grins, and it lights up his whole face. He's such a colorful person, with his rainbow hoodie, purple hair, and a slight pink flush to his cheeks. But when he smiles? My heart just can't.

"We can switch on your microphones manually, so it's not like we can't talk," he says. "But I can't listen in on you anymore, which sucks because some of you are so damn funny."

I laugh, trying to remember if I've said anything amusing.

He claps once. "So that challenge was wild, right? We filmed so much amazing footage, and I promise I'll make a video out of it."

My good mood pops like a balloon. It's just my luck that the first time I get to appear in an Anton video, I get humiliated by Erin Love. Urgh, I can still taste the fake plastic of her pants.

"So you're wondering about that ghost we met," Anton goes on. There's a pained edge to his voice now. "Got to say, that was a bit of a surprise."

He laughs, but it's clear he's putting on a brave face. Poor Anton. All that hard work, ruined.

"But I'm back in control now, and I'm confident *my* game will continue without further interruptions." He pauses, staring into the camera, more serious than I've ever seen him. "I would, however, like to find out who was behind that bad-taste prank. I'm pretty sure this is an inside job of some kind. One of you isn't who they say they are."

I gasp. Erin Love! She's obsessed with money, as fake as cheese puffs, and borderline evil. I'm almost completely sure that this isn't my jealousy speaking. She's probably being paid to interfere with the game or something else nefarious.

"I want you to watch your competition like a hawk. There's ten thousand pounds on the table for information," Anton says.

I snort. I'll take down Erin for free. This game is everything to me. Anton is everything to me. This sort of thing is exactly what Lola does in my stories. If I can make it up, then I can do it for real. You can do anything with love on your side.

"I need you to find out what you can," Anton says. "A-OK?"

"A-OK!" I say back. "I've got this, Anton."

"The next challenge will be announced in an hour. Plenty of time to do some investigating first." He vanishes without saluting us goodbye.

I check my bracelet. The game of tag is back on, and I'm a Chaser. Perfect. I find Erin Love, a.k.a. Erin19, on my map. Her spot's a big diffuse area thanks to her winning that last challenge. The memory of her dragging me to the ground resurfaces, and my bruises throb angrily.

"Whatever she's up to," I say to myself, "I'm going to stop her."

"I knew you'd have my back," the Anton at my side says. "Just like last time."

ERIN

I can always tell when Jesse is worried. His ears turn red. So when I saw him talking to Gray26 outside the museum, the sides of his head a glowing pair of beacons, I knew something was going on. He knows how much I hate it when he keeps things from me. It reminds me of my mother.

That's why, after the van drops me off, I follow Jesse's location on my Friend Finder app. At first, his position moves around the Paddington area as he drives the other contestants to their restart positions. Then it stops. He's less than a mile away in Lancaster Gate, so I go looking for him.

Ten minutes later, I turn onto a street of expensive white houses, each with dozens of windows and several floors. The only color is a phone booth, as red as blood. I don't see any sign of life. I suppose all these buildings are owned by incredibly rich people who live elsewhere, apart from one boarded-up hotel covered in scaffolding.

I call Jesse, and it rings and rings. I lower the phone to my side and listen. I hear something. I hurry around the corner, and that's when I spot him. He's holding the ringing phone, but he's not answering. Then he presses the Call Reject button and returns the phone to one of the pockets in his baggy cargo pants.

Hurt flares like gas on flames. "Jesse?" I call out.

He nearly jumps out of his skin, then quickly leaps behind a van with a hand up to shield his face. "Erin! You can't be here."

"Something's wrong, and you need to tell me what it is. You can trust me." I chase him around the van.

"The only thing wrong is that we can't be seen together. If Anton clocks me on your feed, the game's over for us."

I stop. Oh. I'd forgotten. I was so desperate to find out what he's hiding. But Jesse's not my mother. I shouldn't be judging him by her standards.

"I'm sorry." I sigh, bumping my head back against the van. "I didn't think."

"No. You didn't." He takes a slow breath. "We most likely got away with it. The audio feeds from the smart glasses are still offline, and Anton has enough on his plate, so I doubt he was watching."

"Sorry," I repeat.

"I know you're sorry," Jesse says, his tone clipped like he's still cross with me. "Try to remember how much we need that money. It's the only reason I'm letting my girlfriend do this shit. If there were another way…"

"I know. And I'll get the money."

He sighs deeply. "I didn't tell you because I didn't want to worry you, but I kind of owe this guy a few thou, and—"

"What?" I interrupt. "I've told you how I feel about being in debt, Jesse!"

"You're seventeen, Erin. Wait until *you're* twenty-three, and we'll see how your ideals are holding up in the grown-up world." He doesn't usually talk to me with such venom, but then his tone softens. "It's no big deal, all right? Just make sure you win."

I nod; then—realizing he can't see me from where he's standing—I clear my throat. "I'm going to win. I'm top of the leaderboard, aren't I?"

"See if you can do it without flirting with anyone," he mutters, and suddenly his surliness makes sense. Jesse's jealousy is a constant presence in our relationship. He only has to see me talk to another boy and he starts with the accusations.

"I haven't flirted with anyone." I bristle.

"Every time I checked up on your location in the museum, you were with Gray26."

I close my eyes and force my tight shoulders to relax. I know to walk the fine line between reassuring him when he starts on one and not engaging with his paranoia.

"Is this why you were talking to him outside? What did you say to him?" I ask. It wouldn't be the first time Jesse's embarrassed me by threatening another boy. I won't be able to look Gray26 in the eye now.

"Keep away from him, all right? I don't want you talking to him. I've got to go."

He jogs off across the road. I watch him go with a hollow feeling in my belly. I want to run after him and bury my face in the loose gray hoodie he wears, but I can't. I need to be strong. Grown-up. I can do this.

I look down at my phone and notice that his location is now showing as "not found" on Friend Finder. He's switched off location services. It feels like he doesn't trust me, or maybe it's punishment for talking to Gray26. I tell myself everything will be better after tonight. Only, for the first time, I can't help but worry that nothing will ever be enough for Jesse.

I bottle my feelings up so that I don't cry. Grown-up. In control. I break into a slow trot. By the time I've made it a couple of streets away, I'm holding it together again. Everything's fine. Jesse and I are fine. Every relationship has its challenges. This is the price of not being alone.

An alert flashes on my lenses as I receive an incoming call. My microphone switches on, and Anton's call screen unfurls, along with the words *Private Message* at the top of my field of vision. I stop walking and wait for him to speak.

"Hello, Erin," he says. "It's been a while. How are you doing?"

He doesn't care. It's not like we're friends or anything. We just did a number of online collaborations over a year ago, all monopolized by my mother. Back then, Anton always treated me like a little kid. A lot has changed. My patience when it comes to small talk, for starters.

"Why did someone hack into your game pretending to be Rose?"

"Straight to the point." He laughs, sweeping his purple bangs out of his face. "But I suppose it is why I called you."

I wait for him to clarify what he means.

"I've been trying to get to the bottom of this Rose business. Safe to say, she was a bitch when she was alive, and she's still causing me trouble, so…" He stops speaking. It looks like it's an effort to control the temper we witnessed in Rose's clip. "Don't quote me on that."

"Do you seriously believe the ghost thing's real?" I can't keep the disbelief out of my voice. "Matthew seemed to think it was a filter."

"Of course I don't believe." He scoffs. "But ghosts don't have to be real to kick us in the balls. She—whoever *she* is—made a lot of reputation-damaging allegations. I want to know why."

"Not sure where I come in."

"Gray26 is acting suspiciously. I saw him talking to someone earlier, and it's made me wonder who exactly he is."

"You mean…" I stop myself in time. I was about to say Jesse. But I'm not supposed to know Jesse. "Um, you saw someone on his feed?"

"I want you to follow him for me. Use your feminine wiles to find out what he's here for and if he was involved in the ghost thing." His grin is worthy of a magazine cover: bright, with a troublemaking sparkle to his eyes. He's enjoying this part. "I know you already have it in for him."

I pick at a tear in my cuticle, pulling a strip of skin painfully from my finger. "I do?"

"You didn't save him at the museum out of the goodness of your heart. You want to be the one to send him out of the competition."

At least there's no camera on me so he can't see the surprise on my face. I hadn't realized my intentions were quite so obvious.

"There's twenty thousand in it for you, and I'll stack the contest in your favor. It's a good deal."

I still my hands. It really is a good deal. So why do I feel grimy at the thought of taking it? I don't mind cheating, but to have Anton personally help me? I'm not sure.

"Why me?" I say.

He laughs. "I know you, Erin. Or enough about you. You're clever, cunning...desperate. You're leading this competition for a reason, and I need someone like you on the inside. Someone who's up to this task."

I clench my teeth so hard my jaw aches. God, he's such a patronizing ass. He's calling *me* desperate? But I need the money more than I need my principles. And it's not as if spying on Gray26 doesn't play into my own plans for revenge. "All right," I say.

"Perfect. I'll check in with you soon."

"Is it true?" I say. "What that piece of paper at the museum said? *Was* Rose's death really an accident, or did you buy someone off?"

His eyes crinkle in amused delight. "You're overestimating the reach that my good looks and money afford me. The only thing I bought was a team of the best lawyers, and they...made it all go bye-bye through the proper legal channels. All I had to do was keep my mouth shut."

"That sounds like you hid something from the investigation."

His smile freezes; then his screen vanishes.

He's so full of crap, but I don't have to like him to take his money. I find Gray26 on my map. Anton was right. I didn't help Gray26 win those points at the museum because I felt sorry for him. I want to let him get within inches of the thing he desires most in this world, then crush it beneath my boot and laugh in his face.

Following him is easy but boring. For the best part of half an hour, we circle Hyde Park, avoiding the other contestants. Then a text comes through on my phone. Amber's noticed I have deviated from her plan.

Eyes on the prize.

Side mission, I reply.

No time for that. I have a lot riding on this game.

The wording of her text makes me freeze in my tracks. It's the way she says "I" instead of "we" like she usually does. There's something she's keeping from me, and past experience tells me what that something will be.

An icy feeling of dread courses through me. No. She wouldn't. Would she? I'm hit by the memories of bookie receipts in her pockets, my childhood piggy bank smashed on the floor, my possessions vanishing overnight. I used to believe her when she told me she had it under control. Now I know better than to trust anything she says.

She's the reason I hate liars.

I take a slow breath, then reply: How much?

The pause while I wait for her answer tells me everything I need to know. She's bet money on me winning this competition. Money that we can't afford to lose. I slam my fist into a plastic bus shelter, making the people on the opposite side jump. I can't believe this. Every fucking time. Once, I felt sorry for her. Now I'm just tired.

The truth is, behind the public glamour of my mother's life, there are a dozen maxed-out credit cards. Yes, she gets all sorts of freebies—manicures, facials, highlights, and Botox. If you watch our channel, it looks like we're rolling in cash. But it's a lie. Half the stuff we promote, we need to return. And the money we make from ads gets sucked into the black hole that is her gambling habit.

Her favorite thing to bet on is the celebrities she claims to know personally. *Is so-and-so pregnant? Will that actress go to prison or get community service? Who's going to win* Love Island? Sometimes, she'll stake tens of thousands of pounds, utterly convinced that she has the insider knowledge to guarantee she can't lose. She usually loses it all.

Her reply finally arrives. It doesn't matter. Stick to your part of the bargain and leave the business decisions to me.

Business decisions? Ha. But maybe this is a good thing. If I win, I can take my prize and run, while the money she makes keeps her occupied until I'm far, far away. If I lose, then it's more of the same. Scrounging free tampons from the library because my mother won't buy them, then posing in a thousand-pound bikini.

But I'm not going to lose.

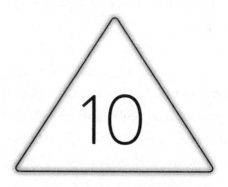

GRAYSON

Rose, Rose, Rose, Rose, Rose.

The ghost has gone, but I can still feel her, hiding in the corner of my vision.

She's haunting me.

When I blink, I see flashes of her face, and my imagination runs away with itself. I picture her smiling. Laughing. Lying dead in Anton's pool house, blood trickling along the grouting between pristine white tiles.

The word *murder* keeps replaying in my head. Murder, murder, murder.

I can't bear to imagine what must have gone through her head during those final terrifying moments. I want to tell myself her death was a tragic accident. An overdose. Slippery tiles. Knocked unconscious. Drowned without knowing what was happening to her.

It's not true.

I need to focus on something that's not Rose. I put Lenny's earpiece in and switch on the mic. I pray that she's listening. "Lenny? Are you there?"

There's a long silence. A rustling. "You're back, then?" she eventually says. "Don't think I didn't notice that you took your earpiece out the moment Erin Love appeared on the scene."

"You've caught me," I say, trying to sound light.

An office chair squeaks as she sits down. "Are you all right? You sound out of breath."

"Just having a minor breakdown." I lean against a lamppost for support and tell her everything. Rose's appearance, her claim that she was murdered, how she's planning to reveal all the suspects in her death. Lenny listens in silence. She's always been a good listener.

I hear her rapping her long nails on a table. "And you're panicking because you're worried you'll be one of her suspects?"

It's like being slapped in the face. "What?" I gasp. "Why would she…? You can't believe I had anything to do with it?"

"If you've ever watched a true-crime documentary, you know it's almost always the ex-boyfriend."

"Thanks for the support," I mumble, scuffing my toe in a sandy path through the park. "But no, how could I have killed her? Anton kept her locked away in his house, and people like me don't get invites to his parties."

I don't know why I'm defending myself. Surely Lenny's not accusing me of murder.

There's an awkward silence, and then she clears her throat. "Do you think it was really her, come back as a ghost to seek justice?" I can't tell if she's mocking me or not. She laughs softly. "Oh, of course you do. So…what happens next?"

It's an impossible question to answer. Something I've always liked about Lenny is she doesn't try to solve my problems for me like some girls do. I'm not a project. But right now, I wish she *would* tell me what to do. Because I have no idea how to get myself out of this mess.

"Mostly, I want to go home." I rub my face, the adrenaline draining from my body and leaving me bone-achingly weary. "But I need to find out why she's creating this game. Why doesn't she just tell everyone what happened to her and get it over with?"

"Maybe she can't remember." Lenny snorts. "Being buried for a year has to mess with your memories."

"I'm not ready to joke about this yet. Or ever," I mutter.

"Yeah. Sorry. Maybe she's hoping this game of hers will force the killer to give themselves away. I mean, it's not like a ghost can go to the police. She needs evidence."

That makes sense. The thing is, I knew Rose. And Rose wasn't someone for games. Whatever this is, it's dangerous. The only safe way to play would be to walk away, but I can't.

I still love her, and I still hate Anton.

"Tell me what to do, Len," I whine. "I'm totally unequipped for this sort of thing."

Lenny goes quiet while she thinks. She's never been one to fill a silence for the sake of it. There's the rustle of a potato chip bag being opened.

"You have to keep playing," she says through her mouthful. "It's the only way you'll ever be able to let her go. Besides, it sounds like she's wrecking Anton's game. You must be enjoying that part."

I smile. A little. My wristband buzzes a warning to get moving again, so I follow the path out onto a busy junction. I wait to cross the road with the last of the evening's commuters on their way home after work.

"All right," I say. "Anton thinks this is an inside job. Maybe one of the other competitors or a crew member knows how Rose is doing this. A ghost didn't string up that money net. She must have had help."

"Ye-ah," Lenny says, drawing the word out. I know she thinks I'm ridiculous for believing that the ghost is real. She no doubt shares Matthew's opinion that it's computer trickery. But she's a good enough friend that she never mocks me for my supernatural beliefs. Much.

"I could start by asking around and seeing if anyone—"

"Uh-uh. You start by making sure you stay in the competition."

"I came second in that last challenge, didn't I? I'm in the top ten on the leaderboard."

"You won't stay there if you don't start playing for real."

I don't want to play. Not Anton's game, not Rose's. But Lenny has a good point. Reluctantly, I open my map with a flick of my eyes. I'm a Chaser, which is good, and there are contestants within walking distance of my position, a few of them Runners. I spot Erin19 but decide against it. Char02 is nearby too, but she's also a Chaser.

"Neil39 or Emma98," Lenny says. "Take your pick."

"Let's go with Neil," I say. "I knew a Neil at school, and he was a dick."

Neil Bayer. I hated him. He'd dated Rose when he was fourteen, and had taken it badly when she dumped him. Thinking about him—thinking about school—brings a pang of regret.

Up until Rose left me, I'd had plans. I wasn't the smartest in my class. I wasn't super popular or particularly cool. But I had an eye, as my art teacher put it. I figured I'd grow up and go into fashion or interior design or floristry. Something where style mattered.

Rose laughed at my ambitions. She was beautiful, and people often thought that meant she cared about her appearance. She could throw on a pair of my old jeans and some red lipstick she got free with a magazine, and people would instantly want to interview her for their street style column. In reality, she only cared about her appearance insomuch as it opened doors for her.

Like that clip of Rose arguing with Anton. *Fuck, Anton, look at me.*

After she died, the school put on a big service for her, and Neil Bayer wouldn't stop noisily sobbing during the readings. It made my marrow boil. Rose hadn't been his, not for a really long time.

"I'm allowed to be sad," he told me defiantly, after I slammed him against the fence in the teachers' parking lot. The service was over, and everyone was supposed to be heading to the football field for our own vigil that would never happen. "She dumped you too."

The rest of our class stood around us in silence as I punched him again and again, his head bashing against the fence as he made no effort to defend himself. That was the final straw with the school after months of me skipping classes, getting into fights, and refusing to engage with the teachers. Being permanently expelled put an end to all my ambitions, but I'd already given up. What was the point of making beautiful things when the one that really mattered to me was gone?

"Grayson?" Lenny says.

I shake off the memories. "I'm here. Tell me what I have to do."

She helps me find my way to the Soho backstreets crammed with people. It's still early, but there's already a buzz to the area. Groups of young people drink cocktails at sidewalk cafés, a mismatch of stylish streetwear and ugly parka jackets. Colorful lights are starting to come on at the front of buildings. I bet it's something special after dark.

When we finally track down Neil39, he's nothing like the Neil from my school. He's much smaller, with white-blond hair that reminds me of a bichon frise. I hesitate. There's something seriously weird about chasing a stranger. So I stand there awkwardly, waiting to see if he notices me.

All of a sudden, he bolts. "Go after him," Lenny says, sounding exasperated. "Catch him!"

I run, but he's already got a good lead on me.

"Take the next right," Lenny tells me. "Wait out of sight, and we'll cut him off."

I do what I'm told. To my surprise, Neil39 doubles back on himself, probably because he was getting too close to the bigger threat of Char02. His spot jumps all over the map, as does mine. The GPS isn't too good around here, with all these tightly packed buildings.

"Stay where you are," Lenny says. "He's coming to you."

"Really? Because it looks like he's on a parallel road."

"That's what he thinks too."

Lenny's right. A minute later, Neil walks right past me. I laugh to myself, then step out of a paved side street and tap him on the shoulder. He jumps as his bracelet countdown activates. He goes to run, but a group of vintage hipster types get in his way. I pin him in a shop doorway with my hand bundled up in his T-shirt. He's smaller than me. It's surprisingly easy.

"Nothing personal," I say. "Sorry, dude."

He struggles, but it's no use. The timer gets to zero, and I release him.

"No hard feelings?" I say.

"Fuck you," he snarls, then stomps off, dropping his smart glasses as he goes.

This is the game, yet I can't help but feel dirty. It's way too intimate, grabbing a person and holding on to them, waiting for their dreams to come crashing down. I tell myself I saved him. Anton's not someone he should be idolizing.

"Good job," Lenny says. "Now go after Emma98."

"Can't I have a bit of a rest first?"

"Stop being such a coward. She's just around the corner."

According to the map, Emma98 is in the same area as Erin19, although it's hard to tell with Erin19's spot being so big. Both of them are Runners, so it's not as if either can tag the other out. Perhaps it's a coincidence. The weirdest thing is, when I get to Emma98's position, I don't see her anywhere.

It's a busy area, with little of the charm of Soho. The crowds are older, many of them heading to the theater or chain restaurants or for pre-club drinks. A group of young men in boring designer shirt, jeans, and smart shoes combos look me over as they pass. I suddenly feel incredibly self-conscious.

I focus on my map and try to understand why I can't find Emma98. "Hang on, I think she's on a five-minute countdown for going out of range?" I say, frowning in thought. "And so is Erin19."

"They must be in the underground station," Lenny says. "The only reason I can think of for doing that is if they wanted to meet without their cams picking anything up."

I hang by a flight of stairs that disappears down into the subway.

There's a tour bus shelter I can hide behind while I wait for them to emerge. A dude in a red jacket keeps trying to hand me a flyer. I nearly buy a weekend pass because I'm that bad at saying no.

Finally, two girls climb the stairs and head in opposite directions. Erin19 I'm familiar with, of course—Emma98 is a stranger. She's slight, with long dark hair tied up in a ponytail and pale skin. She's wearing a gray fedora with a purple ribbon. I'd love to be able to get away with hats, but boys like me in fedoras tend to come across as douchey.

"Grayson, stop staring at her ass and move," Lenny says.

"I wasn't. But point taken." I go after her, having already lost my advantage. She walks fast, with her beige trench coat pulled tight and her smooth ponytail swinging. She weaves through the crowds with impatient efficiency.

Suddenly, she turns. She must have seen me on the map. She backs away slowly with her hands held up. I get a proper look at her. I'm guessing that she's almost my age, but the braces on her teeth make her appear younger.

"Listen," she says. "I can't let you tag me out."

"Leave her alone," Lenny says in my ear, whispering even though Emma98 can't hear.

"It's kind of the whole point of the game," I say, talking to them both.

"I'm not here for the game." Emma98 nearly steps off the sidewalk into the road. A taxi holds down its horn, and several passersby stare at us. Emma98 frowns at me. "Have we met before?"

I haven't met her previously, I'm sure of it. I'm good with faces. "You're just trying to talk me out of trying to tag you," I say.

She doesn't return my smile. "You look familiar."

"Get out of there," Lenny says. "She's not worth it."

"Do you know Anton?" Emma98 continues. "Because I'm a journalist investigating Rose's death. Maybe you can help me."

"Seriously, Grayson," Lenny says. "That girl's bad news."

"I'm leaving now. Don't try to follow me," Emma98 says.

She walks away quickly, looking back at me to make sure I'm not chasing her. A journalist. And she's investigating Rose's death. I'm not sure how I feel about that.

"Len, do you know that girl?" I say, watching her ponytail bob down a pedestrianized street between grand beige buildings.

Lenny doesn't answer. There's rustling at her end.

"Lenny?"

"She was up to something with Erin19. We should be careful who we tag out, that's all. In case they know something about the ghost." She puts on an enthusiastic voice. "There's another Runner not far away. Let's get them instead."

I watch the space where Emma98 vanished. Something very strange is going on here.

"Lenny?" I say. "You've gone crackly; it's deafening me. You there?"

"It's working at my end; why don't you—"

I take the earpiece out and switch off my microphone. Then I go after Emma98.

CHARLOTTE

Erin Love is up to no good. I've been watching her for the past forty-five minutes—in between running from a couple of Chasers and managing to tag out one Runner—and she's *definitely* up to something. First I saw her meeting up with Jesse from the museum, and then, ten minutes ago, she disappeared into an underground station with that reporter, Emma Sano.

My theory is that Erin Love is the mastermind behind this whole Rose's ghost trickery—a rival influencer is an obvious suspect—and Emma and Jesse are her accomplices. I haven't fleshed out the literal details, but I will. My thoughts drift to how pleased Anton will be when I prove Erin Love's deception and save the game.

His fingers lace with mine. "I wish we didn't have to go through all this nonsense," he says. "If I could announce you as the winner right now, I would."

"Tsk-tsk, you can't be seen to have favorites," I tease. "I'm going to win this game fair and square."

"That's my girl." His smile falls. "But not everyone is playing by the rules."

"No, they're not." I watch Erin Love as she pauses to adjust her hair in a store-window reflection. "I wish you'd get rid of her."

Anton doesn't reply. When I glance across at him, he's vanished.

I walk on for a while, using the map to keep an eye on where Erin Love goes. I can't figure out what she's up to. Her route is seemingly random, and she hasn't tagged anyone in ages. I follow her across the cobbled square outside Covent Garden Market. I give her a minute before I go in after her, but all I find are unlit shops and emptiness.

I'm so busy wondering where she's gone that it takes me a moment to process the fact that the shadows are shifting. I watch in horror as dark shapes ooze from walls. Cracks in concrete widen as creatures with glowing eyes squeeze into our world. A puddle ripples, and a figure rises with its arms outstretched. It's *Shadow City*, but real.

I mean, obviously it's not actually real. But it feels real.

"Accomplices!" Anton cries as the video call screen opens. I'm surprised to see that he's slightly disheveled. His hair is hidden under a turquoise baseball hat, and his eyes are bloodshot.

I check my watch. I can't believe an hour has gone by so quickly.

"I'm on to you," Anton says, leaning so close to the camera that I can only make out his left eye and part of his nose. "I'm going to take you down."

Then he throws himself into his chair and picks up a mug before taking a long swig of what I hope is tea.

"Meh. Let's get on with the next challenge already," he grumbles.

"You have probably noticed that you're no longer alone. For the next hour, it's not each other you need to worry about; it's the ghosts. There'll be no Chasers and Runners, just victims."

He wants us to play *Shadow City*.

"You can exorcise them with your bracelets. Make it to the geofenced area by the river—it's marked on your map—and you'll be safe." His voice is dejected, his heart no longer in it. I wish I could give him a hug. He manages a smile. "But be warned: those ghosts will keep on multiplying until they're everywhere, and if one of them touches you…"

Three hearts appear in the top right of my field of vision. He doesn't need to explain. Three lives and I'm out.

"Let's see how many of you can—" His signal abruptly cuts out, and he vanishes. As do the ghosts.

"Anton?" I say. "Anton, are you there?"

My vision flickers, and I think he's coming back, but it's not him.

Rose appears, the big spinning wheel next to her. Her image crackles, jumping from place to place. Then she settles, bright against the seeping dusk.

"What's up, losers?" she says, laughing at us all. "Hands up, who thinks it was Anton who killed me?"

"No. Never! You're such a B-word," I cry, getting some weird looks from a couple of people passing through the deserted market.

My heart's going like a sparrow's. I can't believe she's back. Anton was so sure he'd regained control of the game.

"If it wasn't Anton who murdered me, then maybe it was someone very close to him." Rose spins the wheel, and it noisily turns before eventually stopping on another of the silhouettes. She rips the paper away. "Everyone, I give you my second suspect: Matthew Bright."

She clicks her fingers, and a candid photo of Matthew appears. He's rushing down the front steps of a boutique hotel like he can't get away fast enough. His silly face is panicked and wide-eyed. It's obvious he's done something really, really stupid.

I remember this picture. Some random person happened to take some photos, and they ended up online. Emma Sano interviewed the photographer and wrote a whole article about how Matthew was having an affair. She tried to sell it to the tabloids, even though I doubt anyone really cares who Matthew sleeps with. Except maybe Beatrix.

Emma's whole story was based around how he wasn't wearing any pants in the pictures. Everyone got to see his embarrassing boxer shorts: fuchsia with little yellow rubber ducks on them. My mom bought them for him as a joke Christmas present, and that somehow made the whole thing feel even more sordid.

"Who was he at the hotel with?" Rose says. "Was it an affair, or something else?"

I snort. Of course it was an affair. Why else would he have taken his pants off? A rogue spider?

"In the run-up to my death, Matthew and I were seen arguing on numerous occasions. Let's imagine I knew the truth about what went down at that hotel," Rose says. "What if I threatened to tell Beatrix? Did Matthew kill me to save his relationship and protect his nice little position in Anton's inner circle?"

I think about it. The cheating, I can imagine, but murder? It's not that I don't believe Matthew has it in him to kill. I'm just not sure he's clever enough to get away with it.

"Everyone knows Matthew's pre-Beatrix reputation for sleeping around, but she changed him. Right?" Rose's expression turns monstrous. "Except people don't change, and when they show you who they are, believe them."

She has a point. I didn't buy into Matthew's personality make-over when he got together with Beatrix. They're so different. I could never understand why he'd be with her, unless it was a ruse to get close to Anton.

"Anyway, I have to go," Rose says, smiling again. "Enjoy *my* game, won't you?"

She vanishes, leaving behind the mental equivalent of a really bad smell. At first, I'm unsure what to do. I wait, hoping that Anton will return and tell me everything's fine. But the only icon on my smart glasses that works is the map, plus none of Anton's *Shadow City* ghosts have rematerialized. I suspect he's still locked out of the system.

It's up to me. First off, following Erin Love isn't working. I need to find a way to come at her from another angle. I think about how Emma said she was interested in finding out what happened to Rose. Then she met up with Erin Love. Now a photo Emma tried to sell gets a starring role in Rose's suspect reveal. Emma's involved. I need to find out what else she knows.

So I follow her spot on the map. Since her chat with Erin, she's gone west. This part of the city is disorientating. It can go from beautiful old buildings to intimidating office blocks within the space of a few yards. Emma appears to be inside a building site surrounded by a tall blue fence. The weirdest part? Erin Love and Gray26 are here too, according to the map. I *think* this is a good thing. Three birds, one stone. Or something like that.

I follow the perimeter until I find a gap big enough to poke my head through. The building site is like Doctor Who's TARDIS. It's much bigger on the inside. There are piles of dirt and sand compacted by the treads of heavy vehicles. Metal girders and huge sheets of wire mesh lie stacked up everywhere, and plastic orange fences mark the edges of the deep foundation pits.

I hesitate, unsure if I really want to go inside a deserted building site, and without a hard hat, no less. I bite my lip. Then I remember that Anton could be watching my live feed right now, and I don't think he'd be very impressed at what a coward I'm being.

I imagine that Anton's narrating my progress, making jokes and clever observations. Everything becomes slightly less terrifying. "Obviously you have to investigate," Anton's fantasy narration says. "The footage will be epic."

I nod. My heart hammers as I squeeze through the gap in the fence. The rough wood catches at my hoodie, but I make it through. My teeth chatter. I pick my way past big blocks of concrete and scaffolding poles, turning my head to give my camera a good view of everything. Check me out, being a professional even in the face of danger.

I check the map again. It's hard to pinpoint where either Erin Love or Gray26 are since their location spots are fairly large. Emma's is more precise because she's low down on the leaderboard. I creep closer to her. Then I step out from behind a partially erected wall and meet Erin Love, posing against a digger like she's trying to sell it.

I gulp. "Erin," I say, feigning surprise. "I can't believe you're here."

"I know, it's *such* a coincidence," Erin says. "How are you, bestie?"

"Not great," I say. "You cheating me out of those points at the museum wasn't very nice."

Erin laughs quietly. "You're still upset? I'd have thought your brother being accused of murder would put things in perspective."

"Stepbrother." I sniff. "And Rose wasn't murdered. Her death was an accident."

"You sound very sure. Were you there?"

I feel my blood rush to my cheeks. "I was at the party, yes. You were too, if I remember correctly."

Erin's perfect lips quirk into a faint smile like she's amused by the memory. Then she strolls off, already bored with our conversation.

I run after her. Got to keep my friends close and my enemies closer. "Wait, what are you doing here? Are you following Emma too?"

"The journalist? No." She points as Gray26 trips out from behind a pile of dirt. "I was following him, although *he* was following Emma."

Gray26's face freezes as he spots us. "I was, um, looking for somewhere to pee?" The effort of coming up with that lie was way obvious. "Who are you?"

"I'm a friend of Anton's, and I'm investigating this ghost business for him," I say. "My name's Charlotte."

"Grayson," he says, giving me an awkward little wave.

"Charlotte's also Matthew Bright's sister," Erin says, examining her fingernails. "For full disclosure's sake."

I take a deep breath. "Stepsister. Erin Love is just here for the fame."

Erin grins. "Actually, it's the money I want." She walks off again, pleased with herself. "Let's talk to Emma, then. Seeing as you're both so interested in her."

"No, I'm not…" Gray26 trails off when he no doubt realizes that neither Erin Love nor I are falling for his lies. He follows me. I follow Erin.

Emma's spot is ahead, jumping about in the darkness of what

will eventually be a block of apartments. At the moment, it's all metal supports and concrete slabs and a whole lot of shadowy places where anyone could be hiding.

Exchanging looks, we tiptoe closer and closer and…

"There's nothing here," I say, turning on the spot.

"That's not entirely true." Erin unhooks something from an exposed bolt. It's a tracking bracelet, which, based on my location map, belongs to Emma.

A pair of smart glasses lies crushed on the ground, blood splattered on the broken lenses.

ERIN

I examine the tracking bracelet. It's still active, so it can't have been here for long. Emma must be close by.

"Do you think she's been kidnapped?" Charlotte whispers. "Or worse?"

"This can't be happening," Grayson says.

He's staring down at the smart glasses. There are several drops of blood on the crack-frosted lenses, like someone stood over them with a nosebleed. It's not much blood at all, but Grayson's clearly panicking.

Anton suspects him, and who am I to argue with twenty thousand pounds and a leg up in this competition? But come on. Grayson couldn't scheme his way out of a paper bag. No way is he involved in something as sophisticated as hacking into Anton's game and pretending to be a ghost.

But if Anton wants to pay me to follow him and find out what he's up to, then that's what I'm going to do. He's scared. This could be my chance to get closer to him. The only problem is Charlotte.

I dust off my hands and sigh loudly. "Oh well. I guess she's gone. We'd better go our separate ways before the game restarts."

I wait, hoping that Charlotte will take the hint and leave. She doesn't.

"No. We're going to work together to find Emma," Charlotte says, sounding a lot like a schoolteacher. She looks like one too, with her serious haircut.

"We are?" Grayson finally tears his eyes away from the blood.

"I promised Anton that I would save his game from whoever it is trying to sabotage him with this Rose nonsense." Charlotte looks meaningfully at me, as does the ridiculous drawing of Anton on her hoodie. "Emma is a journalist investigating what happened to Rose, and now she's vanished. She has to be important."

"You mean she's not just another contestant?" Grayson says.

Grayson is claiming he doesn't know who Emma is, yet he was clearly following her. Perhaps there is something to Anton's suspicions, after all.

Charlotte continues. "Emma was undercover at the party where Rose died, but Matthew threw her out." She pauses to gasp loudly. "I wonder if she saw Matthew being naughty."

"She found me less than an hour ago, wanting to know what I remembered from that party and if I'd seen anything odd," I admit.

"What did you tell her?" Charlotte asks.

I shrug. "That I don't remember anything."

"That's *interesting*," she says. "Something else *interesting* is that Emma vanished moments before we got here. Where were you, exactly, when that happened?"

"Where were you?"

Grayson steps between the two of us with his hand raised. "Um, I'm seriously confused, so I'm going to...go."

"Wait," Charlotte and I say in unison. We glower at each other.

"I thought we were a team," Charlotte says.

He shakes his head, swishing his mane of hair. "I'm not interested in teaming up. I've got Len... I mean, I'm a lone wolf. And also, I don't trust either of you."

He has a point. But I'm yet to meet a boy who can't be won over with a flutter of my eyelashes. I force myself to smile at him. "If you want to go it alone, that's fine. I guess I thought we were friends after what happened at the museum."

To my surprise, he doesn't bite. "Friends? Is that why you fixed it so I'd get those points?"

"Ha, so you admit you cheated?" Charlotte cries.

I ignore her and keep my attention fixed on Grayson. "It's not all about the money for me. The thing is...I knew Rose."

"You knew Rose?" His voice changes from steely to wistful in a split second. Got him.

"I collabed with Anton and the Accomplices a number of times. She always seemed nice." This isn't true. Sure, I met Rose, but she wasn't nice. Patronizing and arrogant would be a better description. Poking her nose in where it didn't belong. "I feel like I'm part of this. Like I owe it to Rose to play her game," I finish.

"Liar," Charlotte grumbles. "You never liked Rose."

"And you did?" I snipe, silencing her.

Grayson frowns and shakes his head like it's full of wasps. Just then I notice a *Shadow City* ghost rising out of the dirt behind him. Anton must have wrestled control of the game from Rose and restarted the challenge. I'll save Grayson, and he'll realize he needs me. Smiling to myself, I step forward and lift my arm to swipe the ghost away.

Charlotte gets there before me, leaping past both me and Grayson. With a dramatic slashing movement, she draws a cross in the air and then punches the ghost through the heart. It explodes into writhing black dust that streams into the pink-hued sky.

"You're welcome," she says sweetly, blowing on her fist.

Grayson gapes, wide-eyed, like he can't believe how close he came to being caught by the ghost. "Thanks, Charlotte." He checks for more ghosts, then takes a shaky breath. "I guess it wouldn't hurt if we stick together for a bit."

They walk away together, leaving me silently seething. Charlotte is sharper than she initially appears. I need to up my game if I want to come out on top. We climb through the fence and onto the road. Passing cars have their lights on now, and the reds and whites glow as brightly as the projected display on my smart glasses.

"Let's think about this rationally," I say. "Emma could have gone home, but she didn't strike me as someone to give up easily. We can presume she's still determined to write her article. That means she either ditched her bracelet and glasses to avoid being followed, or someone grabbed her and... What are you doing?"

Charlotte has dropped to the ground and is crawling on the sidewalk. "I'm searching for clues. There might be tire marks or—"

"Get up already. You're being ridiculous!"

She stands up and holds out a finger to me. The tip is red with blood. "In the time it took you to insult me, I found a trail. She must be bleeding, but at least she hasn't been driven off by a kidnapper. This way."

I growl under my breath as Charlotte sets off, her short hair bouncing smugly. We don't find anymore blood, but it doesn't matter. Emma was on foot, walking in the direction of the river—and the end point of Anton's latest challenge. All the contestants are heading that way, not to mention Anton's helpers. Most likely Emma's going there too, hoping to find the next installment for her story.

We fall into an uneasy silence, broken by the occasional appearance of Anton's *Shadow City* ghosts. They're easy enough to exorcise at the moment, but they're becoming more frequent and faster moving. I usually find *Shadow City* pretty tame, but the ghosts are scarier now that darkness is falling.

"We should get to know each other a bit better," Charlotte says, breaking the quiet. "What's your favorite Anton video ever?"

"Um, I haven't watched that many," Grayson says.

Charlotte gasps and covers Anton's ears on her hoodie. "Well, you should. They're hilarious! One of my top moments was in 'Lost in the Maze.' Anton had this huge hedge maze in his old garden, and it was in the shape of his face. Anton and the Accomplices recorded themselves with drones running around the maze, shooting at each other with paintball guns. Matthew got hit in the boy parts. I laughed and laughed."

"You and Matthew aren't close, then?" Grayson asks, wincing.

"Not in the slightest. I literally hate him. I don't know why Anton and Beatrix put up with that big cheat-face."

"Do you have any evidence of his affairs though?" I say, just to be contrary.

"I don't need proof." Charlotte sniffs. "You can smell the lies on him; it's a horrid, sweaty musk. Like Rose's ghost said, people don't change. Hmm, she seemed very angry, don't you think? Maybe she was having an affair with him."

Grayson stops walking at this, and his jaw goes painfully tight. Interesting.

"Did *you* know Rose?" I say mildly.

He hesitates. "No."

Liar.

"Why would I know her?" His voice goes a bit high-pitched. "I'm here for Anton. Love him."

"And yet you haven't seen any of his videos?" Charlotte crosses her arms.

"Um, I have, I… The zorbing one was good. When they went zorbing in Greenwich Park and Anton got arrested."

Again, interesting. He picked one of the few videos where Anton suffered the consequences of his rule-breaking behavior. Rumor has it the fine was massive.

"I always liked the ones with just him and Rose," I say, making my voice and face as innocent as possible. "They were such a cute couple."

"Most of that was faked for the cameras," Grayson says in a soft growl.

He speeds up so he doesn't have to walk with us. Also interesting.

As we get closer to the river, the *Shadow City* ghosts become more and more frequent, although there's no sign of Anton. We're forced to keep turning on the spot to make sure nothing creeps up on us. I exorcise three ghosts and Charlotte gets four, but I console myself with the knowledge that she's a long way behind me on the overall scoreboard. I'm winning, and winning easily.

We pass by an unlit park, surrounded by a low metal fence. I spot something. Crossing the busy road, I lift a torn hat off one of the fence's vicious spikes. It's a gray fedora with a purple ribbon.

"That's Emma98's hat," Grayson says. "What a waste."

Charlotte gasps. "She *has* been kidnapped. Or eaten by a bear."

"Or she's hiding from us in the park," I say. "Come on." I check that there's no police around, then pull myself up and over the fence.

Grayson clumsily follows but Charlotte looks horrified. "That's so dangerous. One slip and it's death by impalement."

"We both made it fine," I say, following a path lit by old-fashioned streetlights. Away from the city traffic, it suddenly feels much more like nighttime. "You stay out there if you want."

A heavy thud announces that she's more or less made it over without serious injury. She runs to catch up. "I went through a phase of watching a lot of old public information videos," she says. "Spike fences are right up there with playing on railroad tracks and falling into quicksand."

"Quicksand?" Grayson says. "Really?"

"It's a misnomer, actually. Quicksand is liquid mud. It's a non-Newtonian solid with a varying viscosity depending on the application of force."

"I'm so glad you're here to educate me." Grayson laughs, but it's a friendly laugh, not the mocking one Charlotte deserves. "You're a bit of a brainiac, or what?"

"I'm a writer, actually. I do a lot of research for my, um, stories." She goes a bit red and stops talking like she's said something she shouldn't have.

I bite my tongue. I'm aware of what a non-Newtonian solid is too. Back before my mother decided to homeschool me so we could concentrate on her channel, I was acing all of my subjects, especially science and math. It never crosses anyone's mind to wonder if I'm smart though. They're usually too busy staring at my chest.

"Did you hear that?" Charlotte says, stopping abruptly.

I squint past the yellow light of the streetlights into the shadowy trees beyond. A second later, someone rushes straight for me and knocks me to the ground.

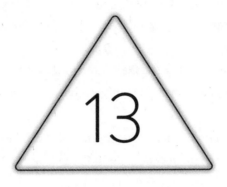

GRAYSON

Erin and Emma98 tussle on the ground, punches and kicks flying. I hover uncertainly. Erin lands a fist on Emma's cheek, and I flinch.

"Stop it right now!" Charlotte shines the bright light of her phone's flashlight on them. "What would Anton think?"

Erin judo rolls away from the other girl and rises to her feet with her fists raised. She appears to be unharmed—and somehow as polished as ever. Emma stands up less gracefully, her previously neat ponytail coming loose. She sways slightly, then tentatively touches a swollen cut on her temple. I turn away from the sight of the dried blood. "Whoa. I didn't hit you that hard," Erin says.

"This wasn't you." She leans against a bench, lit by a flickering streetlight. It turns her into a clichéd detective from a trashy novel, with her trench coat and ugly high heels.

"Why did you attack me?" Erin says.

"I heard voices and thought you might be planning to hit me with a scaffolding pole. Again. I was already swinging when I realized who you were."

. "That's where the blood at the building site came from." Charlotte slaps a hand to her mouth. "Oh my goodness. Was someone trying to kill you?"

Emma shakes her head, then winces. "Truth be told, I'm not a hundred percent sure the pole didn't fall on me by mistake. I thought I heard footsteps but…head injury."

"You ditched the bracelet so no one could find you," Erin says, catching on a lot faster than I ever could.

"Didn't work though, did it?" Emma says.

She looks fiercely between the three of us: first Erin, then Charlotte, and finally me. Her gaze lingers on me. I tuck my hands into my pockets so that she won't see how much they're shaking. It's humiliating that the three girls are keeping their shit together while I dissolve into a puddle of terror and anxiety at their feet.

"I'm surprised to see you again," Emma says to me. "I still haven't figured out where I know you from, but I will."

"I have one of those faces," I say.

"He really does," Charlotte says. "I thought he was Jesus when I first saw him. It's the hair."

Erin and Emma look at Charlotte like she's been sniffing glue; then they both return their glares to me. Usually, having two pretty girls paying me this much attention would be flattering. I get the feeling they both find me lacking in every possible way though.

"Why are you following me?" Emma says. She's addressing us all, but her eyes haven't left mine.

I desperately want to ask her if she's been helping Rose's ghost stage her takeover, or if she knows who is. I want to ask her if she knows a way to talk to Rose because I'd give anything for one last chance to tell her I love her. But if I say those things out loud, I'll have to explain who I really am and why I'm really here. I can't risk anything getting back to Anton.

"Um, Anton's money?" I mumble. "I thought you might know about the, um…"

"About who hacked the game? You're after his ten thousand pounds? That I could believe from Erin. And Charlotte's clearly here because she's an Anton stan."

"I am!" Charlotte says happily. Then she quickly exorcises a nearby ghost that's emerged out of thin air.

"But you?" Emma says.

I nervously clear my throat. Erin comes to my rescue. "Charlotte said you were at the party where Rose died. I didn't see you there," she says to Emma.

"Matthew spotted me taking photos and threw me out," Emma admits.

"Why were you taking photos?" Erin says.

Emma tightens the belt on her trench coat and looks around like she thinks we're being watched. Beneath the glow of the streetlight, her serious frown makes her face shadowy. It's creepy, especially with all those ghosts about. They roam the park, glowing in the darkness. Their programming doesn't have them chasing us yet. It's only a matter of time.

"I used to write about Anton and the Accomplices for my school paper," Emma says. "Like a gossip column, I guess. At first, I was a fan. Then I discovered what they're really like, and the shine totally wore off. I started work on an exposé about the drugs and bad behavior at Anton's parties. But then Rose died and, you know..."

"Is Rose why you're here tonight?" Charlotte says.

"Mostly, I thought there might be a story in the game that would look good on college applications. I didn't expect it to take such a dark turn."

"Do *you* think Rose was murdered?" Erin says.

I shriek as a ghost gets close enough to register my position. It goes from drifting specter to howling monster in a split second. Long fingernails slash at me as smoke billows from its open mouth. Erin exorcises it as I cower in fear. She shoots me a look of such disapproval I want to turn myself inside out.

Emma sighs. "Honestly? I don't know anymore. I always believed her death was an accident. I came here tonight thinking I could fill in the final gaps in Rose's story, not solve a murder."

"What gaps?" I say, lowering my voice to sound more manly.

"That night at the party, I overheard Matthew and Rose arguing. She was yelling at him, saying he had to tell Beatrix the truth. I figured it was about those photos of him in his underwear."

"Then what happened?" Erin says, impatiently observing a number of approaching ghosts. They've evolved. They're coming for us. As I watch one, its face flickers. For a second, it's Rose. Her eyes are burning embers; her mouth is ringed with black and far too wide.

"Shit, we really need to go," I say, backing away.

Emma ignores me. "I don't know what happened after that. I took a photo of the argument, but like an amateur, I'd left the automatic flash on. Matthew spotted me and had security throw me out of the party."

"What time was this?" Erin asks.

She shrugs. "Hours before Rose died. Eight, maybe? That's why the police weren't even interested in my photos. I guess they'd already decided it was an accident."

"We're going to get tagged out by those ghosts," I say. "We need to run."

"We're nearly done," Erin says.

Emma touches her head again, this time thoughtfully. "If it was murder though…" She stops speaking and looks around, like she's heard a noise. There are dozens of *Shadow City* ghosts approaching, ready to pounce, but they're not what has her spooked. She can't even see them without smart glasses.

"What were you going to say?" Erin says.

"Huh?" Emma blinks at her. "This is too much. I keep thinking someone's after me, which is why I was hiding in the building site in the first place. And then someone pushed that scaffolding pole on me."

Charlotte watches Erin closely. "According to the map, the four of us were the only ones in the building site."

"The only ones with tracking bracelets," Erin says, straightening her spine. "Every member of the crew has smart glasses they can use to find us with. They just don't show up on the map."

We all fall silent as this information sinks in. Then a *Shadow City* ghost lunges at me, and Erin exorcises it, but not before my wristband buzzes and I lose one of my three hearts.

"I need to go," Emma says abruptly.

Charlotte blocks her way. "Wait. We should stick together, don't you think?"

Emma makes an unimpressed noise, like a cat with a hairball.

"As you said, you were all in the building site when I was attacked. And I'm sorry if I'm not about to trust *Matthew's* sister when she gave Anton an alibi for the night of Rose's death." Emma jogs away, leaving Charlotte open-mouthed and red-faced.

A moment of silence. "You were his alibi?" Erin says. "You?"

"Anton didn't need an alibi. Because it was an *accident*." She glances at the ghosts and makes a face. "Grayson's right. We should head for the geofenced safe zone."

"Not until you tell us what really happened at the party," Erin says.

Charlotte swallows. "Oh, all right. It was a warm night. Not hot. Kind of average—"

"Skip the weather report."

"I'm *setting the scene*. The story won't have the same emotional depth, but whatever. I arrived at the party with Matthew, but he ditched me in the gardens with the other guests, and I didn't see him for the rest of the night. I didn't see much of the Accomplices and crew, in fact. I was mostly on my own."

"Doesn't sound much fun," I say shakily.

I edge closer to Erin as a ghost approaches with its arms outstretched. I try to exorcise it, but I'm not close enough and forget the moves. I see a flicker out of the corner of my eye, and I briefly think it's Rose. I'm officially losing it.

Charlotte bites her lip, watching the ghosts, then turns back to Erin. "It wasn't long before I bumped into Rose, and she was rude to me, so…that wasn't fun either."

"Rude, how?" Erin asks.

"She called me a pathetic Anton fan. Which maybe I am, although 'pathetic' is kind of harsh."

"What happened next?"

"Um, well, around ten o'clock, I spotted Anton crossing the lawn. He was alone, so I took the opportunity to talk to him. I caught up with him outside the big hedge maze in his garden. He seemed upset, so I asked him if he was all right, but then we heard someone calling for him. He took my hand and led me into the maze. The one that's in the shape of his face?"

"Unimportant," Erin says.

Charlotte continues, "In one of the eyes, there was a cute summer house, and that's where he took me. It was beautiful. Inside, it was this amazing open-plan den. There were cushions and beanbags and a sofa in the shape of a giant pair of lips."

"Did you have sex with him?" Erin asks.

All of Charlotte's blood finds its way into her head. I worry she's about to pop like an overinflated water balloon. "What? How can you…? Who do you think you are? How dare you!" she splutters.

"That's a no, then," I joke, trying to act like my usual goofy self. Hard when I'm surrounded by monsters.

"But you spent the whole night together?" Erin continues. "Not having sex?"

Charlotte wipes sweat from her hairline. "Yes. Until the next morning." She scowls. "I don't see why you're questioning *me*, given your mother was at the party causing a drunken scene."

"My mother always causes a scene." Erin sighs, but her shoulders slump. She looks around, seeming to notice the ghosts for the first time.

"There are too many to fight now." Charlotte gestures to the ghosts. "So excuse me, but I'm out of here."

With that, she sets off at a sprint. Ghosts turn their fiery eyes toward her as she gets close enough to activate them. Their faces contort, mouths split open, leaving ragged skin hanging in strips. They lift their arms with the crack and pop of breaking bones.

"Huh," Erin says nonchalantly. "They've had an upgrade."

In turn, they become Rose, then flash back to gray-faced ghosts. They approach in a tightening circle. Their burning eyes bore into me as their mouths tear wider and wider, revealing nothing but darkness.

CHARLOTTE

I can't believe her cheek! Emma, throwing me to the wolves like that. Insinuating that I covered for Anton because I'm Matthew's stepsister. It's almost as if she thinks I made it up, which I did not. I would never. A few details may have been massaged, but that's a storyteller's prerogative.

The important thing is my time with Anton was special and meaningful and classy, no matter what Erin Love and Grayson think. I wish it hadn't been sullied by this alibi nonsense, of course. But now's not the time to dwell on the nagging doubt at the back of my mind. I need to focus on running from dozens of hinge-jawed ghosts.

At first, my legs are buoyed by the power of love and determination, and I run like the wind. Five minutes later, I realize that this isn't how human musculature works. My calves burn and my lungs constrict. A stitch in my side feels like a shard of my rib has broken off and is stabbing me in the liver.

I have to rest. I can't go on. Then I turn a corner, and up ahead, like a glowing oasis, there's a subway station. My wristband won't have a signal underground. The ghosts will leave me alone. I'll have five minutes before I time out, but it will be enough to regroup.

I barrel through the barriers and shove my way down the escalator. Ghosts continue to appear, floating in midair without any flat ground for them to stand on. I trip off the escalator and scramble along the tiled tunnels, out onto the platform. And then, the ghosts vanish.

There's a train pulling into the platform with a noisy electrical hum. The announcement is drowned out by screeching brakes, and the doors hiss open. I wouldn't usually take a risk like this—I have four and a half minutes left on my countdown—but the next station is one minute away. It will get me closer to the river and give me a chance to catch my breath. *It's not cheating*, I tell myself.

Inside the train, I slide down onto the floor by the doors even though there are seats. The car is way too bright. I must resemble a sweaty tomato. A woman keeps flicking me curious glances. This time around, it's not so exciting having people know I'm playing Anton's game. I try to stay calm, but every time the train wheels clank on the tracks, my heart jumps in my chest.

"Excuse me," the woman says. "Are you part of that game?"

"No," I say. "Not me."

"Oh, I thought your glasses…"

I push them up my nose and smile at her. "Just glasses. Actually,

I'm on my way to meet my dad. I haven't seen him for a while, and he's coming to visit."

"That's so sweet," she says, returning to her book.

All right. I can do this. I close my eyes and do some deep breathing. In for four, out for eight. Feeling more composed, I open my eyes again. It takes me a second to realize that the countdown on my lenses has vanished and I'm back in the game. That's weird. Surely that could only happen if my wristband had a signal, and that's not possible so far underground.

Then it hits me. I'd forgotten about that new plan to increase the free Wi-Fi coverage on the subway.

It's OK, it's OK. *Shadow City* is designed to work for pedestrians, not on forty-mile-per-hour trains. The ghosts can't take shape properly. They rush past harmlessly as blurs at the corners of my vision. We'll reach the next station within seconds, and I'll get above ground.

Only then the train slows. It stops. It waits.

This is more of a problem. Now the ghosts are materializing for real, reaching for me with their horrid fingernails, coming closer and closer. They flicker in and out of existence as the Wi-Fi cuts in and out. I try to exorcise them, but it doesn't work. Why won't it work?

"I need to get off this train," I shout, slapping my hand on the door release button. "Let me off!"

Outside, the tunnel is dark, all wires and filthy concrete. I'm buried belowground, surrounded by endless mud and rock, entombed down here like one of the dead. A ghost stretches its arms toward me, and its mouth becomes this huge gaping black hole that threatens to suck me in. I shriek and shield my face.

Then we're moving again and the ghost rushes away. The commuters watch me suspiciously. It can't be much longer. I need to get outside where I can run. I jiggle up and down, skittish with nervous energy.

The lights on the train flicker, and we're plunged into absolute darkness, broken only by the sudden spark of electricity from the train wheels as we slow to a halt. The *Shadow City* ghosts vanish with the Wi-Fi signal, and my countdown starts. But in the dark, I swear I can hear a ghost creeping toward me, and this one isn't from Anton's game.

This time when I scream, someone else does too, followed by nervous laughter. I want to tell everyone that there's nothing for *them* to be scared of. This ghost is here for me and me alone. Because this ghost is Rose, risen from her grave with peeling skin and empty eye sockets. She exhales fetid breath against my face.

"This is on you, Charlotte," she says. "This is what you wanted."

Another scream tears its way out of me, and it sets off a chain reaction. People start yelling and crying for help. The whole car becomes this cacophony of sobs and shouts. People hammer on the windows. Someone presses the call button to alert the driver, but his reply is nothing but static.

My countdown ticks over, closer and closer to the one-minute mark, and still the train doesn't move; the lights don't come on. I press myself against the divider and squeeze my eyes closed. I can sense her right there, inches from my face. What's she waiting for? What does she want with me?

"You lied," Rose snarls.

"I had no choice," I whisper, hiccuping in my panic.

TAG, YOU'RE DEAD · 129

"All you cared about was yourself."

"That's not true! I never meant for any of this to happen."

The car is a chaos of yelling and fists beating on the doors. I take myself away, into a memory of that night in the maze.

———

"Tell me about yourself, Charlotte," Anton said, closing the door of the summer house. He peered out of the floor-to-ceiling windows to make sure we were alone.

"Well, I'm sixteen, and I'm a huge fan. The biggest."

I told Anton how I loved English and hated math and how I wrote stories in my spare time. I remember I was so nervous being in the same room as him, but you know what he told me?

"Charlotte, you've got this. No one can be you better than you can. You're the only Charlotte here right now, and that makes you the best."

It made me laugh, and I started to relax. Anton went on to tell me how he'd gotten into making game maps for his friends and turned it into a living. He seemed so different from his online persona, and it only made me love him move. In his videos, I'd seen glimpses of the shy, thoughtful boy he really was. But that night I got to meet him for real.

He told me he'd fallen out with his family and how everything he did was to prove himself to his dad. We had so much in common. Both of us had been abandoned by our fathers in one way or another. Both of us wanted someone to see us.

I told him that he was someone to so many people already, and he smiled. "You're the sweetest girl," he said, closing his eyes and resting his head on my shoulder.

It wasn't long before he was snoring away. I put my hand under his and he squeezed it, and everything was perfect.

That's what I'm playing for. That's what I have to lose.

———————

"You have everything to lose," Rose's ghost says.

"No," I reply. "You're not real. You can't hurt me!"

The lights come on and I'm alone. Well, I'm in a subway car full of a dozen panicking people, some of whom are crying, some of whom are trying to smash the windows with their briefcases. But Rose is gone.

My timer stops as the signal returns, barely in time. The train shudders and starts to move as the ghosts reappear. Seconds later, we're pulling into the platform. I press the Open Doors button repeatedly until the car releases me. I dare a quick look over my shoulder at the now-embarrassed passengers trying to act like nothing happened in the tunnel in the dark. They return to their seats or hurry off the train, wiping their eyes and smoothing their clothes.

I push my way through the crowds on the platform and hurry up the escalators, pausing to exorcise a particularly persistent ghost. I burst out of the station into welcome fresh air, and the second I've got my bearings, I set off at a run. The ghosts are getting faster, but I can outrun them.

Like Anton told me, I've got this.

15

ERIN

I leave Grayson gaping at the ghosts, and I run. I'm not sacrificing my place in this competition for anyone, especially not him. Maybe he'll make it; maybe he won't. That's his problem.

I'm sprinting toward the river when suddenly everything stops. The ghosts freeze with their talons outstretched and their jagged teeth bared. I slow to a walk. As I pass the ghosts, they distort like optical illusions that only make sense when you look directly at them.

Among them all, balanced on his ridiculous Segway and holding a tablet, is Matthew. His faux-hawk is flat, and he appears to be breaking out in hives—there are several raised blotches on his neck, red where he's been scratching. I prefer this messy version of him. At least it's real.

He gestures at the frozen ghosts. "Makes things easier for you, right?" he says, his voice raspy.

"I was doing OK by myself."

"I suppose you were," he admits. "But it's early days."

I cross my arms and wait for him to tell me why he's interrupted the game to speak to me. I'll play my part for the cameras, flirting and laughing. But there are no cameras here now. He's frozen the game for a reason, and I'm betting it's because he doesn't want Anton finding out about our conversation.

He clears his throat. "I wanted to talk to you about this Rose nonsense," he says. "I saw you following Emma98 and meeting up with my sister. Why are you getting involved in this?"

"Anton asked me to."

He does a double take and nearly drops the tablet. "Anton?"

"Didn't you know that? I thought he told you everything."

I shouldn't stir the pot. It's what my mother would do, and I'm nothing like her. But Matthew's an easy target, so convinced of his own importance that he can't comprehend not being at the center of everything.

"No, he doesn't," he says. "Anton's losing it over the interruptions to his game. I haven't seen him so worked up since…"

"Since Rose?"

He changes the subject. "What does he want you to do?"

"Find the person who's behind that ghost." For some reason I don't admit that he's specifically asked me to spy on Grayson. I'm not letting anyone, especially not Matthew, get in the way of my plans.

Matthew's jaw twitches. "You need to walk away from this. Focus on the game and forget everything else."

"I can manage both," I say with a shrug.

"I don't think you understand. Take a look at your map and find Alic91. She's just down the road."

I do what I'm told. "Who is she?"

"Nobody." Matthew types on his tablet. As I watch, her spot vanishes. He lowers the tablet to his side. "I can edit you out of the competition in seconds, like I did Alic91."

Blackmail? Not happening. I take a step toward him and place a single finger on his chest. He swallows heavily. "Only you can't," I say. "I'm not a nobody. I'm top of the leaderboard, and people would notice if I vanished. I suspect your boss would be very unhappy with you."

His face goes still and loses its usual expressiveness. I know I've struck a nerve.

"I'm Anton's business partner. I don't work *for* him. What makes you think he'd pick you over me?"

I laugh. "To annoy you?"

He manages a hint of a surprised smile. "Fair enough."

"What's it to you anyway, whether I get involved or not? Unless you killed Rose."

His smile vanishes. "Of course I didn't kill Rose. I'm trying to protect Anton from having his name dragged into this drama again. Because that's my job—being the voice of reason while he sends teenagers to investigate a ghost."

"You believe she's real now?"

"Don't be ridiculous." He runs a hand through his hair and takes a deep breath. "This won't end well for you, you know?"

"Is that a threat?"

He doesn't answer the question. "Why did you enter? You hate this whole online world."

This is unexpected. Matthew seems completely self-absorbed. It feels weird that he's noticed my lack of enthusiasm when it comes to fame.

"It's a lot of money," I say.

"Ahh, right. Money. And I imagine Amber had plenty to do with that part."

I shrug.

"I'm surprised she didn't enter herself."

"She tried to," I admit. "The age cutoff is twenty-one though."

Matthew shudders. "Thank god." He fixes me with an appraising look. "You could win this, you know?"

The unspoken part of his sentence—you could win this *if you stop poking your nose where it doesn't belong*—is clear. I hold his stare and don't back down.

"All right. Your choice. I'll give you ten seconds before I unpause the game." He winks at me. Urgh. "Ten, nine, eight—"

I don't stick around to hear the rest of the countdown. I shoot Matthew one last dirty glare and break into a sprint. I've made it most of the way to the path running along the edge of the river when the ghosts shudder back to life. I easily weave between them though. My bracelet buzzes, and I step into the geofenced area. I'm safe, and the ghosts are gone.

I pause to catch my breath, then send a surreptitious text to Jesse. We need to talk.

I find a bench overlooking the river and wait for further instructions. The pavement is wide and lined with trees. Behind me, a four-lane road is packed with traffic, but the river's more peaceful. Several barges are moored near to an ugly concrete bridge. A river bus powers past.

I'm one of the first contestants here. I can see a couple of others: two girls chatting by a coffee truck and a boy resting on the ground with his head in his hands. No sign of Charlotte or Grayson.

Five minutes later, I get a text from Jesse. I'm busy setting up for the next challenge. Can't get away.

My heart sinks. So much has happened since I last saw him, and he still can't find the time to even chat. Suddenly, I'm hit by a wave of red-hot anger. I need him and he's ignoring me. So I text him something that I know will get his attention: Matthew came to speak to me. He was flirting with me.

This isn't entirely true. A wink is hardly a proposition, and Matthew winks at everyone. But I'm feeling hurt that Jesse's pushed me into entering this competition and then abandoned me to the wolves. I guess I want to make him feel bad for a second.

He texts me almost immediately. Turn right and keep walking.

I head along the river, passing a lifeboat station along the way. Suddenly, I'm grabbed from behind and pulled down a flight of unlit steps leading to a basement bar. My signal goes out of range. Before I can get my balance back, Jesse spins me around and kisses me hungrily like we haven't seen each other for weeks rather than hours.

He pulls back, and I look up into his hazel eyes. "I missed you," I say.

"What did that son of a bitch say to you?" he says.

"Matthew? Oh, nothing really. He doesn't want me sticking my nose into this whole thing with Rose."

"Rose? Why *are* you sticking your nose in?"

"Anton asked me to. He thinks someone has set up this Rose ghost act to sabotage the game. He suspects that Grayson boy from the museum."

He shakes his head dismissively. "The ghost thing is a stupid distraction. Forget it. You should be concentrating on the competition."

"The one that I'm winning? Besides, Anton offered me money to keep tabs on Grayson. Twenty grand. I couldn't say no."

He thinks about this. "Twenty grand is nothing compared to a hundred."

"But a hundred and twenty is better than a hundred."

"You're evil. I love it." He kisses me again, more hurriedly this time, and then pulls away. "What else did Matthew say to you? You said he was flirting?"

"He winked at me, that's all."

His hands form fists at his sides. "I don't trust him with you. He'll hit on you, and you won't be able to say no."

"What did you say?" I step away from him. *I won't be able to say no?* I've said no to more people than Jesse's dated in his entire life. I'm not some naive little girl who would have her head turned by a pretty boy like Matthew. Is that seriously how Jesse sees me? "What the fuck, Jesse? I can handle Matthew."

"I bet you can." He laughs, loudly like it's the funniest thing ever. "Like mother, like daughter."

I hold both hands up. "Whoa. No. You don't get to say that sort of shit to me."

"I'm sorry," he says, reaching for me. I catch the smallest roll of his eyes as he does. "I'm sorry. I'm sorry. I'm sorry."

I yank my hand free of his. Maybe it's this stupid competition; maybe it's the way Jesse's been too busy for me all night until I mentioned Matthew. But it feels like a flashlight's pointing at the cracks in my relationship , and I'm too tired and cold and scared to deny that they're there.

Jesse's jealous streak has always made me uncomfortable, but I told myself it was a sign that he cared. Now I feel as much of a possession as I do with my mother. A thing that needs to be controlled. An object to be owned. And I'm...done.

I back away from him, raising a shaking finger. "You need to grow the hell up, Jesse," I say, my voice quiet and dangerous.

"I'm sorry. Come on."

I duck away from his arms and run up the steps.

"Erin," he calls after me. "Don't walk away from me. Fine! Screw you, then. Run to your little friend, *Matthew*. See if I care. Bitch!"

Each word is a bullet. There's so much viciousness in his voice, hatred, even. My legs feel wobbly beneath me. My heart beats like a tiny bird, quivering in my chest. But in my belly, there's a rising pool of rage.

Suddenly, my eyes are fully open, and I can see my relationship with Jesse for what it really is. A way out of one life that would have led me straight back to more of the same shit that I was trying to escape in the first place. Jesse, like Amber, wants to mold me around his own life. Only, I'm getting tired of being the daughter or the girlfriend. I want to be me, not the final piece to someone else's puzzle.

I wipe a tear and I walk away. I spot Grayson, and a weak little part of me wants to run over to him to see a semifriendly face. But I don't know anything about him, not really. He's not my friend. I don't have friends. I turn in the opposite direction.

I'm going to show Jesse that I'm not the girl he thinks I am. I don't need him; I don't need anyone.

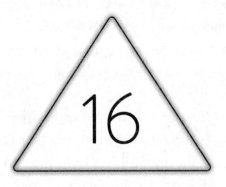

GRAYSON

I smell the river before I see it. It's the stench of low tide, when the rot hidden beneath the water is revealed. Thick mud teeming with worms and fish shit and dead algae, not to mention the crap that people toss into the river—plastic bottles and takeout wrappers. Safe to say, the gleam has worn off for me when it comes to this city and this game.

With two of my three lives gone, I emerge onto the embankment and find that dozens of contestants are already here. I'm not in the mood to chat though. There are too many thoughts tap-dancing in my brain, and my heart's keeping time. So I wander along the river while I wait for the challenge to start.

I'm lurking under a bridge like a troll when I spot a familiar face. It's Jesse from the museum. I freeze, thinking he's spotted me, but then he hurries down a flight of stone steps onto the riverbank. I should get out of here. He accosted me after seeing me win those points from Erin, and it was only the approaching police that saved me from an awkward conversation.

Except he's up to something. I approach the steps where he vanished and peer over the river wall. There's a little stony beach down there, lapped by small waves. Vertical wooden beams make a hidden space beneath my feet, like the darkness beneath a pier. Jesse's on the beach, fiddling with a metal box. I can't figure out what it is.

His phone rings, and grumbling, he answers. "Yeah, I'm doing it now," he says. "I was busy... No, stop. You're not paying me enough to order me around."

I lean over further and try to get a better angle on the box. Jesse looks up, and I barely manage to duck out of sight in time. That was dangerously close. I'm about to walk away when he says something that catches my attention. "Don't worry, everything's ready for Rose's next appearance."

I stop.

"I'm not asking questions. I make a point to stay out of rich-person bullshit, especially when dead girls are involved. I'm merely pointing out how I'd have asked for more money if I'd known what this favor would entail."

He hangs up the phone. I don't push my luck. I jog toward the rest of the contestants before he realizes I've been spying on him.

I discover that a crowd is blocking the sidewalk. Everyone is craning their heads to see down the river. Most are contestants, but there are several confused passersby in there too. "What's happening?" I say, squeezing to the front.

"We're not sure," a girl says. "I think the challenge involves that boat."

I can hear classical music. Approaching along the river is an old-fashioned tugboat, with black wooden sides and a tall red chimney wrapped in strings of lights. There's a small lifeboat suspended above the deck, next to a cute little cabin in which the driver stands. On the roof, there's a speaker spewing out the music.

"That's Tchaikovsky's 'Swan Lake,'" someone says.

As the boat chugs closer, I realize that it's pulling something behind it. A cluster of small white plastic boats—maybe a dozen of them. I stand on the first rung of the fence and squint. The boats have long swans' necks.

"It's like that video of his." A contestant gasps. "The one where the Accomplices chased each other in swan paddleboats?"

"Don't think I saw that one," I say.

"It's one of their most famous stunts." The girl shuffles away from me as if my lack of fandom knowledge might somehow taint her.

The truth is, I have seen that particular video a dozen or more times. It was the stunt that led to my argument with Rose that saw us split up. See, at the end, Anton and Rose pedal off together on one of the boats, surrounded by postproduction hearts. She denied there was anything going on, but three months after we'd split up, they started dating for real.

The boat pulls up to the bank, deafening us with the music. Three men emerge onto the deck and mess with some ropes. Then the crowd shifts as a small but determined person comes pushing their way through. It's Beatrix, her face pale and panicked. "Wait!" she yells at the driver of the boat. But her voice is lost to the music.

The men untie a floating ring of buoys, and the swans drift free. Then the boat powers away, leaving the swans bobbing sadly in the dark water. A couple run aground on the mud. One is picked up by a current and carried away, tipping in the wind and gradually filling with water.

"This is a disaster," Beatrix says. "Thanks to Rose, Anton's having trouble with his connection, and he hasn't explained the challenge yet."

"To be fair, I'm not sure swan boats on the Thames were ever going to end in anything *but* disaster," I muse.

She glances at me, and her eyes crinkle in recognition. The color of her irises is even prettier beneath the streetlights. I shouldn't stare, but I can't help myself.

"Don't," she says, suppressing a laugh. "I have been the number one critic of this challenge, but literally no one listens to me."

"I couldn't do your job," I say, forcing myself to look at her grubby Converse instead of her face.

"I mean, family isn't really a job. But it would be nice if I didn't already know I'll get the blame when it goes wrong." She grimaces at the swans, then turns away with a shudder. I follow her out of the crowd. "I'd better not get arrested," she says sadly.

"You ever consider saying no to him?"

"He's my brother and I love him," she says. "Don't you have someone you'd do anything for, even if it meant getting into trouble?"

I think of Rose. "Yeah, I suppose so," I say.

She sighs and chews on the end of a braid. Then she spits it out like it tastes disgusting. "I'd better get going. See if I can fix this mess. The challenge was supposed to be over before anyone got a chance to call the police."

"We're sitting swans," I say, nodding at my own joke. "You know, like ducks?"

"I got it, Grayson," she says, rolling her eyes. "But thanks for the clarification." As she leaves, she bumps her hip against mine.

142 · KATHRYN FOXFIELD

I smile after her, and for five seconds, the world feels slightly lighter. Then Rose's ghost appears through my smart glasses, and I remember why I'm here. Beatrix stops midstep and puts a hand to her mouth.

"Hello, losers," Rose says, smiling gleefully. Her voice is crackly and disjointed, as is her face. But she's still beautiful. "I wanted to say hello and see how you're doing."

"Oh no," Beatrix says. "Not now."

"What do you think about Matthew? Is he our killer, or will it be the next suspect?" Rose paces, a finger to her lips like she's thinking.

I hold my breath and wait for the announcement.

Rose flicks her hair, and the movement is so familiar that it tears at my heart. Then she spins her big wheel of suspects, leaving it clackity-clacking its way around and around as she talks. "There's a big Anton community on GossApp; I'm sure many of you are members. Back when I was alive, the Anton fans on GossApp used to love talking about me. You should have heard the things they used to say."

Out of the corner of my eye, I see a light sweeping across the side of the closest bridge. It shows words moving over the concrete. It's not just a trick projected on our lenses. The words are really there, for everyone to see.

I wish Rose would go away.

She's such a bitch.

Someone should wipe that stupid smile off her face.

"All these comments were written by a single poster," Rose continues as her wheel slows. "AntonsGirlXOXO. But they weren't the only things she said."

The comments on the bridge vanish, replaced by one that reads: DIE, DIE, DIE.

"AntonsGirlXOXO really didn't like me, back when I was alive. She loves Anton though. What do you think? Did she kill me because she wanted Anton all for herself?"

The wheel clicks as the needle jumps between segments, slowing, slowing. Rose rips the black silhouette from the wheel to reveal her next suspect. "How are you going to explain this one, Charlotte?" Rose says. She laughs, her voice crackling like flames, then vanishes.

Charlotte. Matthew's little sister. Wow, that's a surprise. A murmur ripples across the rest of the contestants on the embankment, growing louder. Someone points. The crowd shifts. I see Charlotte. She looks like she's hyperventilating. She stands there shaking with tears flooding down her face, as more and more people turn to stare at her.

The right thing to do would be to go over and reassure her. But I can't stop thinking about Jesse. The words on the bridge are being projected from where I saw Jesse, down on the riverbank. This is what he was setting up. He works for Anton, but he's the one helping Rose stage her appearances.

I don't know how or why, but it's him.

I jog toward the place where I saw Jesse, and it saves me. Because moments later, several police vans pull up, and shrill whistles sound. I hide under the bridge as all hell breaks loose. People scatter in every direction as police emerge from the vans and run at us. When the contestants realize that their land-based exits are blocked off, they clamber over the wall and drop down onto the riverbank.

There's screaming and slipping and splashing. People pile onto the swan boats, several on one, tipping it from side to side. One boy clings on to the neck of a swan, his feet trailing in the water, as two girls pedal for the opposite side. The police yell and try to stop contestants from running into the river.

I can't get caught. I'm wary of the police after that time I went off the rails and broke Neil's nose at Rose's memorial service. I can still remember being dragged into a squad car, crying my eyes out, while half my school watched. The powerlessness and the regret hurt more than my bruised fingers. So I slide off my glasses and pull my sleeve over my bracelet. The game's offline. Anton won't notice.

I slip unseen onto the riverbank, but there's no sign of Jesse. A noise behind me makes me turn. Too quickly. I lose my footing on the mud, and the only way to go is down.

CHARLOTTE

I have to get away. From the police, from the pointing fingers, from the regret. My secret's out—splashed across the bridge in glowing letters—and I don't know what to do.

I run through the panicking crowd of contestants. I dodge shaky flashlights and shouts and screams. I'm buffeted by people trying to escape in every direction. A rogue elbow catches my temple, and I stumble, grazing my palms on the river wall. I've barely gotten my balance when someone else slams into me from behind.

I tip over the wall. I try to hold on, but momentum has hold of me. I do a forward flip and fall face-first toward the mud and water below. I hit my head on something when I land—a piece of driftwood, a lump of discarded metal, a big rock? Whatever it is sends sparks flying across my field of vision.

I scramble to my feet, but a combination of dizziness and the slippery ground makes it impossible to stay standing. My hands and legs sink into thick stinky mud, and I can barely move. The icy cold seeps into my clothes as I crawl toward the water. There's a swan boat nearby on the shore that's drifted apart from the others. It's my only chance.

I stagger toward the swan and shove it hard. It slides surprisingly easily into the river. I throw myself at the hard plastic. I slip and end up hanging from the swan's neck. It tips to one side; its beak skims the water.

Another contestant is trying to climb aboard too. A boy. He's shouting at me, kicking out, trying to push me off. I can't focus on him, never mind fight back. My head throbs in agony, and it feels like I'm going to black out.

The swan catches on a current, rocking from side to side as water splashes down my hoodie and soaks the legs of my jeans. The river's so dark, and the opposite bank is so far away. My thoughts are splintering, and I'm losing sight of what's real, what's a horrible nightmare. The boy on my boat grabs my hood and tries to throw me off. I scream, but it's lost in the chaos.

Other contestants are trying to cross the river on the boats, but there are too many people. The swans crash into each other with the sounds of splintering plastic and shrieks cut short. A bright light heads our way along the river. The police must have called the Coastguard.

"Get off," the boy in my boat yells, and there's something familiar about his voice. "You're going to sink us."

He grabs at me again, so I kick out at him with all my strength. My foot connects with his chest. Another swan bumps into mine, and I flip over. I grab out for anything that might save me, but there's nothing except water. The swan's heavy base clunks against my head, and I go under.

It's so cold I can't breathe. Everything comes to me in flashes and gasps. The current catches me and spins me around. I catch glimpses of a dozen people shouting and splashing, lit up brightly by the Coastguard's spotlight. No one's coming for me though. The water swallows me up, and I can't fight it any longer.

There's a memory. *The* memory that brought me here, to this watery abyss.

I'm standing at a buffet table, watching everyone else enjoy themselves. This party—Anton's party—isn't as much fun as I'd hoped it would be. Most people are so out of it that their voices have become shrieks and their movements uncoordinated. Matthew is nowhere to be seen, and he's the only person I know, so I'm alone.

I'm picking at a cocktail sausage when Rose appears to my right and helps herself to a bottle of water. She's as beautiful and as unapproachable as always. She gulps the water down in one long swallow, then wipes her lips. Her skin is perfect, and her red-lipped smile is ice cold.

"Charlotte, isn't it?" she says. "Matthew's sister."

"Stepsister-to-be," I reply.

"Same difference." She screws the lid on the bottle and tosses it in with the unopened ones. "Surprised you're not mingling. Trying to discover where Anton's bedroom is or stealing his toothbrush."

"I don't know what you mean," I say coldly and turn to leave.

"Do you go on GossApp?" Rose says, making me pause. "I think you do. There's one poster on there who says terrible stuff about me. Really vicious, personal stuff."

"Oh?" I manage to say, even though my throat is drier than my mom's roasts. "I haven't seen anything mean."

"You haven't? The posts are seriously unhinged. Personal, even. So I asked my friend to look into it. My friend's a coder, you know. Coded *Shadow City*. Finding out an IP address was child's play to them."

She can't know. It's not possible. I've always been so careful.

She gets close to me and drops her voice to a whisper. "Imagine my surprise to discover that the person trolling me was none other than Matthew's. Little. Sister."

My heart plummets to my knees. "What…what do you want?"

Rose laughs. "Why would I want anything from some pathetic Anton fan?"

I grit my teeth. All I can think is how much I hate her. She's so beautiful and so popular and so mean. She doesn't deserve Anton. She doesn't deserve to be one of the Accomplices.

She helps herself to an olive, popping it delicately into her mouth. "I've read your stories too. I know about your little crush on Anton. Shame it'll never, ever happen. Why would he look twice at you when he has me?"

"That's a horrible thing to say." I gasp.

She laughs and marches off with a swing of her glossy curls, leaving me fighting tears. A couple of the other guests look at me, so I duck behind the pool house to pull myself together.

That feeling. Shame tinged with burning hatred. It's unbearable. I take out my phone and write that comment on Rose's GossApp fan page: DIE, DIE, DIE. It isn't enough to kill the feeling though.

———

The memory ejects me with a sudden rush of coughed-up dirty water. I'm lying facedown on a concrete ramp that slopes into the river. The wall of a huge building with too many unlit windows looms over me. There are no lights, only the moon.

I cough again, and it turns into a retch. All I can taste is filth and regret. Then I see him.

It's a person tangled in weeds. He's lying on his stomach with his limbs splayed at funny angles. He must have washed up here like me. I crawl to him, shivering and shaking in my heavy clothes.

"Hello?" I say. "Are you another contestant?"

He's not wearing a tracking bracelet. I tentatively poke his arm, but he doesn't move. Another memory surfaces. In it, I'm struggling to stay on my boat as a boy tries to throw me into the water. The details are hazy.

What I do remember is kicking the boy. And then he went quiet.

"Are you all right?" I whisper.

I carefully roll him onto his back. I fall onto my seat with a gasp. It's Jesse, the driver from the museum getaway. His face is so pale and his eyes so empty. So *dead*. There's a wound on his head, but it's not bleeding, not anymore.

I don't scream. I can't scream.

I stand up and back away, bile burning my throat. Was he the boy I kicked? Did I kill him?

No, this isn't real. I back up so far that I bump into a pair of rusty metal gates. I stumble as they creak ajar behind me. The mud under my feet becomes concrete. Then I turn and run.

I shoot out straight across the road without looking. A black van slams on its brakes. I stand there and gape as it screeches toward me. It stops just in time, its bumper against my legs.

The door flies open and Beatrix climbs out. The headlights of the van illuminate her from behind, turning the hair that's escaped her braids into a glowing halo.

"Charlotte? What are you doing?"

"I…I'm…" I can't get the words out. I can't tell her that a man's dead, not when Rose identified me as a suspect. What if everyone thinks I murdered him? What if I *did*? I can barely remember anything that happened in the water.

Beatrix is watching me like I'm a monster, like I might attack her at any moment. Perhaps I am a monster. Sirens approach as if making a point. "I saw the things you wrote about Rose," Beatrix says.

Of course she did.

"I didn't mean to hurt her! I didn't like her, but it wasn't real life. I didn't think anyone would read it."

"I looked up your username. AntonsGirlXOXO? I saw what you wrote on GossApp this afternoon. Was that real?" Tears are glistening on her lashes. She looks so heartbroken. "You said Matthew was sneaking around behind my back, getting up to no good."

I shake my head. "I had a fight with Matthew, and I wanted to get back at him. What I wrote wasn't real," I whisper.

The sirens get closer, but I'd happily take being arrested over this feeling inside me. Concrete, hardening in my belly.

"Go," Beatrix says. "The police are picking up contestants, and there's no way I'm taking you anywhere in my van. So go."

"But…" I glance over my shoulder at the metal gates hiding Jesse's body.

"Now!" she yells.

So I run, and I try to pretend that a person isn't lying dead yards away on the banks of the river. I try to pretend that none of this is my fault. But it's a lie, and I don't think I can run fast enough to escape, not this time.

ERIN

My phone buzzes with a message from Anton HQ.

Lay low and await instructions. MY game isn't over until I
say it's over.

Anton is losing control of his own creation. Rose is stomping
him into the ground and leaving the scraps to the police. I can't help
but laugh out loud, making some tourists ogling the river glance
nervously at me.

From my spot on the bridge, I watch the Coastguard's boats cir-
cling in the water. A helicopter sweeps past overhead with glaringly
bright lights. On the embankment, contestants are led into waiting
ambulances or sit wrapped in silver blankets that reflect the reds
and blues of silenced sirens.

I figure that more than two dozen people have been rounded up by the police. That leaves about twenty-five of us unaccounted for. From my perspective, the game's dead in the water. I can't see how Anton is going to resurrect it now. It's a shame. I really wanted that money.

But at least this whole experience has freed me from Jesse. I'm happy, honestly.

I keep prodding at my heart, like tonguing the gap left behind after you lose a tooth. It hurts and feels weird. But at the same time, it's a good kind of pain, clean and sharp. Now that he's gone, I can see that my relationship with Jesse wasn't much different from my relationship with Amber. Both of them wanted to control me, and I clung to them both because I believed I needed someone.

Truth is, Jesse asked me out knowing who I was and what I did, then set about systematically trying to change me. He was always berating me for how I dressed, how much makeup I wore, how I styled my hair. He'd get jealous if I was photographed with another man. He'd accuse me of flirting if I so much as spoke to a boy. Bikini photo shoots led to a whole week of sulking and accusations.

On one side, I had Amber pulling me toward the glamour and vanity of her world, forever disappointed that I didn't quite measure up. On the other, Jesse would have found something to be jealous of even if I'd washed off the makeup and dressed in a sack. *It's not fair that the sack gets to touch your body,* he'd have complained.

I laugh at the thought. What a loser.

Even still, my treacherous heart aches at the thought that I'm alone. It whispers that, without Jesse, my escape route is gone. *Coward,* it says. It knows I won't run without him. I'm too weary to keep fighting without someone to hold my hand.

You don't need anyone, I tell myself. If I say it enough times then maybe it will be real.

I join the onlookers peering past the police barricade on the embankment. I look for Charlotte or Grayson. I don't see them though. What I do see is the words projected on the bridge, cycling through their pattern that ends with DIE, DIE, DIE. Charlotte's not as boring as I thought she was.

I look over the river wall. A projector sits by the water, abandoned by its operator. The ground's all churned up by feet and boats. That's when I spot someone farther down the river, crawling out from under the bridge supports. He's covered head to toe in mud, so it takes me a second to realize it's Grayson.

No way. He *made* it? I watch as he sneaks past the projector and tries to climb up the steps, but he has to go back down when a couple of paramedics walk past. Instead, he tries to scale the wall. He's beyond muddy. It's disgusting.

"What are you doing down there?" I call to him.

He pauses and sweeps his filthy hair out of his face. His expression is troubled, but when he sees me, he smiles. "Fancied a paddle, you know? Can you pull me up?"

"I'm not touching you. You look and smell like a sentient poo."

He laughs at this. "For a second, you almost sounded human, Erin Love."

I glare at him and point past the bridge. "There are some more steps over there."

I scrape the dirt out from underneath my nails as I wait for him. He eventually finds the steps and emerges, walking stiffly with the claylike mud weighing down his clothes. We head away from the embankment as quickly as his condition will allow. He squelches with every movement, and I keep catching wafts of rotten eggs.

I gag as a particularly unpleasant smell hits me. "You're going to need your little friend to bring you some clothes," I say.

"What friend?"

I raise an eyebrow.

He exhales. "Oh, all right, you got me. But I lost my earpiece in the mud. And my phone."

I silently offer him mine, noticing as I pass it over that Amber's tried to call me a dozen times. Grayson wipes his hands on the sidewalk before taking it from me. I wait on a bench while he makes his call. We're in a shiny built-up part of the city, surrounded by financial companies and expensive sandwich shops. Everything's closed for the night, giving the street a deserted, end-of-the-world vibe.

"No, I'm OK. I lost my phone." Grayson glances at me and lowers his voice to a whisper. "She already knew about you. I didn't tell her anything."

I close my eyes and pretend that I'm resting.

Grayson moves farther away so that I can't hear his conversation. A few minutes later, he returns my phone. "She's bringing me some clothes and a burger," he says. "She's getting you one too."

"I don't eat dead things."

"More for me then."

It's a fairly long walk to the subway station where she's meeting us. We head into an upscale part of town packed with expensive bars full of media types. The subway station's on a street of what seem to be mostly high-end home-goods shops. Even though we arrive late, there's no one here. We wait outside, a puddle of dirty water gradually forming around Grayson. He smells of rotting vegetation.

There's still no word from Anton, and our smart cams and bracelets remain offline. At least it means we can meet Grayson's friend in the open, rather than having to risk an enclosed underground space where our cameras won't pick her up. Fresh air is the one thing stopping me from puking right now.

Eventually, a girl in a black hoodie appears from behind us. It's the same jogger who tripped me up. She's wearing a mask so the only part of her that I can make out is her dark eyes.

"So, introductions," Grayson says. "Lenny meet Erin, Erin meet Lenny."

"For goodness's sake," Lenny grumbles, shoving a bulging carrier bag at Grayson. "What happened to not telling her my name?"

He blinks. "What's she going to do?"

"I could tell Anton about her," I say, sitting down on the curb and stretching out my calves. "You're not allowed to have help."

They both gape at me.

"I didn't say I was going to." I shrug. "Just that Lenny has a point."

"Stop using my name," Lenny says.

"Relax. The whole system's down, so you're not being recorded."

Lenny continues to stare at me, then turns to Grayson. "There's a phone in the bag. I'll call you later."

"But it *is* interesting that you're helping him," I continue. "What's in it for you?"

"Not doing this." Lenny walks off, stomping down the road in her ugly-ass sneakers. She pauses to glance at Grayson, then huffs dramatically and quickens her pace.

Grayson's bewildered expression follows her. "Did I say something?"

"You really are clueless, aren't you?"

"Um, yes?" he says. "Do you think I should go after her? I mean, we're not dating, so maybe that's a bit too much, but I don't want her to—"

"Yes, go after her!"

"You're right. I'll be back in ten, yeah?" He carries the bag she gave him by one handle. One of the burgers spills out as he jogs after her.

I sit there on the dirty sidewalk and ignore the whispers as a group of men in nice suits are forced to weave around me. Rain starts to fall in a fine mist. I turn my face up to the sky. It's strangely peaceful. But it's not too long before my moment of calm is interrupted by the sound of a taxi pulling up. A door slams. The *tap-tap* of high heels approaches. Amber clears her throat.

"You're ignoring my calls," she says.

"And you're tracking my phone's location."

Amber is wearing an outfit almost identical to mine. Wet-look leggings and a T-shirt that she's pulled down off one shoulder to reveal a leopard-print bra. Her hair's like mine too, only bigger. And her makeup's heavier, accentuating her swollen upper lip and her rounded cheeks. Nearly everyone who passes by ogles her. Unlike me, she seems to enjoy the attention.

"Why are you sitting down there?" she says, fluffing her hair. "Someone might take a photo of you looking all homeless person."

"Unlikely," I say. "Besides, the game's probably over."

"That's not what Anton said." She waits for me to ask when she spoke to Anton, but I don't. "I was worried, so I gave him a call. He's adamant he's going to stop this Rose nonsense. In fact, he was on his way to intercept the culprit. That's good news, isn't it?"

"Yeah. I don't suppose your bet will pay out if the game's canceled."

Her expression goes ugly, but then she pulls it back with a forced laugh. "Don't joke about that sort of thing, Erin. Now, come on, let's get you tidied up. Your hair's an awful mess."

I thrust both hands into my hair and scrub at my scalp, feeling the tangles forming around my fingers. Then I drag a hand across my lips. It comes away pink with lipstick.

Amber gasps like I've torn out her intestines and used them as a scarf. "What are you doing?" she cries. "Oh my god, this is a disaster."

"I'll never be enough for you," I cry, much louder than I intended. A sob makes its way into my voice, which surprises me.

Amber holds out both hands like she's placating an angry bear. "Have you eaten anything? I have some dried apple slices in my bag."

"I don't want any apple! I don't want any of this. I just want…"

What *do* I want? I honestly don't know anymore.

"We'll fix your face and hair," Amber says gently. "And I'll buy you a coffee to perk you up. Why don't you have some caramel syrup as a treat? You're getting a lot of exercise running around, after all. Then we'll talk tactics. We can still win this, Erin."

Numbly, I let her help me to my feet. I try to convince myself that this is what I want. Security over freedom. In six months, I'll be eighteen, and maybe things will be different by then.

Deep down, though, I already know that nothing changes unless you force it to.

GRAYSON

"Wait up!" I jog up to Lenny and give her shoulder a friendly squeeze. She pulls away. "What's wrong?"

"You don't take anything seriously, do you?"

She has no idea. Sometimes, it feels like if I don't laugh, I'll fall to pieces.

"I'm trying to help you," she continues. "But you're not even trying. Turning your mic off, inviting Erin Love along to meet me?"

"She's just another contestant. It's no big deal—"

"She's *Erin Love*," Lenny interrupts. "She tried to tag you out of the competition, remember? She's pals with Anton Frazer. Do you want him to find out why you're really here?"

My smile fades. "I haven't told her anything," I say.

"Other than my name?" She raises an eyebrow, the one with a metal bar through it. I don't say anything. "For pity's sake, Grayson.

I want you to keep playing this game. Because that's what you want. But you need to focus."

"Sorry, what were you saying?"

The bad temper melts out of her expression, replaced by mild exasperation. I'm suddenly conscious that I must smell terrible. Falling into that mud was not my greatest moment, but it was so damn slippery and…well, let's not go there.

At last, Lenny breaks our gaze. "Have you heard anything from Anton?" she asks.

"He sent us a message saying the game's not over. Maybe that's wishful thinking on his part though."

"And Rose's ghost? How's *her* game going?" It's clear from her tone that she doesn't think the ghost is real.

"You'll never believe this. The last announcement from Rose revealed Charlotte as the third suspect. I didn't see that coming."

Lenny laughs. "That's because you're naive and overly trusting." Her phone buzzes; a series of notifications are coming in at the same time. She frowns at it. "I should go. I wouldn't worry about the game not continuing though. Evil always finds a way."

"But I'll miss you if you go," I say, sticking out my bottom lip.

"Quit it. That phone in the bag's an old one of mine. I put some credit on it. If you need me."

"*If* I need you? You're all that's keeping me from complete disaster."

"This is true," she says. She smiles wryly. "Remember that night we got caught in the middle of that fight?"

Of course I remember. It was the moment when I realized Lenny was going to be my friend and not just some cute girl who bought ice cream from the shop I worked in.

———

I was working a late shift at Softly Scoops It. Lenny had been coming in for a few months. She'd sit in a booth and drink a milkshake while typing away at what I later found out was some AI program she was developing at college. Sometimes, when it was quiet, we'd sit and chat. She was nice to talk to, and I'd started opening up to her about Rose.

That night, she'd barely had time to take out her laptop when this fight broke out between two grown men who both wanted the last waffle cone. Spoons were used as weapons, chocolate sauce was sprayed on the walls, people skidded on pools of melting gelato.

I pulled Lenny behind the counter, and we ducked down out of sight while the fight raged on. She was biting her lip, which I mistook for terror. "What's your favorite flavor?" I asked, attempting to keep her mind off the danger we were in.

"Um, mango sorbet?" she replied, shielding her head as a stool came flying past our hiding place.

"Even after witnessing this display of civil dis-sorbet-dience?" I asked.

Her lips parted in surprise, then a slight smile made it onto her face. "My first impressions of you were totally wrong."

"I look like I'll be funny, don't I? And then I open my mouth."

"I guess I thought you'd be one of those good-looking guys who believes he can smile people into thinking he's a nice guy."

I laughed. "I'll take good-looking because the rest of that was… yeah."

Right then, a massive dude wielding a broken chair leg launched himself over the counter. I'm ashamed to say I nearly fainted in fear.

Lenny was amazing though. She took charge of the situation and talked the guy down. By the time the police arrived, everyone was eating ice cream together.

Lenny and I have been best friends ever since.

———

"You going to fix this whole thing for me tonight too?" I ask her now.

"That part's up to you." She gives me a little push. "Get on with it, then. I have things to do too. It's not the Grayson show, you know?"

She heads off, but she pauses to flick me the middle finger. I grin after her. I'm on her good side again.

I find the spot on the sidewalk where I left Erin, but she's not there. Her burger is on the ground, and dejectedly I pick it up. I slip onto a side street and change out of my filthy clothes, into a pair of Lenny's skinny jeans and one of her sweaters. As I'm emerging, I spot Erin. She's in a hair salon with a woman who looks almost exactly like her.

There's no one else in the shop, and three of the workers are swarming around Erin as she sits regally in a chair. The other Erin orders them about while holding a champagne glass.

A bell announces my entrance, and everyone looks up. "Sign says closed," the other Erin says.

She sounds like Erin too. Close up, though, I can see that she's considerably older. Erin's mother, Amber, I realize. The other half of her channel.

"I was after Erin, actually," I say, slumping into a leather chair with my legs over the arm. "We've been hanging out during the game."

Amber's lips twitch into the bitchiest smile I've ever seen. "I'm aware. But she's got me now. So…shoo."

I spin in the chair and ignore her. I unwrap the burger and take a massive bite.

Erin—the real one—makes a displeased noise. "Don't you breathe on me with your meat breath."

I chew quickly and swallow more than is comfortable. "So what's the plan?"

"I don't have one," Erin says.

"Why would you two need a plan?" Amber sniffs. "You can't win this game together."

"You're done," a hairdresser says, showing Erin a three-sixty of her head with a mirror. "Happy?"

"Rarely," Erin says.

"She's perfect," Amber says. "I'll post about your salon tomorrow, if that's OK. We've got things to do tonight."

The man grins at her. "Of course, of course. We're so grateful for your support."

"Of course you are," Erin says, climbing down from the chair and sashaying to the door.

I follow her outside while her mother stays to exchange a few words with the shop owner.

"You all right?" I say.

"I don't know," Erin says. It's weird. Her time in the salon appears to have preened and cleaned the spark out of her.

The shop door dings as Amber steps outside. "I'm sure I'll see you around during the game," Erin says abruptly. "Bye."

That was weird. Guess I'm on my own, then. I've walked ten yards down the road when I feel fingers close on my arm. Sharp nails dig painfully into my skin. "I'm on to you," Amber snarls. "You must think I'm stupid."

"What have I done?" I say, laughing nervously. I glance at Erin, but she's engrossed in her phone.

She gives me a nasty smile. "Boys like you think they've got us fooled. You're a nice guy. Friendly, self-deprecating, unthreatening. But I know what's hiding beneath the surface. Secretly, you hate women. Making us the enemy helps you deal with the fact that you're a nobody. A nothing."

"Um, if you're worried about me and Erin, she's really not my type."

She looks me up and down and shudders. "Gross. But I suppose there are plenty of girls with low self-esteem out there. Erin is not one of them. Now fuck off."

A cloud of perfume lingers after she's rejoined Erin outside the shop. She shoots me a final disgusted look, then hurries her daughter away.

"That was seriously weird," I mutter to myself.

I can't for the life of me understand why Amber has it in for me. Maybe she's overprotective and does this with every boy Erin meets. But something about her tirade felt kind of personal. And I can't shake the feeling that there's more going on here.

I'm sure I haven't met Amber before. I'm almost *completely* sure.

CHARLOTTE

Here's a secret: Jesse knew I lied about Anton's alibi.

He was working security at that party where Rose died and I had my moment with Anton. He knew that Anton wasn't with me all night.

The real story starts the same as the one I told Grayson and Erin. Anton's hand on mine and his soft snores. Me drifting off to sleep with his head against my shoulder. But that's not how it ends.

———

I woke up close to midnight, curled up on the sofa. Anton was gone. The summer house was silent and dark. I ran through the maze, the path lit by strings of fairy lights tangled in the hedges. When I found my way out, most people had disappeared inside the house. I didn't join them though. There was too much on my mind.

I sat in a swing seat, the warmth of a patio heater already chasing off the scariness of waking alone. I hid in my imagined stories until I fell asleep. In the morning, everywhere was crawling with police cars and an ambulance. Someone had found Rose in the pool. She was dead.

"Charlotte, where the hell have you been?" Matthew called out, running to me. He looked like he hadn't slept all night, and he smelled of sweat and stale alcohol. "You can't wander off alone."

"I wasn't alone," I said. "I was with Anton, actually, but he—"

Matthew interrupted me with a laugh. "Anton? *You* spent the night with Anton? Yeah, right."

"I did! We went to his summer house in the middle of the maze and fell asleep, and it was lovely."

At that moment, a man in a cheap suit strolled over to join us. He had a notebook in his hand and smelled like coffee, so I figured he was one of the police officers.

"I couldn't help but overhear," he said, pen poised above the notepad. "Do you remember what time you and Mr. Frazer left the party together?"

"About ten o'clock, I think," I said.

"And he was with you all night?"

I was torn. I could only account for Anton's whereabouts for the hour we were awake. But I couldn't backtrack with Matthew standing there. He'd have thought I was even more of a loser than he already did. I just nodded.

The rest of the morning was a confusing whirlwind. There were more questions, and my mom came to pick me up, yelling at Matthew for taking me to a party where a girl died. But no one questioned my story.

I went home and I waited for Anton to call, but he never did, and Matthew refused to pass on my messages. It was for my own good, he said. I couldn't give up, so I went to the house. Anton was gone. Jesse was there though, collecting a box of stuff from the studio. I asked him where Anton had moved to. I told him we were friends, but he laughed at me.

"Oh, you're the girl who told the police Anton spent the night with you." He sneered. "Except I saw him leaving the maze before midnight. Busted."

———

A surge of nausea washes the memory away. I lean out over the bridge wall, thinking that I'm going to throw up. But I don't. There's nothing left inside me. I'm empty, physically, emotionally, morally. The things I've done and the lies I've told make me ashamed to call myself Anton's number one fan. I don't deserve him.

I can't stop shaking, and it's not just the cold from being soaked to the skin in wet clothes. It's fear and guilt on top of hypothermia. I'm feeling as terrible as it's possible for a girl to feel when Rose's avatar appears through my smart glasses. Turns out it *is* possible to feel more terrible after all.

"Change of plan," Rose says. "Look who's here."

She clicks her fingers, and a video of Anton plays. Anton is tied to a chair with a gag in his mouth. He's struggling, and the chair's bouncing all over the place. Then it topples to the side. The gag loosens enough for him to start yelling.

"Help me," he cries. "A million pounds if you help me."

His eyes widen at something off-screen. He wiggles around, attempting to shuffle away, but he's too slow.

"The ghost's not—" The video cuts off.

I stagger off the curb and accidentally step into the road. A bus horn blares out, startling me into leaping aside.

"Do you want him back?" Rose purrs. "The winner of *my* game gets Anton to do whatever they please with. Take his million pounds, throw him in the Thames, marry him for all I care. It doesn't matter to me as long as the truth comes out. Find my killer and I'll let him go."

"You're a monster," I whisper, my teeth chattering.

So many of my daydreams have started this way, with Anton being kidnapped and me—well, Lola—the only one who can save him. But Lola always knows what to do. Whereas I don't know where to start.

"All you have to do is keep on playing, and Anton's yours," Rose continues. "And if no one wins him or one of you tries to call the police? Well, I guess I'll take him with me."

I clutch a hand over my mouth. She's threatening his life. Anton's life. The city flows around me, noisy and smelly and oblivious. I want to yell at everyone. Make them stop and listen. *Anton is in danger. Why don't you care?*

"I've narrowed down the players to a select few," she says. "Are you ready to play, *Accomplices*?"

The way she says that word—*Accomplices*—sounds like an accusation. There's a new hatred in her voice that she was keeping masked before. This is no game. Games are playful and fun, not threatening and dangerous. Jesse is *dead*. Anton has been kidnapped. And I am totally, utterly, completely out of my depth.

"I'm sending you the coordinates for the next challenge," Rose says. "Let's say twenty minutes? Anyone who doesn't turn up won't get to play anymore, and you really don't want to miss out on the fun we're going to have. Take a bus if you want. But the old rules apply—go out of range for more than five minutes, and it's over. Ticktock, ticktock. Don't keep Anton waiting."

She vanishes with a maniacal laugh.

My map activates, and I can see the location of Rose's challenge. It's not far from where the van dropped us off after the museum debacle. I can make it there in twenty minutes. I have something to focus on, something to take my mind off Jesse and his dead, staring eyes. I'll have to face up to what happened in the water at some point, but right now, Anton needs me.

I flag down a taxi, giving the driver the address. It's only after the taxi drops me off that I realize exactly where I am. I was here earlier, watching Erin meet up with Jesse. I follow the spot on the map to an abandoned building fronted with scaffolding and blue plastic netting that obscures most of the facade. The ground floor is boarded up, but there's a gap through which I can make out the closed front door.

There's a group of people outside. Grayson, Matthew, Beatrix, Erin Love and Erin's mother, Amber. I shuffle across the road, trying to keep my shivering at bay. Everyone falls silent and stares at me, except for Amber, who is engrossed in her phone. I can smell her perfume from yards away.

Matthew has a look of injured confusion on his face. "Was it true?" he asks in this small voice unlike his usual bullish shout. "You're the one who posted those mean comments about Rose?"

"It was a joke," I say very quietly.

Erin laughs. "It is kind of funny."

Everyone gapes at her, and she holds up her hands, backing away.

"I can't believe that I defended you every time people said you were a loser," Matthew says.

"Who said I was a loser?"

He shakes his head at me. "Unbelievable. You only care about yourself, don't you?"

I shrink under the intensity of his disgust. I never thought I'd care if Matthew hated me. Turns out, I do. And he only knows half of what I've done.

A bright flash briefly wipes clean the rest of the world. When I blink away the light, I realize it's Emma and her camera.

"Stop taking my picture!" I hurriedly wipe at my eyes.

"What are *you* doing here?" Beatrix says. The look she gives Emma is pure hatred. Emma did nearly destroy Matthew and Beatrix's relationship, I suppose. Seems unfair to blame the messenger though.

"Refusing to slink off with my tail between my legs," Emma says resolutely. She sounds more in control than she looks. The bump on her head is horribly bruised and half her hair is free of its ponytail. "Someone needs to get to the bottom of all the lies."

"And a teenage reporter for *St. Bernadette's School Press* is clearly the right person for the job," Matthew says. "Go home, Emma. You're out of the competition and in over your head. Again."

"This isn't one of Anton's parties. You don't get to throw me out this time, and I don't see any of your fancy lawyers around to scare my parents. Besides, Rose texted me an invitation, so…I'm staying."

"Ghosts don't send text messages," Erin says, quietly enough that not everyone hears.

"What now?" Matthew makes an exasperated face.

"I said, 'Ghosts don't send text messages.' Whoever summoned us here, it's not Rose."

Matthew shakes his head. "I never believed it was."

"No, it has to be her," Grayson says.

"Who are you really, Gray26?" Matthew snaps. "Why are you even here?"

Grayson clamps his mouth shut and doesn't say anything else. Matthew has a point. Rose—or whoever it is hiding behind her computer-manipulated face—invited us here for a reason. We all knew Rose. We were all at that same party where she died. Except for Grayson. So who is he?

A distant bell chimes on the hour. "Are we going in or what?" Amber barks, looking up from her phone.

The others traipse up the steps toward the hotel entrance. Matthew tries the handle, and the door swings open. I wait down on the sidewalk though. This whole situation is so, so wrong.

Erin pauses on the threshold, and I think she's going to say something mean. But for once, her voice is missing its usual sharpness. "We're in this together, Charlotte. We can't back out now," she says, then ruins what was almost a nice thing by continuing to speak. "Basically, we're all fucked."

I take a deep, wobbly breath; then I follow her through the door. It doesn't matter why the others are here or what they think of me. Anton is the only one who matters. He's literally all I have left.

ERIN

This is the shittiest hotel I've ever been in, and I've seen my fair share of shitty hotels. I'm sure that it used to be grand, with gold leaf on the plasterwork and velvet drapes. Now there are big strips of wallpaper peeling from the walls, and the stair carpet has been ripped up, revealing bare wood speckled with black mold.

There are wires snaking across the ceiling, leading to lights that don't do much to brighten the place. What little furniture there is has fallen into disrepair. A coffee table with a broken leg leans against a wall, with a vase full of dead flowers sitting on top. A rug is so threadbare that I can see the hessian backing along with a large dark stain.

I approach the front desk. Perched on the chair with her hand on an old-fashioned telephone is a mannequin. Marker pens have been used to garishly color in her face, like a child's attempt at putting on makeup. A red wig sits askew on her plastic head. On the desk in front of her, there are two wristbands and two pairs of smart glasses.

Emma and Amber put them on. Amber adjusts hers in a tarnished mirror, checking her reflection from several angles. I catch Matthew staring strangely at her. He's always been weird around Amber. At first, I took it for dislike. Now I'm not so sure.

"Why has Rose sent us here?" Charlotte whispers.

"The hotel was meant to be the location of one of Anton's challenges." Matthew gestures to the mannequin. "She has nothing to do with us though."

"Whoever brought us here has set this up to reveal the next suspect," I say, grimacing. "We're dancing to a psychopath's tune. Tra-la-la."

"We've got no choice but to play. It's the only way to save Anton," Beatrix says.

"Some people are only here for Anton's money," Charlotte says, directing her judgment at me and Amber.

I almost make a crude joke about Charlotte's intentions toward Anton, but there's a new desperation to Charlotte, like she's barely holding it together. I'm guessing she's taken a dip in the river, because her clothes are wet and dirty, and she's shivering with cold. It's no fun mocking her when she's already at rock bottom.

"I'm here because I want to find out who is doing this to us," Matthew says.

"It's Rose," Grayson says. "I know it is."

Emma takes his picture, making him hurry off with a hand over his face. He leads us into a lounge with shabby sofas and clean squares on the wall where pictures used to hang. There are more mannequins, all female with red hair. They're splayed out on the furniture. Some have been crudely dressed in designer clothing; others wear costume jewelry that reflects the light from a dusty chandelier.

"This is up there with the creepiest things I've ever seen," Grayson says. "Pretty sure we're in a horror movie."

"In a world where mannequins come to life after sunset," Beatrix says in a decent impression of a movie voice-over.

Grayson laughs nervously and tries to smile at her.

"Dead rich, dead pretty, dead dead," she continues.

"Can we take this seriously?" Matthew interrupts, and Beatrix stops with a roll of her eyes.

"Are they supposed to be her?" Charlotte says, chattering her teeth in my direction.

"Like Erin would wear fashions from three years ago," Amber grumbles. "Or plastic diamonds."

"I don't think that's the point they're trying to make," Matthew says.

Emma snaps another photo. The flash splits the darkness to reveal the grime on the floor and the mannequins' smudged makeup. It's strangely unsettling, especially considering the mannequins really do look like me.

Their cold hard faces are fixed in full-lipped pouts. Their pink skin is shiny and bloodless, and their limbs are arranged into unnatural positions that accentuate how not alive they are. They're as fake as I feel in my newly applied makeup, with my hair stinking of hairspray. Like me, they have no choice except to let others style and pose them however they want.

"What's the point of this?" Amber complains.

"You tell us," Matthew says.

"You first." She pushes past him to head upstairs.

We traipse up the creaking stairs, lit by flashes from Emma's camera. The bursts of light pick out dusty oil paintings. Crumbling brickwork reveals the wooden bones of the house beneath. There are several doors up here, all closed.

"What was the challenge supposed to be?" I ask Matthew.

"Never have I ever." He sighs. "Anton thought it would be a break from the running around and would make good content."

"Huh." I push the first door open. More mannequins, posed on a bed with lacy sheets. "Never have I ever eaten cheese."

"You haven't lived," he says, managing a crooked smile. "Never have I ever…um…"

"Never have I ever cheated on someone," Beatrix says, which surprises me. The mood in the room goes icy.

"Neither have I," Matthew says, but Beatrix has already left the room. He rounds on Charlotte. "This is your fault. That comment you posted on GossApp today has her doubting everything I say."

"I said I was sorry," Charlotte mumbles. Pretty sure she's said no such thing.

Matthew gets close to Charlotte, leaning down to speak right in her face. "Never have I ever screwed over my family."

She gulps heavily. I think she's going to cry. "You're not my family," she whispers. "You're the son of the man who stole my mother from me."

He makes an irritated-sounding noise and points at her meaningfully. Then he pushes past to the upstairs landing where Beatrix is waiting and kicks open the next bedroom door. This room is different. As well as the mannequins, there are pieces of paper stuck all over the walls. I squeeze past to take a closer look.

"What? That's theft!" Amber cries, shoving me aside. She snatches the papers from the walls and crumples each one up, trying to block us from seeing what they are.

I pick up one of the discarded balls and unfurl it. It's a final notice for a credit card in Amber's name. The letter's been ripped into several pieces, but someone's taped it together and used pink lipstick to draw a ring around the total. It's over twenty thousand pounds. *Each* bill is for a similar amount, adding up to hundreds of thousands. One is a notice of default on the mortgage.

No wonder she's so desperate for me to win Anton's money.

"Get out," Amber shouts. "This is personal information."

Matthew pulls down a bank statement with a low whistle. "I'm impressed."

Amber snatches it from him. "Shut up, or I'll tell everyone *your* secrets." She whips around on Emma. "And get that camera out of my face. Always sticking it where you're not wanted."

Emma laughs. "Believe it or not, I haven't bothered taking your picture before now."

Amber glares at her. "You were in our faces at that party too. Then Matthew threw you out. Pretty embarrassing, wasn't it?"

"The party where Rose died?" Grayson says.

Amber ignores him and goes back to gathering up paper. All I can do is numbly watch as she rampages around the room, armfuls of bills clutched to her chest.

I am cold empty plastic.

The flash turns everything white, and I'm pulled into last year, when debt collectors were calling us up every day and scary men kept turning up at the house wanting to speak to Amber. That was the first time I realized how much of a problem my mother has. That was when I decided it was up to me to fix things for her.

I didn't have much to trade on. My looks, my body, my age. I'd had my photo taken enough times to know how to pose, so I figured it would be easy. Not that different from the bikini photo shoots I'd done so many times. I mostly sold them as one-off pieces of art to uber-rich men who contacted me through social media.

I was careful to always hide my face so no one would be able to prove the pictures were really me if they ended up on the Internet. I never met anyone in person. I told myself it was just meat, and I pretended that I was the one in control.

Amber never asked why the men stopped turning up at the house. She didn't ask where the money to pay off the debt collectors came from either. She had to know though. Where would a sixteen-year-old have gotten all that money from?

I never spoke to anyone about what I'd had to do. One person found out, but they never told. I made sure of that.

GRAYSON

We all know who Rose's next suspect is going to be. When Rose appears with her spinning wheel and that knowing smile, I'm almost ready. Seeing her standing there, even if she's made of light and computer code, still takes my breath away.

I can't accept that it's not the real Rose. The way she slouches with her weight on one leg. All her little habits, like how she sweeps her hair from one side to the other. How can she be so much like Rose and not be Rose?

No. Matthew and Erin have to be wrong. It's too painful to accept that this has all been a trick.

"How are you enjoying my haunted house?" she says, taking a bow.

"What do you want from us?" Beatrix says.

"Let Anton go!" Charlotte cries.

"Let's meet our next suspect, shall we?" Rose says. She spins the wheel, as noisy as ever. She's drawing it out. Playing with us.

It's obvious the next suspect is Amber. I'm presuming Rose knew about her financial situation and was threatening to tell on her. For all her faults, Rose didn't like lies.

Like before, an embedded video screen opens. This time, it's a recording taken in Anton's kitchen. The camera's been left running after filming some stupid eating challenge or whatever. Rose is there, making a cup of tea, quietly humming to herself. She's so alive and so beautiful. I swallow, watching as she jabs aggressively at the tea bag with a spoon.

"Fetch me a cuppa, will you *Rose*. Be a love, *Rose*," she mutters. A smile twitches on her lips. She makes a hacking noise and spits into the tea. "Screw you, Anton."

I laugh out loud. It's good to know she hated him. It's also heartbreaking to know that she hated him.

She's happily stirring the spit tea when a redhead storms into the shot. I was expecting Amber. But this girl is younger. Prettier.

I look across at Erin, and she's gone as still as a mannequin.

In the video, Erin goes straight over to Rose and shoves her hard. "What the hell do you think you're doing?"

Rose steps back and examines her striped sweater where Erin touched her, dusting it down with a look of mild irritation. "Questioning my choices in life, if you must know."

"My mother's problems are none of your business," Erin yells. "Stay out of it, Rose."

It's weird seeing Erin so worked up. I remember her temper when I rescued her from that crate at the museum. Despite her cold exterior, Erin's blood runs hot.

"It is my business when her seedy loan shark friends turn up here, isn't it?" Rose says coolly. There's a pause. "Oh, you didn't know that? Sweet."

"What did they want?"

"Er, money? Being loan sharks. They tried to intimidate me into paying them. I guess they were banking on me giving a shit about Amber. Which I don't."

"There's not giving a shit, and there's threatening my mother with *social workers*? You don't think things are bad enough already?"

Rose sighs dramatically and folds her arms. "I heard about your side hustle, Erin. You're sixteen for fuck's sake. You shouldn't be selling photos of yourself online to fund your mother's gambling habit."

Back in the tatty hotel bedroom, Emma gasps softly and glances at Erin. She snaps a photo. Erin pretends to not notice though. She continues staring straight ahead, her chin defiantly lifted.

The video keeps rolling. "It's none of your business," Erin snarls.

"It is my business when I have to work with you and Amber. You're a child, and she isn't fit to be a parent."

"You can't call a social worker on her. She's not that bad. She really isn't."

"You're a coward," Rose says. "Why are you protecting someone who doesn't give a shit about you?"

With no warning, Erin swings a punch. Rose staggers backwards, raising her fingers to dab at a bleeding lip.

"Stay away from me, and stay away from my mother," Erin says quietly, her face twisting into something vicious. "Come near me again and you're dead."

The video ends.

Grinning, Rose points at the wheel as it slows and stops spinning. She tears the silhouette off to reveal two faces—Amber *and* Erin.

"Like sisters." Rose laughs. "But which one is really calling the shots?"

"This is bullshit," Amber snaps. "Who the fuck does she think she is?"

"There's a special prize hidden in one of the rooms," Rose continues. She purses red lips at us and blows a kiss. "The mannequins will show you which way to go."

I glance at the mannequins and try to figure it out. I've got nothing.

"Smile for the camera, Erin." The ghost flickers and disappears. We all stand here, waiting for someone to speak.

"What are the photos of?" Charlotte finally says. "Were they… you know?"

"Fuck off, Charlotte," Erin snarls.

"I wasn't being mean. I just don't understand," Charlotte says. She goes quiet, chewing her lip.

Amber grabs her daughter's arm and pulls her outside the room. The rest of us crowd around the door and watch them. Emma stands poised with her camera.

"This could ruin me," Amber hisses, loud enough that everyone can hear. "How could you be so stupid?"

"They're your debts." Erin snatches her arm from Amber.

"They're private. You dragged me into this sordid mess by threatening to murder Rose days before she died for real. And the photos she was talking about? Didn't you think about my reputation?"

"That's all you care about, isn't it?" Erin cries. "How *you* will look."

"Was this your plan all along? To cast me as a terrible mother?" She slow claps her daughter. "Congratulations, Erin. You win."

"I was trying to help you!"

"For the last time, I don't need your help. Especially not that kind of help. How could you be so stupid as to let Rose—of all people— find out about your little photo shoot? Now the whole world will find out how much of a—"

"Whoa, time out." Matthew interrupts, placing himself between the two. "Amber, you're being seriously uncool right now."

Amber laughs hysterically. "Is this you looking for a signed picture? I'm sure she'd be happy to sell you one for the right price."

I don't usually agree with Matthew, but right now I want to punch Amber on Erin's behalf. What kind of mother lets her daughter feel responsible for fixing her financial problems, then turns on her when the truth comes out? Amber should feel ashamed, but only of herself.

Erin swallows heavily and fixes her mother with a cold stare. "We're done," she says, her voice shaking. "As soon as this is over, I'm leaving."

"Where exactly are you planning to go?" Amber laughs. "Oh, wait—you're planning to run away with your little boyfriend, Jesse? Ah, you thought it was a secret? How adorable."

Jesse. Erin and *him*? I can't for the life of me understand why a girl as beautiful and as sharp as Erin would ever go for Jesse. It doesn't make sense. Charlotte's surprised too. She lets out a gasp and clamps a hand over her mouth.

A flicker of hurt crosses Erin's face, but she pushes it away. "You knew about me and Jesse?"

"He picked you up because you looked like a meal ticket, Erin. And you let him use you because that's what you do."

I can't listen to this anymore. "You're the one using her," I say. "You're pathetic."

Everyone looks at me in surprise. Like they didn't realize I had it in me. I've surprised myself too.

Amber tosses her head. "And here comes another boy wanting a piece of my daughter. But don't worry; I'm sure there's plenty to go around."

"Stop it," Matthew says. "That's enough."

Amber looks him up and down, then turns to Erin. "They don't care about you, not really. They'll use you and throw you away, and it's me you'll come crawling back to."

"No, I won't," Erin says in barely a whisper.

"We'll see," Amber says before leaving the room with a swish of her hair. Her heels tap down the stairs.

Erin smooths down her T-shirt, and then, ignoring all of us, she sets about ransacking the bedroom. She picks up every mannequin and tosses it down, limbs popping out of sockets, wigs sliding off shiny plastic. After she's done with the mannequins, she pulls the pillows off the bed and flips the mattress.

When she's turned over every piece of furniture in the room, she starts on the next. The rest of us silently follow, no one knowing what to say or do. We stand there watching. She's too calm and methodical to be taking her temper out on the hotel. She's looking for something. It's times like this I wish I were smarter because I have no idea what's going on.

"What's she doing?" Beatrix whispers.

"Finding the special prize that Rose talked about," Charlotte says, her teeth chattering. "The photos she sold to pay Amber's debts."

She's gone really pale. I guess she's spooked like the rest of us, but I can't help wondering if something else is going on too. She was acting odd when we got here, all shaky and skittish. But since Erin and Jesse's relationship was revealed, she's gone as white as death.

Matthew grimaces at Charlotte. Then he silently hands her his leather jacket. "The ghost said the mannequins would show us the way," he says. "I don't get it."

Erin finishes searching the upstairs and goes downstairs. Outwardly she looks calm, but her eyes have this panic in them that's not been there before. We follow her into the living room. This room is warmer than the rest, with a fire burning in the hearth. The mannequins bask in the light of the crackling flames, without a care in the world.

Erin turns on the spot. "Where is it? I've searched everywhere."

"Rose blew us a kiss. She was wearing red lipstick," Charlotte says, small in Matthew's oversize jacket.

"Rose always wore red lipstick," Erin says.

"But only some of the mannequins are. It's a clue." Seeming to pull herself together, Charlotte walks over to the one mannequin in the room with red lips and follows its outstretched arm to the mantelpiece. She pulls an envelope from the face of a carriage clock.

Erin freezes, her chest heaving. Charlotte hesitates with her fingers on the envelope's flap; then she tosses the whole thing into the flames.

"Hey, that could have been important," Emma says, springing forward. The envelope is ash now.

Charlotte shakes her head. "It wasn't." She walks out of the room toward the front door. The rest of us follow.

Beatrix clears her throat. "Um, people? Who set this up? Because it wasn't a ghost."

It's a good question.

Charlotte's bottom lip wobbles. "Jesse," she whispers. "He was here earlier. I was following Erin, and I saw them meet outside. There was a van here too. He must have unloaded the mannequins and set everything up."

Erin nods. "She's right. I guess someone—Rose's fake ghost—was paying him to sabotage Anton's little game from the inside." She gives a sour smile. "He did always love money."

It fits with what he was up to at the river, I think. That call I overheard, where he mentioned Rose. The projector.

Charlotte takes a deep breath and lifts her head. "I need to tell you something else about Jesse," she says, and then the lights go out.

CHARLOTTE

Jesse is all I can think about. I was more or less holding it together right up until Amber revealed he was Erin's boyfriend. And now he's dead. Because I killed him. Poor, poor Erin.

In the dark, the memory is all there is. My foot kicking out. Water filling his lungs, no strength to struggle. Limp fingers, white skin.

Just like Rose.

My mind fills in the blanks. The lives not lived and the years stolen away. It's what I do—make up stories. Both Rose and Jesse are nothing but stories that will never happen. Wedding parties, gray hairs, big family Christmases like I've always dreamed of.

In the dark, I'm surrounded by their untold stories, and I can barely stand.

"Where are the lights?" Emma says.

I try to move toward her voice, but I bump into something. A cold dead hand strokes my cheek, and I scream. I can't see her, but I know it's Rose. Her fingers are so stiff; there's nothing but bones left after a year in the ground.

I try to fight her off, but she tangles her arms around me, tugging at my hair, pressing her fleshless skull against my face. I struggle and scream and kick.

"Charlotte, stop," Matthew says. "Calm down."

A warm hand feels my face, then finds my hand. He pulls me free. Plastic clatters to the ground. The mannequins; it was just a mannequin.

Flashes of light from someone's phone flashlight are blindingly bright. They sweep past me, but I can't make out my surroundings.

"There's no handle on the front door," Grayson says.

"The windows are boarded up," Beatrix says. "This is a fricking nightmare."

"We'll have to go back upstairs." Matthew releases me. "Climb out via the scaffolding."

The bobbing flashlight beams move away from me, and I hear footsteps on the stairs.

"Wait, can't you kick the door down?" Beatrix says. "You spend most of your life in the gym, Matthew."

"And you watch nothing but baking shows and can't cook for shit," he mutters.

Someone laughs. Erin, I think. She has a cruel, sharp laugh, like Rose's was. In my head, I'm back at that party, and Rose is calling me a pathetic fan. "You will never, ever get to be with him," she taunts. "He wouldn't look twice at you."

Suddenly, I'm surrounded by people laughing at me. Matthew, Beatrix, Erin, Grayson, Emma. Even Anton.

"You really are pathetic," Anton says. "As if I'd want you."

I try to breathe, but my lungs won't work. I can't get any air. My chest is so tight that I think I'm turning to plastic. I'm becoming one of the mannequins, with their smooth, lifeless skin and staring eyes.

"Join us," Rose whispers in my ear. "You'll never be alone again."

She sweeps something across my collarbone. It's cold against my skin, and it jangles slightly. I think it's one of the gaudy necklaces from the mannequins. I reach up to touch the dangling jewels, only it tightens around my neck. Tighter and tighter, like she's twisting it. The metal settings cut into my skin. I really can't breathe.

I hear the others traipsing up the stairs, their voices growing fainter. I want to call out to them, but I can't make a sound. I claw at my neck and try to get my fingers under the necklace, but it's too tight. My chest burns; my brain conjures sparks that fly across my vision. My legs sag beneath me.

There are hurried footsteps, then a bright flash of light. The necklace is suddenly gone as if it were never there. I suck in a desperate gasp of air as I drop to the ground.

Another flash, farther away this time. I crawl toward it. The light came from the lounge, where the fire burns low. There's a person kneeling in front of the grate, scraping at the embers with a poker.

"What are you doing?" I rasp, finding that my voice is small and painful.

Emma gasps and spins around, taking my photo as she does. "Charlotte? I thought everyone was upstairs. I was…um…that envelope."

"It burned," I say. "I made sure."

"Damn it," she grumbles. "Since when do you care about Erin Love?"

"Because it's the right thing to do," I say. Truth is, I don't give a damn about Erin Love. But looking at those photos would have been wrong, and for all my faults, I'm not that much of a bitch.

Breathing is getting easier. I stand up and find that my legs are shaky but strong. My neck stings where I clawed at it, but my head is clear. The ghosts are gone.

And I have to do the right thing by Jesse.

Now that I've calmed down, I manage to find my own phone flashlight. It guides me to the top of the stairs before the battery goes, but I can hear the others. In one of the bedrooms, moonlight streams in through an open window. There are people on the scaffolding, climbing down to the street.

Erin sticks her head inside. "There you are," she says, offering me her arm. She's gray-faced and looks exhausted.

By the time we've made it down to the street, only Grayson is waiting for us. He gives me a weird look and opens his mouth to speak. But then we're interrupted by Emma clattering her way down the ladder with her camera bobbing around her neck. I feel my own neck. It really hurts.

"Where are Matthew and Beatrix?" she asks.

"They went to find the rest of the crew," Erin says, her tone clipped and cold. "They think Jesse was involved in setting this up. I've tried to call him, but the bastard's not answering."

"Do you want to talk about it?" Grayson says gently. "Any of it?"

"No," Erin replies quickly. "I want to find whoever it is behind all this and kill them."

Emma raises both eyebrows. "Literally?"

"Shut up, Emma," Erin snarls; then she sags a little and sighs. "I'll try Jesse's phone again."

"Do I know Jesse?" Emma says.

Erin scrolls through her phone and shows Emma a picture of them together. Erin's smile on the screen claws at my heart. I have to tell her. I can't tell her.

"This is Jesse?" Emma says, taking the phone. "I've seen him before."

"He was at the museum," Erin says.

Emma shakes her head. "Before tonight. Before Rose." She frowns and hands the phone to Erin. "I'll have to look at my old photos and see if anything jogs my memory."

"Why does it matter?" Grayson says, scratching his head. His hair is stiff with dry mud. "Am I missing something?"

"He knows what's up with this ghost thing, right? But no one's asking why he's involved," Emma explains.

"Money," Grayson says. "Probably. Isn't it always money?"

Erin nods tightly. "With Jesse, yes."

Emma claps once. "So we find him and we find Rose's supposed ghost too," she says. "And we find out why we've been dragged into this mess."

I take a deep breath. "I need to tell you something," I say.

They all turn to me, faces shocked like they'd forgotten I was here.

"Jesse is—"

"What's with your neck?" Emma interrupts. "Did you scratch yourself?"

My neck is seriously sore, actually. I tentatively touch it again. "I think I had a panic attack and tried to strangle myself," I mutter.

Erin pulls at my hoodie. Her expression starts off impatient, then turns to concern. "You're all cut up and bruised. You did this to yourself?"

"Maybe?" I say, wincing. "I don't really remember. Everything's kind of hazy. I mean, I thought it was Rose at the time, so…"

"Rose?" Grayson says. "Why would Rose want to strangle you?"

"You'll all want to strangle me in a minute," I say, sitting on the sidewalk. Everyone stares at me in silence, waiting. I take a deep breath and wipe the tears from my eyes before they can fall. "Jesse's dead. I think I killed him."

24

ERIN

We stand inside a gated yard by the river. An expanse of scarred concrete stretches down to the water, too small to be of interest to developers. It's empty except for various pieces of litter lying among washed-up algae and weeds, everything coated in dirty yellow foam. Totally the sort of place you could imagine finding a body.

Except there's no body.

"Jesse was right here. I don't understand," Charlotte says. She's stopped blubbering now, which is a relief. I was one sniffle away from grabbing her by the shoulders and shaking her. *Stop being so pathetic,* I wanted to yell, although I'm not sure if it would really be aimed at her or at myself. I haven't had the best hour, and this Jesse thing is the icing on a really shit cake that I couldn't even eat since I don't eat cake.

"There's nothing here," Grayson says, letting out a big breath. He looks beyond relieved that we don't have to deal with a corpse.

Am *I* relieved? I'm not sure. It doesn't feel real without a body. Maybe it's not real. I kick a can, and it clatters down toward the water.

"You're saying someone moved the body? Why?" Emma says, unimpressed. Her camera hangs loosely from one hand, its corpse-photographing potential spoiled. "Unless it was to get rid of evidence," she goes on slowly.

"Maybe he's at the hospital?" Grayson says. "Are you sure he was dead?"

Charlotte clutches her head with both hands. Her hair's drying in a puffy blond thatch. "Oh no. What if I imagined it? I don't know what's real anymore."

"How could you imagine an entire corpse?" I say.

"My whole world is imaginary," Charlotte mutters through her hands. "Sometimes I go entire days without anything real happening. Who's to say this is even real?"

"For god's sake. Amateurs," Emma mutters. She shakes her head.

I gaze out across the oil-black water. It's funny. I'd planned out my entire life to revolve around Jesse, and now I'm struggling to imagine a future in which I am the center of everything. I'm a satellite untethered from its orbit, hurtling out into the blackness of space, cold and alone. It's Jesse's gravitational pull that I already miss. Not him.

Maybe that part will come later, when I start to remember the things I loved about him. I try to conjure them up in my heart—his warm arm slung over my shoulder, the way he'd buy me special clothes that I only wore when I was around his house, how he'd want to start a fight with any man who looked at me. Only, none of those things were really about me.

I laugh softly to myself. I can't even pretend that I'm sorry he's gone.

"Why would you want to kill him?" Emma says, making me jump.

"What?" I say.

"I was talking to Charlotte." Emma eyes me suspiciously. "Charlotte, focus. Tell us everything you remember."

"Um, I was running from the police," Charlotte sniffles. "But someone knocked me over the wall on the riverbank, and I hit my head. It got a bit hazy after that, but I remember climbing onto one of the swans."

"Where was Jesse?" I say.

"Well, someone climbed onto the swan with me. It was tipping over, so they wanted me to get off. I thought it was another contestant, but perhaps it was Jesse." She focuses on her feet, shuffling her sneakers in the grime. "I don't know for sure."

"Why would Jesse get on a swan?" Emma says. "Why would he be on the riverbank in the first place?"

"He was operating the projector. For Rose's appearance," Grayson says. "I saw him before all hell broke loose."

"Why didn't you tell us that earlier?" Emma says.

Grayson winces. "Because my brain's made of cauliflower?" he says sheepishly. "And there were these mannequins, and the lights went out, and—"

"Forget it. Charlotte, you were on a swan with Jesse or someone you mistook for Jesse. What happened next?"

"I kicked him and he fell in the water. Then I think I got knocked semi-unconscious because I don't remember anything else until I woke up here, next to his body. The simplest explanation is that he was the person I kicked."

"Is it? Because, if you did accidentally kill him, why would someone else want to cover it up?"

I think for a moment. "To protect Anton. A death during his game wouldn't look good, not after Rose. Someone could have moved the body, hoping no one traced Jesse back to the game and to Anton."

Emma snaps her fingers. "You could be on to something. Charlotte, did you see anyone else?"

"Beatrix was here," Charlotte says, sniffling.

"Beatrix?" Grayson asks. "Seriously?"

Charlotte nods. "She was on the road outside. I ran out in front of her van, and she had to stop."

"A van that she could have removed the body in," I say.

Grayson chuckles. "I'm finding it hard to believe that Beatrix has body disposal on her CV."

Charlotte, Emma, and I look at each other. He's so naive. Taken in by a pretty face. None of us know Beatrix, not really. The kooky act for the cameras is as put on as my own plastic persona.

"Beatrix wouldn't," Charlotte says. "Would she?"

"She's Anton's sister, and she'd do anything to protect him," I say.

Everyone is silent, thinking their own dark thoughts. I take advantage of the quiet to run through what I know about Jesse's involvement in this big mess. It's pretty clear he's been working against Anton and helping stage the Rose shit. Which explains why he was hanging around the abandoned hotel when I tracked him down.

I squeeze my phone so hard in one hand that I think either the screen or my fingers will break. He set me up. Jesse positioned those mannequins to look like me and my mother. Pinned her taped-together bank statements to the walls. Tucked a photo of me into a carriage clock, ready for anyone to find it. I never told him about those photos.

I'm tearing myself apart inside, wondering what else he lied about. Did he genuinely care about me, or was it all about how he could use me to make money? It doesn't matter now, I guess. The important thing is that Jesse wasn't working alone. Someone was paying him to set up this whole charade.

The question is who?

I'm hit by an abrupt surge of nausea. "I have to go," I say. "Don't follow me."

At the gates, I look back. They're all watching me, but no one has moved. No doubt they're waiting until I'm out of sight before they laugh at me. Emma will add this to her story. Princess Erin, selling dirty photos to protect her mother, heartbroken at her boyfriend's death. It's the climax everyone wants to see. The pretty, famous girl brought down a peg or two.

I angrily wipe at my eyes. *They're not my friends*, I remind myself. I don't give a shit about them. Not Charlotte, with her mean comments giving way to kindness when it actually mattered. Not Grayson, always trying to make me laugh even when he's suffering inside. I don't care what they think of me.

I slide down against the wall of an apartment building and put my head on my knees. I'm alone and that's a good thing. I can depend on myself. I don't need anyone else.

It's a few minutes before I hear footsteps. Part of me is hit by this surge of desperate hope that it's Grayson or Charlotte coming to check on me. Only it's neither of them. It's Emma, and Emma isn't one of us.

"Everyone's wondering the same thing." Emma leans casually

against the wall. Her shrewd expression gives her away though. For someone so young, she's as cold and determined as a shark.

"Did you kill Rose, Erin? You must have been scared those photos would come out."

"Rose was never going to tell anyone," I say quietly.

"Maybe you killed her to protect your mother's secret, then."

I stare her down. I don't have to justify myself to her.

"You know, you're going to have a starring role in my article, so you should use this opportunity to put across your side of the story."

"You have no shame, do you? This story of yours could destroy my mother's reputation."

"It's sweet how you still care what happens to her. From what I've seen, she hasn't been much of a mother to you."

I can't argue with that.

"Couldn't have been easy, growing up with a parent like her. Then you finally find someone you think is on your side, only for him to die."

"I split up with Jesse earlier tonight," I say before I can stop myself.

"You did, huh? Was it a big argument?" She takes a hand out of her pocket, and I notice she's holding a voice recorder. "When did this happen, exactly? It must have been right before he died?"

I narrow my eyes at her.

She smiles with all her teeth, revealing the colorful elastic stretched between her braces. "On the way here, I started going through my photos from tonight, looking for him." She takes her phone from her pocket. "This one from the embankment is interesting."

I squint at the picture. "Jesse's not in it."

"No, but Charlotte is." She zooms in on a blurry figure with short hair and a bright orange hoodie.

I take the phone. It's Charlotte, all right. She appears to be crawling across the mud toward a swan boat, which matches the story she told us earlier. There's no sign of Jesse anywhere in the shot. There is, however, another boy down on the banks. He's smaller than Jesse, with curly blond hair. He looks a bit like Sean23 from the museum.

"I'm wondering if Charlotte was confused and it was actually this boy on the boat with her," Emma says. "Or was she lying?"

"Why would she lie?"

"Guilt makes people irrational. Perhaps she really did murder Jesse and made up the story about accidentally kicking him to convince us that it wasn't murder."

"Why would Charlotte want Jesse dead? I don't think she even knew him."

"Perhaps he saw something at that party. The one where Rose died." Emma takes the phone back, smiling knowingly. "Or someone else entirely killed Jesse. Someone with a reason to hate him."

I meet her eye defiantly. "I didn't hate him, and I didn't kill him, if that's what you're insinuating."

Her smile widens. "I wasn't insinuating anything, only stating the facts. Either way, I'm going to look at my photos from the party and see if I can't spot him in the crowd. Maybe it will turn up something incriminating."

My mind drifts to that night. Rose's last party and the first time I met Jesse.

———

I went there looking for Rose. It was a few days after our big argument, and I couldn't stop thinking about how she knew about the photos I'd been selling and Amber's financial situation. I was convinced she was planning to call a social worker, which would have spelled the end of *Amber and Erin Love*...

And it would have destroyed my mother.

My plan was to confront Rose more calmly than during our previous discussion and persuade her to let it drop. Things obviously didn't work out that way. For starters, I couldn't catch her on her own. I saw her talking to Charlotte at the buffet table, but afterward, she headed over to speak with Amber, then disappeared for a while. At some point, she must have argued with Matthew, overheard by Emma. I didn't see any of that though.

I spent half the night hiding from boring conversations with Anton's acquaintances, all of whom either wanted to book me for jobs or ply me with alcohol. My reply to everything was, "Ask my mom," which was always enough to put them off on both counts. Mostly, I sat on the patio by myself and waited for Rose to reappear.

When I saw her next, much later in the night, she was talking to a small group of crew members I didn't recognize. One was a tall white boy with bleached hair. The second was a scowling Black girl with a shaved head. The third was Jesse. He didn't look like much to me at that point. Skinny, serious, messily dressed. He was also a lot older than me.

I waited for Rose to stop talking, and then I followed her. Only, when I rounded the garden studio, she was gone.

"Lost something?" Jesse stepped out from the shadows, a bottle of beer lazily hanging from his fingers.

"No, I... It's nothing," I said.

"What's a nice party like this doing with a girl like you?" he said, smiling like he knew what a crappy line it was.

I rolled my eyes at him. But I had to admit to myself that he was better looking up close, especially when he smiled. There was this confidence about him. He didn't need designer clothes and perfectly styled hair to feel comfortable in his own skin. It fascinated me in its alienness.

"Want a beer?" he said, offering me his half-drunk bottle.

I immediately revised everything I'd been thinking and decided he was disgusting. "Your mouth is home to a billion bacteria. So, no. I don't want to drink your backwash-contaminated beer."

He laughed like he wasn't expecting this response. His laugh was real. I was used to people being weirded out by the strange things I'd say, but he didn't seem put off at all. It felt like he was intrigued by me, and not just by my looks.

He eyed me with interest. "What about kissing?"

I shuddered. "Kissing transfers like eighty million bacteria. I'm not kissing you either."

"I wasn't going to try to kiss you," he said with a wry grin. "Take you to movies, maybe. But you're totally out of my league, so…have a nice night, I guess."

I was about to leave, but I hesitated. Strange men hit on me all the time, but his mixture of confidence and self-deprecation felt different. Most boys I met hid their lack of self-confidence behind an arrogance as overwhelming as Matthew's aftershave. I wanted to find out more about him.

"I like movies," I said shyly.

"Guess you could give me your number, then?" he said hopefully.

I was typing it into his phone when his face changed. His serious, grown-up expression was back as he noticed something over my shoulder. "I need to have a word with someone."

"Who?" I said, but I couldn't see anyone.

"Just so you know, I'm a very good kisser," he said, taking his phone from me and rushing away. "Bacteria and all."

———

The memory dissipates, and I'm left grappling with the realization that it was Jesse's adultness that attracted me to him. I didn't have a dad, and Amber wasn't exactly much of a mom. I was desperate for someone to look after me for once, and he took advantage of that.

Emma is holding out her voice recorder, waiting for me to speak. But I have nothing left to say. I clamber to my feet. When Emma doesn't move her arm out of my way, I swat the recorder out of her hand. It clatters into the road.

"You don't know who I am or what I'm capable of," I snarl. "You'll leave me alone, if you know what's good for you."

"What the hell?" Emma says as I walk away, but I keep my eyes forward. The past can't catch me. I won't let it get close.

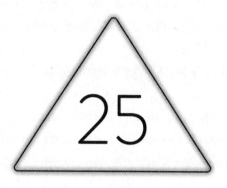

GRAYSON

Charlotte kicks at a pile of foamy river slime. As if Jesse's body is magically hiding underneath, rather than squirreled away. But by whom? Someone who's trying to protect Anton? That's what the others think, anyway. I don't know what to think.

Everything's such a mess. Rose's ghost, as she promised, is revealing everyone's secrets, and the whole damn web of lies and death is growing and growing. Matthew and his supposed affair, Charlotte and her trolling, Amber's finances, and Erin's desperate attempt to keep her family from ruin. Top that off with Emma snooping around, and like I said, it's a mess.

It's going to get messier.

Both Charlotte and I straighten up as Rose's avatar crackles into life. My stomach pitches. All I can do is watch her play her game and see where it leads. I know where it will lead.

"Accomplices," she says with none of her usual amusement. She sounds kind of breathless. It's like she's nervous, which is very unlike the Rose I knew.

"What does she want now?" Charlotte says. "Hasn't she done enough?"

"It's time for her to announce her next suspect," I say numbly. I should have tried harder to find her. Now it's most likely too late. I've dodged the bullet four times now. Surely it's my time against the wall.

Rose lifts a handwritten letter. Yup. This is it.

I close my eyes. I knew this was coming. I'd resigned myself to it. It still makes me want to hurl myself into the Thames. I wait, but she doesn't speak. I open my eyes, and the ghost is standing there, staring at the letter.

"What's she waiting for?" Charlotte says.

"I don't suppose the killer wants to confess? No, I guess not," Rose says quietly. She clears her throat and starts to read. "*Dear Rose. I can't stop thinking about you, and it's driving me crazy.*"

"Oh, a love letter," Charlotte says earnestly. "That's so sweet."

"*I can't get your face out of my mind,*" Rose continues. "*The way you didn't even look back when you walked away has broken me. I love you so much, but I'm nothing to you.*"

"A kindred spirit," Charlotte says, placing a hand on her heart. "A fellow lover of language and romance."

"*You've ripped my fucking heart out and tossed it away like it's nothing. Is that what I am to you—nothing? Something to be shitted on?*"

Charlotte's smile fades into a toothy grimace. "Oh. You know, that's not actually a real word," she whispers.

I think I'm going to throw up my internal organs.

Rose's hand is shaking, and the letter rustles. "*Why won't you answer your phone? I need to talk to you. I keep thinking that if you'd listen to me, I could make all this better. I want to put my arms around you, and then you'll remember what we had.*"

"Shit," I say, adrenaline forcing me to pace, otherwise I'll explode. This isn't good. In fact, it's a total nightmare. Every word claws deep gouges in my heart.

"*You made a promise,*" Rose says. "*And you broke it, like you broke me. Please, Rose. I can't do this. I need you. I love you.*"

She lowers the letter and spins her wheel. I want to tear the smart glasses off and run away, but there's no point. Everyone else is seeing this. Charlotte is rapt, with a hand resting on her own heart. The wheel slows. Clicks. Stops.

"Everyone, meet my ex-boyfriend." She rips away the featureless silhouette. The picture is a recent one. "Grayson Holt," she declares.

Charlotte's mouth falls open. "Seriously?" she says. "*You* dated Rose?"

"We split up five months before she died," I say quietly.

She nods as she processes the information. "You know, I didn't have you down as a poet. But that letter was actually very romantic. Some of it."

I think she's trying to make me feel better after Rose's reveal. I'm presuming I look as hollowed out as I feel. I knew Rose would get to me at some point—everyone always suspects the ex—but it hurts much more than I was expecting. Yes, the letters and texts and voicemails that I sent her right after she dumped me are pitiful. But having her show other people the things I wrote is brutal.

I remember writing that letter, barely able to catch my breath through my tears, my knuckles bloodied from where I'd slammed them into a door earlier that day. Inside, I was tearing myself to pieces, but when I tried to write those feelings down, I couldn't find the right words. It came out like I was some pathetic crybaby who couldn't accept his relationship was over.

"What do you think, people?" Rose says. "Did Grayson come to that party to murder me in revenge after I dumped him?"

"Did you?" Charlotte says.

I numbly shake my head. Shame is filling me from head to toe. That letter made me sound so desperate and wretched. No wonder she didn't call me back. No wonder she dumped me in the first place. Who'd want to be with someone like that? I sit on the wet ground and put my head in my hands.

"You don't need to be embarrassed," Charlotte says. "Putting your heart out there and being vulnerable isn't something to be ashamed of."

The fact that she's trying to reassure me makes it even worse. I open my mouth to laugh it off like I usually would, but a hiccuping sob escapes. I bite my thumb to stop myself from crying.

"Our next challenge is in Highgate Cemetery," Rose says. "I love it there. It's so romantic, don't you think, Grayson? Oh, and I've left a gift for Grayson on the front gates."

At least this stops me from crying. I can't think what she's left for me, but I'm guessing it being made public will prove as traumatic as her reading my letter out loud. I need to get to the cemetery before anyone else and make sure that I'm the one who finds it. I move to stand, but then my hand falls on a hard object, hidden in a pile of washed-up trash. I surreptitiously move it with two fingers. A phone.

"Are we going to the cemetery?" Charlotte asks, eyeing me with such pity I can't bear it.

"I'll catch up with you," I manage to say. "I need a minute to get myself together."

She hesitates, clearly unsure if she should leave me alone or not. She does though. Girls rarely know what to do when a boy cries; it makes them too uncomfortable. Thanks, patriarchy.

I wait until she's out of sight before retrieving the phone and brushing it off. It's wet and filthy, but the screen lights up when I press the power button. I'm presuming it belonged to either Jesse or the person who removed his body. The background is the default blue. The owner didn't bother to customize it or, it seems, set up a pass code lock.

I open it and flick through the photos. There aren't many, but I do find a couple of Erin. Jesse's phone, then. He doesn't have email set up or any social media. There are some text messages, but nearly all of them are from Erin, asking where he is and why he's not calling her.

The last one from her reads: Matthew came to speak to me. He was flirting with me.

He followed it up forty minutes later with: Fuck you Erin.

That message must have been sent right before he died. Erin didn't reply.

I check the calls. Jesse wasn't good at adding contacts to his address book. Other than the calls to and from Erin, most are numbers without names. I'm about to pocket the phone when something familiar catches my eye. I'm not good at remembering digits, but this is different. This number is Lenny's.

"Why was he calling Lenny?" I say.

I try to figure it out, but it makes no sense. How could Lenny have even met Jesse? My head jumps between possibilities. Jesse spying on us contestants in advance of the game. Jesse investigating Lenny on behalf of Anton after she stepped in to help me.

Lenny couldn't have been in on it. She wouldn't do that to me. *I know Lenny.*

But do I? She has so many secrets, something I always wrote off as her being independent and busy. Now I'm questioning all those times she couldn't meet for ice cream because she had schoolwork to do and all the times she deflected my questions about her past.

I can't believe she's part of this though. I tell myself Jesse must have been contacting her against her will. She probably didn't tell me because she didn't want to worry me. No way is my best friend deliberately lying to me.

Then the phone rings, and I bat it into the air in surprise. I catch it and focus on the screen. It's Lenny's number. Shakily, I answer the call and silently hold it to my ear.

"Jesse?" Lenny's voice says. "Where are you?"

I stay silent, listening to her soft breathing on the line. "Jesse, you there?"

She hangs up.

I stare at the phone for a few heart-shattering moments. Then I tuck it into my pocket and head for the cemetery.

CHARLOTTE

I get how Grayson feels. When Rose revealed the comments I wrote on GossApp, I felt the same. Humiliated and ashamed and like I couldn't look anyone in the eye. I should have done more to reassure him that his secret really isn't that bad. We've all lost our heads over love at some point.

If I had reassured him, then maybe I wouldn't be alone with my own thoughts again. I always used to love my ability to slip into a daydream, anytime, anyplace. But now the thoughts come uninvited, clawing their way into my consciousness, like they did at the mannequin hotel. It takes all my concentration to keep my mind focused on the real world.

I wait at the bus stop on a wide empty street. The occasional car passes, but mostly it's me and a hundred dark places where anything could be hiding. I try to act like I belong. Like I get buses alone at night all the time. My head keeps drifting to thoughts of Jesse, only it's my face on his corpse's body.

It was real. He was real. I didn't imagine it.

As the bus pulls up, the wind whistles past me, carrying with it the smell of river water. I quickly scramble on board, into the bright artificial light and promise of safety. I sit on the top deck with a few others—a woman eating a stinky burger, a drunk man in a posh suit who sways in his seat, and a pair of girls giggling behind their hands as they eye me.

I check my reflection in the window. I'm a mess after my dip in the river—damp, muddy, goose-bumped with cold. I futilely pat at my hair, but it's no use. And I'll have to meet Anton looking this terrible when I find him. Just then, I see movement behind me. I presume it's another passenger getting on the bus, but when I look over my shoulder, there's no one there. Weird.

I return to picking dirt out of my hair. The person behind me moves again.

"Hey, what?" I turn to the laughing girls, but they've lost interest in me and are watching videos on their phone. "And I'm officially losing it," I say to myself.

I lick my thumb and use it to remove a splash of mud from my chin. There's movement in my reflection again. A person slumps into the seat right next to me. I feel the seat jerk. I freeze with my hand on my face.

And then they lean forward in the seat so that their reflection appears next to mine. It's Jesse, with empty eye sockets and river weed spilling out of his mouth. "You think you look bad? Look at me," he gurgles.

I scream and try to scramble away from him, smacking my

head into the window in the process. I pin myself into the corner, only there's no one in the seat next to me. There are still only five of us on the top deck, and the others are watching me suspiciously from a distance. I check beneath the seats. All I see is an expanse of grubby flooring and litter. It must have been a dream. I dare another glance at my reflection. There's no sign of Jesse. All the same, I'm officially uneasy. When the bus pulls up at the next stop, I hurry downstairs. The girls' laughter is a sudden sharp noise as I disappear from view.

Outside in the cold, I check my map. I've traveled farther than I thought, so perhaps I did fall asleep and dream of Jesse. That has to be the explanation. I screw up my face so tight that I feel a rumbling vibration in my ears. It doesn't rid me of the sleepy daze threatening me with more intrusive thoughts though. I shouldn't be alone.

I fumble with my phone and call Matthew because who else is there? He answers after six rings. "Charlotte?" he says, sounding surprised and a bit scared.

Hearing his voice brings a feeling of relief. The vastness of the city shrinks slightly to a more manageable bubble.

"I wanted to say…I'm, um…"

"Me too," he says quietly. "Where are you?"

"Near the cemetery. Just around the corner."

"I'll drive around and pick you up." He hangs up.

I sit on a bench and try to stop thinking about Jesse. I rub my neck. It really hurts, and my brain is super woolly. Nothing makes sense. My thoughts keep jumping all over the place.

One second, I'm imagining I'm in the water and Jesse's trying to steal my boat, so I kick him away. Then his face changes, and it's Sean23 who I'm kicking. He swims off and is heaved into a

210 · KATHRYN FOXFIELD

coastguard's dinghy, safe and sound. I don't know if I'm imagining that because I don't want to accept that I killed a person, or if it's what really happened. The water was so cold, and I was so confused and scared.

Next, I'm on the ramp, crawling out of the river. It's freezing, and my vision is closing in on me. But Jesse was there; I'm sure he was. And he was dead. At least, I think I'm sure. But now he's gone, and the way Emma was looking at me? She thought I'd made it up. What if I did?

My memories jump again. I'm in the mannequin hotel, and I'm panicking in the dark. Rose's ghost is there with me, wrapping her cold fingers around my throat. No, that's not right. I touch my neck again. A ghost didn't do this to me, and I'm pretty sure I didn't do it to myself either. Which means someone else—someone real—was in that hallway with me, in the dark, and they tried to kill me.

"Charlotte?"

I jump as Matthew hurries to my bench. His van is parked on the road, headlamps bright.

"You looked like you were in a trance. Didn't you hear me calling your name?"

I shake my head, tears prickling my eyes.

"Jesus, what happened to your neck?" he says.

"It was in that hotel with the mannequins. I don't actually know what happened."

"Shit. I should have waited until the rest of you got out, but we thought you were right behind us." He rubs a hand on the shaven back of his head. "We thought that we could catch up with Jesse and find out what the hell he's up to."

"Did you find anything out?" I whisper.

"No. Most of the crew has packed up and gone home, and no one's seen Jesse."

"Oh," I say. I open my mouth to tell him the truth, but the words won't come. It was one thing confessing to Erin, Grayson, and Emma. It's another admitting it to Matthew. He'll hate me all over again, and I can't handle that right now.

"He's a weird guy," Matthew continues. "I wasn't that stoked about bringing him on board again, but Anton wanted to stick to the original crew. Half of them don't want anything to do with him these days, so we had to take whoever we could get."

"That's weird," I say. "I can't believe they wouldn't want to work with Anton."

"Not really, considering he ditched them without a second thought after Rose died."

"He did? Oh."

"Jesse was really eager though. He'll do anything for a paycheck, you know? He's not good with money. He's always wanted to be a musician, and he must have plowed thousands into it."

"Matthew," I say. "I need to tell you something."

"I guess it's no surprise that he'd be involved in this Rose thing. If someone paid him, then he'd do it without a second thought."

"Matthew! Jesse is dead."

Matthew gapes at me. "D…dead?"

"He was killed," I say, missing out the part involving me. "But then someone took his body away. We don't know who it was, but…"

I'm about to say that Beatrix was there at the river, but then the passenger door on the van opens, and Beatrix climbs out.

"We're going to be late for the next challenge," she says, her hands thrust deep in her cardigan pockets. She glances between us. "What's going on?"

"Nothing," Matthew says quickly. Not sure why he's keeping it from Beatrix or why he's gone so still. He's looking at her funny. Like he's realized something about her that has him scared.

"We should go," Beatrix says.

Matthew checks his watch. "Yeah. Come on." He jogs to the van.

Beatrix hangs back, still staring at me. "Why can't you leave him alone?"

"What do you mean?"

"I mean, you're always pointing out that he's not your real brother and saying how much you hate him. Yet the second you need help, you expect him to come running."

"That's not true."

"No? Whose jacket is that you're wearing?"

"I fell in the river, and I was cold."

"Exactly. You use him because, no matter what, he always has your back. You're horrible to him, Charlotte. And one day he'll give up on you." She watches me icily as I open and shut my mouth, lost for words; then she moves to leave. "It would be better if you walked to the cemetery. It's around the corner, and the back of the van is dirty."

For a second, I'm furious and hurt. But then it hits me that she's right. I am horrible to Matthew, and I don't know why. I've been so consumed by jealousy that he got to live with Anton that I didn't stop to consider his feelings. Not even once. All along, he's been trying to be my big brother, and all I've done is yell at him and be mean.

In the van, Matthew raises both hands in a shrug as Beatrix tells him I'm not coming with them. Smiling brightly, I wave him off. I manage to wait until they're gone before I burst into tears. There's no time to be self-indulgent though. I wipe my eyes and make my own way to the cemetery.

By the time I get there, the van is already parked, but the gates of the cemetery are closed, so I don't know if they've gone inside. My eyes fall on a plastic envelope cable tied to the bars. At first I think it's a missing dog poster, but then I realize it's a torn piece of paper. I pull it out of the envelope and squint at the messy handwriting.

I know you're sleeping with him, it reads. *I saw you together in his pool.*

Rose said she'd left a gift for Grayson on the gates. I wonder if this is another extract from one of his letters and what it could mean. Did Grayson suspect Rose of having an affair while they were still together?

And could that have made him angry enough to kill her?

Hearing a noise behind me, I quickly tuck the piece of paper into my pocket and yank the plastic envelope off the gate. I stuff it under a bush. Something tells me that trusting any of the others would be a mistake. From now on, I'm going to be holding my cards close to my chest.

27

ERIN

My mother is bathed in the glow of a streetlight. She leans up against the cemetery fence with her hair swept over a shoulder. She rearranges her T-shirt and pushes her breasts higher in her bra. Everything's a performance with my mother, down to the way the shadows fall on her face.

She's not waiting for me. I don't warrant any of her current preening. I hide out of sight to find out who she's meeting. I don't have to wait long. Minutes later, Matthew bounds over. They talk, accompanied by angrily gesticulating arms.

The argument doesn't last long. Matthew spots Beatrix emerging from their van with a cardboard box and immediately puts a few feet between him and Amber. He shoos her away and goes to intercept Beatrix.

I wait until he's out of sight; then I step out of my hiding place and approach my mother.

If I surprise her, she hides it well. "Erin, darling. I was worried."

There's a slight slur to her voice. No one else would notice, but to me, it's clear she's had a few drinks.

"What are you doing?" I say.

"Rose invited me to play this game with you, so here I am." Her laugh is like breaking glass. "And someone has to keep an eye on you, don't they?"

She reaches to smooth my hair, but I duck away. "What are you doing with *Matthew?* You've been weird with him all night, and that discussion you just had clearly wasn't friendly. Is something going on between you two?"

"It's nothing," she says breezily.

Usually, I'd argue and get nowhere. Only, I've had enough of letting people lie to me. I try a different tack. "You're right," I say.

"Right about what?" Her lips purse in confusion.

"Of course there's nothing going on between you and Matthew. What would he want with *you*, anyway?" I say.

"Oh, Matthew wanted plenty with me."

That was easy. She's so predictable. I fold my arms and wait.

"Fine. We kissed, if you *must* know. I hope you're not too jealous."

Of her and Matthew? What a joke. I raise an eyebrow. "When was this? Back when he was a seventeen-year-old child?"

Her smug expression falls at the corners. "He was eighteen, so get off your high horse already."

"Did Rose find out?"

"Yes, Rose knew." She sighs. "That picture of Matthew leaving the hotel caused a big drama, and she figured it out."

"That was you? *You* were having an affair with Matthew?" Wow. What was he *thinking*?

"It wasn't an affair," she says reluctantly. "We met for a drink and went to my room, only he panicked and ran away before anything happened."

I believe her. She wouldn't make up a story in which a man didn't want her, even to save her own reputation.

I eye her closely, looking for signs of guilt on her overly smooth, expressionless face. "Did you kill her?"

She laughs again. "Why would I want to kill Rose?"

"Because it would have ruined you if she'd revealed the truth about you and Matthew, never mind your financial situation."

"Like I said, *nothing* happened with Matthew. Besides, she was never going to tell, or call a social worker, or give me up to the press."

"No?" I say. "Because from what I saw, she hated you."

Amber looks at me slyly. "She didn't hate you though, did she?"

The truth hits me like a bucket of icy water thrown in my face.

Rose kept those secrets to protect me. First Amber's almost affair with Matthew, then her financial problems and her poor parenting. I wish I could rewind time and ask Rose why. Ask her what I ever did to deserve that. But the last time I saw her, all I cared about was making sure she kept her mouth shut.

I nod slowly, trying to take it all in. I've never felt so much disgust for my mother. It's not the Matthew thing. It's everything else. The selfishness, the lack of accountability for the things she's done, the manipulation and lies.

I move to walk away. Amber scurries to block my path, a sickly-sweet smile tightening her plump lips. "Erin, wait. Come on, darling. We both said some things we regret earlier, in the heat of the moment. Can't we put it behind us?"

I don't trust myself to answer. It's a trap that will lead me right back to the beginning.

"I'm a mess, Erin. But my own mother wasn't a kind woman, and it started me out on the wrong foot." Her voice takes on the rehearsed rhythm of someone who has practiced this same speech a thousand times. "I was never good enough for her. When I got pregnant with you at seventeen, she cut me off. If I made some bad decisions along the way, please know that I did my best."

I've heard it all before.

"You have no idea what it was like, Erin," she continues, her voice wavering. "I did *everything* to give you the life she didn't let me have. All you've ever done is throw it in my face. I wish I knew what I was getting so wrong."

And there it is. The twist where everything goes from being her fault to mine. I laugh softly, which confuses her.

"I'm trying, Erin. I'm going to keep trying because you're everything to me. *Amber and Erin Love* is everything to me."

This is what always happens. She attempts to plaster over the cracks in our relationship with sugary words. Pretend that everything's fine. Go back to normal. But it's not my normal. It's hers. It's always about her.

I keep walking, stepping past Amber without another word. She tries to argue, but Rose gets between us. Or Rose's avatar, at least. We fall silent and wait for her to speak. "Me again," she says, sounding bored. She spins her wheel with no fanfare. "Want to meet our final suspect?"

I wait for the wheel to stop spinning. There's one more person left to have their secrets laid bare. Beatrix.

Rose smiles. "We were like family: me, Anton, Matthew, and

Beatrix. But of course, Beatrix really *is* Anton's family. His little sister, to be precise."

Beatrix has always seemed so quiet if you ask me. Happy to blend into the background with her pigtails and constant smile. But I suppose there are unanswered questions too. Like what was she doing by the river where Jesse's body lay?

"Beatrix would do anything for Anton, but he wouldn't give her what she wanted. A starring part in his videos. That was my role," Rose says. "And I can tell you, this used to make Beatrix *very* jealous."

It's true that Rose used to be the star in Anton's stunts. I never knew that Beatrix was jealous. She's always seemed so happy to be the kooky, giggly one. The adoring little sister and Rose's best friend.

"Here's the thing," Rose whispers. "Beatrix was the one who found my body. Only the timelines don't add up. It took her a whole hour to call the police, so what was she doing during that time? Interesting fact—a member of the staff saw her carrying a bucket of cleaning products at close to four a.m., and it's said that the pool house smelled of bleach when they fished me out of the water."

"Covering up the evidence," I say to myself.

Rose swishes her hair. "Your job, Anton fans, is to figure out what Beatrix was up to. Was our under-the-radar Accomplice simply house proud, or was she trying to hide something more sinister? And who was she protecting—herself or someone *extremely* close to her?"

Matthew or Anton. Beatrix would do anything for either of them.

"We're going to have a little treasure hunt," Rose declares. "If you've played any of the *Shadow City* minigames, you'll know all about 'Sleeping Ghosts.'"

I don't have the time—or the interest—to play *Shadow City*, but I did my research. I know this game.

"Anton has hidden a hundred virtual bones in the cemetery," Rose says. "Your total at the end of this round was supposed to determine his top four. Now it will decide whether you get to stay in the game long enough to rescue Anton."

"What's the prize?" I say, frowning. There has to be a prize. It makes me extremely nervous that she hasn't told me what we're playing for.

Rose drops her voice to a dramatic whisper. "But be warned: Do. Not. Scream."

She vanishes to the soundtrack of a woman screaming like she's in a horror movie. Wearily, I make my way toward the cemetery gates, Amber tottering several yards back, too cool to be seen with me. I bump into Charlotte and Emma outside the entrance.

"Erin, you're here," Charlotte says, pulling me into their secretive huddle. Her hand is surprisingly warm. "Emma says she's found something."

Emma glances around nervously. When she speaks, her voice is a whisper. "I looked through my photos from the party where Rose died and—"

We all jump and turn at a rustling in the undergrowth. Emma gives a panicked shriek. A head and shoulders appear.

"Grayson," I snap. "Could you not creep up on us outside the deserted cemetery?"

"Sorry," he says sheepishly, picking a leaf out of his hair. "I didn't want to face everyone after…that letter. So I hid. In a bush."

"You're such a weirdo," I say.

He shuffles out, refusing to look any of us in the eye. I can feel the embarrassment radiating off him. It's understandable. That love-hate letter was painfully pathetic. But at the same time, there's something sweet about caring so much for someone that you completely fall apart when they leave you. This night couldn't have been easy for him.

I punch him on the arm. "Welcome to the suspect club," I say.

He rubs his bicep and tries to smile. It comes out as a pained grimace.

Right then, there's a scream from deep inside the cemetery. A second later, Matthew bursts out of the gates.

"I don't know where Beatrix is," he cries. "She ran off into the cemetery, and I was looking for her when I heard her scream."

Rose has raised the stakes in this game of hers, and Beatrix is the prize we're playing for.

GRAYSON

The cemetery gates creak as I squeeze through. Flanked by tall trees and four pillars standing like sentinels, a wide path winds its way into darkness. Nearby, there's a small wooden gatehouse with shuttered windows. Beyond, the path branches off into densely wooded areas dotted with dozens of tombstones.

"Why the heck did she come in here alone?" Emma says.

"I was chasing her," Matthew says breathlessly. He glares at Erin's raised eyebrow. "Not like that. She was upset because we had a stupid argument, and she ran off. We need to find her!"

"Maybe she just tripped?" Charlotte says hopefully. I hope that she's right. Beatrix is one of the good ones, even if she is dating that idiot with the muscles. I hate the thought that something's happened to her. It's enough to push my own problems to the back of my mind, if only for a few minutes.

"Or whoever's behind Rose's ghost has got her, and based on the shit they've been pulling, I don't trust them not to hurt her!" Matthew says.

"Rose is behind Rose's ghost," I say quietly. I'm trying to convince myself at this stage.

"If someone took her, they can't have gone far. Let's separate and find her," Erin says.

Matthew nods and points shakily at a box. "We brought some flashlights for the original game, so everyone grab one."

We each take a flashlight and turn them on. The faint light isn't as comforting as I'd hoped.

"Wait, shouldn't we stick together?" Emma says, eyeing the darkness nervously.

Matthew ignores her. "Charlotte and Emma, you're with me. Erin, Amber, and Grayson, you go that way." He points into thick foliage where there's barely a path.

"As if." Amber laughs. "Erin and I will come with *you*, Matthew."

Matthew's jaw hardens, but he gives a tight nod. "Fine," he mutters. "Emma, Charlotte, you go with Grayson."

"Seriously?" Emma says, glaring at me. "We get *him*?"

Charming. It's like being at elementary school again. Always the last to be picked for a team.

Matthew jogs away with the Loves at his heels. That leaves me, Charlotte, and Emma.

"Don't worry," I say. "I'm tougher than I look."

Emma gives me a glare of disgust. "Let's find Beatrix and get out of here," she says.

"What do you think's happened to her?" Charlotte whispers, sticking close to me as we walk.

"She's probably fallen over a bush," Emma grumbles. "I can't believe we're in here searching for her when…"

I glance at her. "When what?"

"Nothing," she mumbles, speeding up. Her eyes dart anxiously around.

A distant scream makes us stop.

I turn on the spot, sweeping my flashlight's insubstantial beam of light at my surroundings. Bushy trees have already risen to surround us. Among the overgrown foliage are a number of mostly obscured graves. Long woody creepers cling to tree trunks like tentacled monsters. Overhead, fine branches are skeletal fingers that reach down to scratch at my hair.

It's creepy as fuck.

Dead leaves feel squishy underfoot as we trip between shrubs left to grow wild. Small patches of sky are visible through the canopy, bleeding slashes of moonlight onto the ground.

I see something on one of the long-abandoned graves. I bend down. It's a femur, glowing with an eerie light. I touch it with a shaky finger and realize it's not actually there. It's a projection via my smart glasses. The bone vanishes, and my score goes up by five points.

"Not fair," Charlotte says. "You got there before I could."

"Seriously?" Emma says. "You still care about points?"

"I care about Anton," she says.

As I straighten, I notice that Emma's picked up a heavy branch to brandish as a weapon. I'm not sure what she thinks she might meet in here. "Careful where you're waving that thing," I joke.

She doesn't laugh, just tightens her fingers on the branch. "You never know what you're going to find," she says quietly.

"And yet here you are, doing all of this for a school newspaper," I say, not meaning it to come out quite so sharply.

"And here *you* are. Trying to prove yourself to your dead ex-girlfriend," she says. "Therapy would be safer. Come on. I think Beatrix's scream came from over here."

She rounds a corner and comes to a sudden halt. A ghost is drifting a few inches above the ground like a cloak hanging on a peg. Its fiery eyes are closed, as if in suspended animation.

Charlotte screams, then immediately claps a hand over her mouth. It's too late. I have enough time to glare at her before the ghost shudders and awakens, fixing those burning eyes right on us. Then it unhinges its jaw and launches itself with claw-hands outstretched.

"Run!" I yell.

In retrospect, shouting wasn't the most sensible idea because the noise summons more ghosts. The three of us race down the paths, ducking aside as slashing claws try to swipe at us. Every time Charlotte screams, more ghosts seem to join the chase.

"Stop flipping screaming," I say from between gritted teeth.

"I can't help it." Charlotte sobs. "It's a reflex reaction."

My heart beats so hard I can hear it. There's a visceral terror to being chased, even though the ghosts aren't real. I'm hating every second of it. But this game is my only link to Rose. I need to see her again. I need to hear what else she has to reveal about her murder. I'm so close.

"Can't you exorcise them like before?" I gasp.

"That's not how *Sleeping Ghosts* works. You have to outrun them for two minutes."

So I run, uncoordinated limbs tangling, constantly on the verge of falling. Emma's faster than me, and Charlotte throws herself over tombstones and through bushes with a seemingly unstoppable determination. Soon, they've put several yards between me and them. They don't have to outrun the ghosts; they just have to outrun me.

I'm forced to duck as another ghost lunges. I roll to the ground, kicking up stinky leaves and lumps of mulch. When I scramble to my feet, the two girls are gone, racing off into the trees. A ghost dives at me with its cloak streaming behind it. Smoke billows from its open mouth.

I race under a stone archway with big Egyptian pillars on each side. I find myself on a curved path around a crescent-shaped row of mini stone houses. There's another ghost up ahead, so I move to double back, but that's a no-go too. I'm blocked in. All I can do is press myself into a dark gaping doorway and stay as silent as possible.

I figure I'm a goner, but then the ghosts slow down and vanish. I made it. Somehow. I push myself out of the doorway and, as quietly as possible, follow the path, taking more care to watch out for the ghosts. I haven't gone far though, when my foot squelches in something. I shine my flashlight at the ground.

The mud's wet, but I can't see where any water could have come from. Then I notice dark splashes up the pale stone wall next to me. Blood. There's so much of it, sprayed in long spurts across the bricks. My stomach churns as my mind conjures images of blood spreading across white tiles, so much of it that it trickles along the cracks.

I lift my flashlight higher. Written above a doorway are the words: WHERE WAS ALL THE BLOOD?

I stagger backward, nearly slipping on the mushy puddle. I want to believe it's a trick, that the blood's not real. But it smells like a butcher's shop, gamey and metallic. There's a trail of bloody handprints smeared onto the walls, as if someone was dragging themselves along. I follow the trail with my shaky flashlight beam. It leads down some stone steps descending beneath an arched entrance. A metal gate stands slightly open.

"Hello? Beatrix?" I whisper, but no one answers.

I creep down the steps. The handprints become less frequent. Through the archway, there's a long tunnel with little alcoves off to the sides. Each is full of square plaques, some of which are missing to reveal coffin-sized holes in the wall. It's a catacomb or a crypt— I'm not sure of the difference. Somewhere dead people are kept.

I think about turning back, but I can't abandon Beatrix if she's in trouble. I advance slowly. A shuffling noise makes me pause. There's something hiding behind a brick pillar. Not a ghost. Whatever this is, I can hear it breathing.

I creep closer. The breathing stops. They know I'm here. I freeze. I want to run away, but I am too scared to move. Suddenly, a shape leaps out from behind the pillar. I stumble backward and fall. The figure screams, brandishing a chunk of rock like a weapon.

There's so much blood. Thick red drips run down their face, and more is soaked into their clothes. Their hair—two long braids—is sodden. It takes me longer than it should to realize that it's Beatrix.

"Whoa, whoa, it's me. Grayson," I say. A message flashes on my lens. *Winner, winner, winner.* I'm briefly furious with Rose. The girl I knew would never play such a mean trick.

Beatrix lowers the rock. "It's you," she whispers. Her chest is heaving. "I was so scared."

"Who did this to you?" I take her hands, even though they're sticky and slippery. "Where's the blood coming from? Are you hurt?"

How can she *not* be hurt? It doesn't make sense.

"It's not my blood. I got a message with some coordinates, but when I got there, someone had rigged a bucket of blood to fall on my head. I panicked and hid down here because I didn't know what to do." Her voice cracks and she starts to sob.

"It's OK. I think the game's over." I help her sit against the wall, and use my sleeve to wipe some of the blood from her face. There's so much that I can taste its bitterness in the air.

"What's going on, Grayson?" she says. She's shivering. I push her soaking hair off her forehead. She rests her head against my chest, her temple against my sternum. I wonder if she can feel how fast my heart is beating.

"There was a message on the wall. *Where was all the blood?* I guess you found it," I joke.

She sits back and tilts her head so that her throat's exposed, the only clean part of her. "I found her, you know? The water was pale pink with her blood."

I clench my teeth. I don't want to picture Rose dead, but I can't help it.

"And Rose's ghost was right; I didn't call the police immediately. I didn't know what to do, so I went to find Matthew first. And that decision haunts me to this day, even though she was already dead, and I couldn't have helped her even if I'd called an ambulance right away."

"What about the cleaning products?" I choke out. "You were seen carrying cleaning products that morning near the pool house."

She fixes me with this hurt, surprised look. "I walked past the pool house, but I didn't go in. Anton got drunk and was sick in his studio, so I cleaned it up before anyone else saw. That's what I do. I take care of my mess of a brother, night and day."

She starts to cry, resting her forehead against her blood-soaked knees.

"I'm sorry," I say. I put an arm around her shoulder, and she nestles into me. "I really wasn't accusing you. I'm… Tonight has been a lot."

"I know," she says, her voice muffled. "I didn't mean to take it out on you. It's not your fault."

I stretch my legs in front of me. The tunnel is so narrow that I can almost touch the opposite side.

"Why are they doing this?" Beatrix says, getting her tears under control, save for the occasional hiccup.

"Revenge, I suppose."

"You still think it's Rose, don't you?"

I don't know how to answer that.

"Whoever it is, they were right. I was jealous of Rose." She sighs sadly. "God, it feels like they're taunting us. Trying to humiliate us."

I nod. I had the same thought. Only that doesn't sound like Rose. Either she came back different, or… No, I don't want to think about this.

Beatrix shakes herself and fakes a businesslike expression. "We should find the others. Matthew won't be happy that I went off by myself—and look what happened!" She gestures to her blood-soaked clothes.

"It's hardly your fault."

"I doubt he'll see it that way." She sighs. "We had an argument."

"What about?"

"Nothing important. I don't like the way he looks at Erin Love.

I can't help but think there's something between them. Have you noticed that?"

I can't say that I have. "You don't need to be jealous of Erin. You—" I can feel my cheeks heating. "Well, you're…you know, OK."

She raises an eyebrow, smirking at me. "That made me feel so much better."

"Beautiful. I meant to say beautiful."

She bursts out laughing, both of us blushing furiously. "That's high praise coming from the boy who dated Rose Tavistock."

I remember we've not really spoken since Rose outed me with that horrific love letter. "I'm sorry I lied to you."

"I'm not angry," she says quickly, "but I'm slightly confused about why you're here."

"Revenge," I say truthfully. "I wanted to ruin Anton's contest. It's not fair that he gets to start over when it was his world that got her killed."

"It was her world too, you know?" she says, watching me closely for my response.

I smile ruefully. "When I met Rose, she had braces and frizzy hair, and her favorite thing in the world was reading. It was only after Anton got his hands on her that she changed."

"That's not how I remember her. She was always so confident and together, the whole time I knew her. Every man she met fell at her feet." Her face suddenly darkens.

I nudge her knee with mine. "If it's any consolation, I *literally* just fell at your feet. In terror, admittedly. But it's something."

"You're ridiculous." She returns my smile, then narrows her eyes at me. "But I'm pretty sure your girlfriend wouldn't approve."

She says *girlfriend* like it's a question.

I clear my throat. "Um, no girlfriend," I say. I don't know why, but it feels like a betrayal. Rose is dead. Even if it is her ghost, I need to accept that I'm never getting her back. I have to let her go. My whole body sags into the ground at the realization.

Right then, the gate bangs open, and a flashlight beam finds us. I look away from Beatrix's gold-flecked eyes in time to see Matthew standing in the tunnel. "What the hell have you done to my girlfriend?" he cries.

CHARLOTTE

In all the panic, I drop my flashlight. Which sucks because this cemetery is full of seriously sharp branches determined to gouge out my eyes and rip out my hair. It takes me ten minutes to fight my way through the undergrowth, but I make it. There are slashes of light ahead, so I walk toward them.

Voices reach me before I see anyone. Arguing voices. I skulk in the darkness and listen. It's Matthew and Beatrix.

"Don't give me that rubbish," Beatrix says. "You're the one who should be feeling guilty, not me."

"Pretty sure it was you cozying up to Grayson in a dark tunnel, but whatever you say," Matthew snaps back.

Beatrix and Grayson? I didn't see that coming.

"I was scared, and he was being nice. You, in comparison, haven't even asked if I'm OK."

232 · KATHRYN FOXFIELD

"He's Rose's ex! The one she used to complain about. Remember that creepy as fuck song he wrote for her? How did it go?"

"Matthew, stop it—"

"*Rose, I love you. You are my life. I'm so pathetic; I can't let you go,*" he croons. "Grayson is serious serial killer material."

"I'm not talking to you when you're in this mood." There's the sound of breaking twigs as she moves through the trees.

Matthew shouts after her. "And yet again, you're walking away from me. Perfect, just perfect."

"I'm covered head to toe in blood, Matthew. I need to change my clothes."

"And *why* are you covered in blood, Beatrix?" he cries. "No, let's talk about *that*. Because you were pretty damn angry with me when I was being accused of murder. But when it's you, I'm supposed to accept that it's all lies?"

"I didn't kill Rose!"

"Neither did I!"

They go quiet for a long moment. An owl hoots in the distance. I think about leaving them to their bitter little tiff. It's not very nice to be spying on them, but like a car crash, I can't look away. They're as bad as Mom and Dad right before they split. I always thought Matthew and Beatrix were the perfect couple.

"You seriously think it was me?" Matthew finally says.

"You do nothing but lie to me," Beatrix snaps. "Who were you meeting in that hotel when you were photographed in your underwear? How am I supposed to trust you when you refuse to tell me the truth?"

"Nothing happened!"

"Then tell me who you were with. Was it Erin Love? Because I've seen the way you look at her."

"Erin? Don't be ridiculous."

He starts to move again. Their voices get quieter as they storm through the cemetery, sniping at each other. I try to follow them, but it's kind of difficult without a flashlight. I trip over something big and hard, yelping as my toenail bends back. I steady myself on a tree. Matthew and Beatrix have gone quiet.

"What was that?" Beatrix says.

"I don't know. Probably that bloody amateur reporter again. And now you've given her even more material to screw us with."

"Me? You're the one who…" When she speaks again, her voice is small. "And, yet again, I'm expected to grin and accept it. One of these days, I won't be able to hide your mistakes from the world, Matthew, and everyone will find out about the things you've done."

"What the hell does that mean?"

Beatrix starts crying. Her noisy sniffles are all I hear for a good few seconds.

"I'm sorry," Matthew says more gently. "Let's not argue."

"Promise me," Beatrix sobs. "Promise me that when Emma goes through her old photos from that party, she's not going to find pictures of you with Erin Love."

Matthew doesn't answer right away. "I'm getting sick of Emma's photos," he says at last. "She's too nosy for her own good."

Their footsteps move off. I go in the opposite direction before they catch me listening in on them because that would be hard to explain. I catch a brief glimpse of another flashlight nearby, so I head for it. But it vanishes into the darkness, and I start to doubt it was ever there.

I stumble onward with the light from the moon and my bracelet's faint glow to guide me. This part of the cemetery is so overgrown that it's become a jungle, with tombstones that tower over me and gnarly trees that look like evil monsters. I keep jumping at rustling sounds in the undergrowth. It's probably nocturnal rodents, but I can't help but think I hear footsteps creeping up behind me.

I stop. The footsteps stop too. Maybe I was imagining them. I pick up the pace. A branch cracks. I spin around, but it's too dark to see anything but threatening trees surrounding me in all directions. I try to find the path again, but I've lost my bearings. I feel for a gap, but there are spiky hedges and low branches everywhere.

Another branch breaks, and this time when I freeze, the footsteps don't stop. Someone is heading right for me. *Crunch, crack, rustle*—they're moving fast now, breaking into a run. I can hear their labored breathing as they fight their way toward me. Brief flashes of their flashlight cut apart the darkness.

I try to force a path through the hedge, but the old knotty wood refuses to yield. I drop to the ground and attempt to use my bracelet to light my way. I think I've found the path again, so I crawl as fast as I can. It ends in a tall statue of an angel. I pull myself up and run, but ivy tangles around my feet. Everywhere I turn, there are more tombstones and more trees. I can't see a way out.

I trip over a rock and fall heavily. The footsteps are right on me now. The flashlight's weak beam skims across the dozens upon dozens of ancient headstones crammed in together like rows of teeth. All I can do is lie there between them, whimpering and bruised, waiting for whoever it is to find me.

Then there's a sound like stone scraping on stone, and a scream, and a loud cracking noise. Something falls right next to me, smashing old headstones, shaking the ground beneath me.

Pebbles skitter—one strikes me on the leg—and then everything falls silent. Even the creatures in the bushes have stopped moving around.

I push myself onto my knees. There's a flashlight lying beyond the closest row of graves, and its beam shines past me, striking ivy-covered stone. I can't hear breathing anymore. I can't hear anything but my own heart thundering in my ears. I know that if I look beyond the graves, I'll see something I don't want to see. So I don't look. I just kneel there, waiting.

I'm not sure how long I'm there for. Eventually, I hear crunching footsteps, followed by Matthew's voice. "Oh my god. Someone, help," he yells.

"Matthew?" I stand up, trying to look only at him. Even still, I can't help but see pieces of smashed stone on the ground. One of the stone angels has fallen from its tomb and lies broken. A wing. A face. A pale arm speckled with blood.

Matthew yelps and jumps away from me. "Charlotte, what are you…? What happened?"

He's joined by Grayson running toward the sound of our voices. He skids to a halt. He claps a hand over his mouth and turns away. Erin and Amber are close behind him; they're finally joined by Beatrix. She's changed into Anton merch from her van—a green hoodie and rainbow baseball cap. Everyone stands in a semicircle with their flashlights lighting the fallen tombstone.

"It's Emma," Matthew eventually says.

I make myself look but only for a second. It's enough time to see a trench coat soaked with dark blood. I look away again. "Is…is she dead?" I say, which has to be the stupidest question in the history of questions. Of course she's dead.

Grayson stoops next to the body. He touches his fingers gently to her neck, then snatches them away. His expression says it all.

"Someone murdered her. I heard them push over the statue." I catch a glimpse of Emma again, and saliva floods my mouth. "We need to call the police."

Grayson nods and stands. He pats his pockets. "I have a phone. Somewhere."

Beatrix places a hand on his arm, stilling him. "No police, remember? Or Anton dies."

"Anton," I say quietly. Beatrix is right. We can't call anyone.

We silently stand there, staring down at Emma's crumpled body for what feels like forever. I watch the others. Grayson, his dark eyes wide and worried. Erin, looking young and scared for the first time. Amber, as expressionless and unreadable as stone. Matthew, fidgeting like he wants to run and keep on running. Beatrix, tears clearing tracks down her grubby cheeks.

I'm hit by a thought. Someone killed Emma, and that someone has to be in this cemetery.

What if Emma's killer is one of us?

30

ERIN

"Where were you all when this happened?" Charlotte says, staring shrewdly at each of us in turn. The naive fangirl is gone, and in her place stands someone far steelier.

Nobody answers her question. The wind whistles in the trees. It's cold and dark in the cemetery, like we've taken a wrong turn and left noisy, full-of-life London behind. Everyone but Charlotte is shivering.

"According to the ghost, one of us is a murderer," Charlotte says firmly. "Someone killed Rose. And now the same person has killed Emma. Maybe Jesse too."

"I thought *you* killed Jesse," Grayson says, crossing his arms. The sleeves of his sweater ride up to reveal his slim wrists dotted with goose bumps. His jaw quivers as he tries to stop his teeth from chattering. It's clear he's trying to look brave.

"What?" Matthew takes a shaky step toward Charlotte. "You killed Jesse? What happened?"

Charlotte winces. "I don't know what happened. Jesse may or may not have been on a swan boat with me, and I may or may not have kicked him. All I know for sure is that I washed up next to his body. I may have been mistaken about it being him in the water with me. Or perhaps I am the killer. I don't think we can rule anyone out."

"You can rule me out," Amber says. "Why would I want to kill Emma?"

"To stop her from telling people about your financial problems and broken relationship with your daughter," Beatrix says. I'm not sure what I've missed, but Beatrix's hat-covered hair is dripping blood down her new hoodie.

Amber makes a "so what" face. "All of you know about that," she says breezily. "Am I going to kill you all too?"

Charlotte doesn't react. "Emma noticed something in one of her photos from the night Rose died, but she didn't have time to tell us what it was. What if it involved Jesse? What if the killer murdered both Jesse and Emma because they could identify him or her as Rose's murderer?"

It's a good theory. I remember Emma saying she was going to look for Jesse in her photos from the party. Next thing we know, she's dead.

Charlotte raises an eyebrow at Amber. "You were at that party."

"Most of us were at that party," Amber says. "Besides…" She holds out gleaming talons. "I got my nails done today. I wouldn't risk breaking one pushing a filthy statue onto someone."

Everything else that comes out of her mouth may be a lie, but this I can believe.

Charlotte turns her gaze to Grayson. "Everyone here was at that party except you," she says. "Where were you the night that Rose died?"

"I was probably working at the ice cream shop or at home," Grayson says, his voice still shaky. "I've never even been to Anton's house."

Amber raises an eyebrow. "So you never dropped by to harass poor Rose—sorry, I mean try to win her back? Those love letters confirmed everything I already knew about you."

"You don't know me," Grayson says coldly. "But for some reason, you have it in for me."

"I know enough. For all we know, Emma's photo would have incriminated you." She sniffs, then glances at Emma's body. Making a face, she gets out her phone to check her socials.

"Were you with Amber when Emma died?" Charlotte asks me, but her voice is lacking the usual nastiness she likes to direct at me. At some point between the mannequin house and now, Charlotte and I have drifted into a truce of sorts. Never thought that would happen.

"We had an argument. I left her by herself." *Amber's not a killer.* The trees rustle. *Isn't she?*

"So you don't have an alibi either, then," Beatrix says, staring daggers at me. With the blood trickling down her face and onto her clothes, the effect is almost intimidating. "You were at the party where Rose died. She knew about your mom's financial troubles and the photos. Speaking of which, did Emma manage to dig up those photos of you? Was she going to publish them?"

"In her *school* paper?" I fold my arms defiantly. "I was sixteen. If Emma had tried to publish them, she would have been the one in the wrong, not me. I'm not ashamed of my past. Or my body."

This is a lie. I don't know what I would have done if those photos had come out. I think I'm safe now though, and the relief is like fresh air. But the guilt at feeling this way is stifling.

I clear my throat and lift my chin at Beatrix. "It could have been you too. You were jealous of Rose and angry that she knew the truth behind Matthew's so-called affair."

Both Matthew and Amber look sharply at me. I'm not planning to drop them in it though. Not my style.

"I didn't kill her," Beatrix says coldly.

Matthew steps between us. "Beatrix would never do anything like that."

I swear Beatrix rolls her eyes. I begin to wonder if we've been underestimating sweet, helpful little Beatrix. There's a bitter, vicious side to her that she keeps well hidden, except when she looks at me.

"What about you, Matthew?" Charlotte says. "You argued with Rose over those photos of you in your boxers. And you were the first person to arrive after Emma died. You must have been close by."

He nods. "I heard a noise, and I ran over." He hesitates. "You were already here. Didn't you see anything?"

"No," Charlotte sighs. "I was rolling in the bushes being a coward."

"It's kind of suspicious," Grayson says slowly, like he's not sure if he should speak.

"You're right. On paper, I'm a strong suspect. I hated Rose, I have no alibi for any of the murders, and I was literally on the scene of both Jesse's and Emma's deaths. You'd be right to suspect me, but I didn't do it," Charlotte says.

We all fall silent. Six suspects, all of us with reasons for wanting Rose dead. None of us able to prove where we were when both Jesse and Emma died. Seven suspects if we include Anton, whose life hangs in the balance if we can't identify the killer.

"Can we talk about what we're going to do?" Grayson says abruptly. "About Emma. We can't leave her here. What about an anonymous call—?"

Rose interrupts. Her avatar appears, bright against the darkness. My stomach pitches with guilt when I remember how she tried to protect me from Amber, and I was too angry and scared to see it.

"We're nearly finished," she says quietly, slouching on one leg with her hands bunched in her sleeves. She seems fainter than before, so faint that she's almost colorless apart from those red lips. "I've told you almost everything now. I'm sure you can figure out where our final showdown has to happen."

"The place where you died," Grayson says quietly.

"The scene of the crime. Let's make things interesting, shall we? I'm going to tell you a bonus secret. The police missed something. There's a clue waiting for you to find it, behind one of the statues in the pool house."

She vanishes. "Wait," Grayson says, desperately reaching for her. "Where are you going?"

"I'm sure she'll be back again," I say.

"Will she?" He sweeps a hand through his crusty hair and stares at the space where she stood. There are tears in his eyes. "What if that was the last time?"

"Let's finish this," Charlotte says. She picks up Emma's dropped flashlight and sets off.

I'm the last to leave. It feels wrong to leave Emma here, broken and alone. I want to tell her that I'm sorry, but the words don't come.

I silently promise that we'll get her home, and find her killer, and make sure she's not forgotten. Then I walk away.

Hampstead's Billionaires' Row goes on forever. It's a constant treadmill of impenetrable gates and security codes. Shiny cars in the driveways, tall hedges, and sharp fences. These houses are home to royalty, art collectors, and businesspeople. Most are worth millions.

We finally reach a gap in the perfection. Anton's house is set back from the road, behind a tall prisonlike wall. It's stood empty since Rose's death, and the shine has washed off in the rain. Beyond the wall, the trees are wild and spindly. The keypad is hanging from frayed wires.

The gate has been pushed open against a thick carpet of mulch and dead leaves. There's bright yellow paint on the edges of the metal. I spot Anton's Lamborghini sitting in the driveway, the door flung wide open and deep scratches gouged along the side. This is where he came looking for the person behind the ghost. This is where they've been holding him.

Our feet crunch on gravel as we approach the house. It's an overly grand modern building that's all straight lines and glass. The upstairs is surrounded almost entirely by windows. Anton turned half the first floor into a massive entertaining space. We filmed there many times, and then there were the parties. But I never liked it inside the house. Too many annoying people.

The gardens were always more peaceful. They surround the house on three sides. The hedge maze is to the left. The studio, pool house, and various other outbuildings are to the right. Up against the rear of the house, there's a big patio and gardens, with lots of secluded nooks sheltered by topiary. I used to spend Anton's parties hiding somewhere I wouldn't be pestered.

The front door is open, so we step inside. A huge chandelier glows brightly. It's a testament to how rich Anton is that he's continued to pay the household bills despite no one actually living here. I doubt he even noticed.

Everything remains as it must have been the night Rose died. The rugs and curtains are dusty; the tables are coated in grime. Pictures on the wall hang slightly wonky, but maybe they were always that way. What I remember most about this house is the excess. There were TVs and game consoles in almost every room. Unopened gifts from potential sponsors left lying around.

"Take a new phone when you leave," Anton would say. "I've got dozens."

Amber would take two and sell them on eBay.

"I'm going to powder my nose," Amber says, bringing me back to the here and now. She clicks her fingers. "Erin, come on."

"What? No! It's like you don't even listen to me."

"Ohhh," she says mockingly. "Whatever."

Her heels click off across the hall, and for a second, I want to run up behind her and shove her as hard as I can. I hate myself for my temper.

"I'm going to look in the gardens," I say abruptly. "Call me if anyone finds Anton. Or Rose."

Before they can protest, I leave the rest of them in the house and circle the outside of the building to reach the gardens. Everything is the same as before but different. The hedge maze is so overgrown I can't see the entrance. Long branches reach upward and outward from the once neat firs like a hundred grabbing arms. The topiary breaking the patio up into discreet areas has metamorphosed into monsters.

I notice that there's a light on inside Anton's office, where he used to edit his content and film his gaming play-alongs. I push open the door. The place is a real mess. Otherwise, it's similar to the space my mother and I use to record our videos. Our studio is set up like a cozy bedroom. Anton's is more of a gamer's den.

At one end of the room, there's a green screen surrounded by lights that look like umbrellas coated with reflective material. A camera stands on a tripod watching the empty space. On a desk with a racing car bucket seat, there's a computer and gaming equipment. Plus more cameras pointing at the seat.

The fan on a computer softly whirs, and the desk is lit by the blue glow from inside the computer's transparent case. I push the mouse, and the screen flares into life. Someone's been here—recently.

"Is this where you were broadcasting from?" I say out loud.

It makes sense. I've used face-replacement software plenty of times for a laugh. You can make it look like you're a member of your favorite band or a character in a movie. With a high-end computer and no morals, you can even superimpose faces onto porn stars. Or clone someone's real voice if you have a recording of them.

I imagine Rose's ghost was created by filming someone in front of the green screen, then replacing their face with a computer-rendered version of hers. That would explain why the avatar had a slightly unnatural feel to it and why her voice wasn't quite right. I can remember Anton using a similar technique to make his *Shadow City* ghosts move like real people.

I say Anton, but of course I mean his team. Because that's something I learned about Anton when I collaborated with him. He has the big ideas, but he's too lazy to do the boring work. He employs others to do that. This means that dozens upon dozens of people knew his passwords—he always kept them taped to the side of the computer in case he forgot. Amber and *I* knew his passwords.

I doubt he's changed any of them. Like I said, lazy. From this office and these computers, whoever was behind the ghost could have accessed the servers used to host both *Shadow City* and Anton's game of tag. They could have uploaded their recordings of "Rose" and changed the programming to take control of the game from right under Anton's nose. By the time he realized, it would have been too late.

Which would have been why he came here, looking for whoever it was who'd brought Rose back from the grave.

I head into an adjoining space. It's a storeroom full of camera and sound equipment and props from Anton's old videos. There's a box in the middle of the room, and on top of it is a photograph.

It's a picture of Anton's team. Anton's in the middle, of course, his mouth wide in an over-the-top smile-shout that reveals all his teeth. On one side, Matthew and Beatrix stand, arms linked. Matthew is grinning down at Beatrix. Beatrix is sticking out her tongue. On Anton's other side is Rose. She's looking straight into the camera, a faint smirk on her lips.

Around them are more than a dozen members of the staff, from camera people to the general drudges who arranged stuff like meals and tidied up after the Accomplices. Jesse's there, on the sidelines like he doesn't quite belong. I feel a pang, but it doesn't hurt as much as it should. Someone paid him to set this up. One of these people in the photograph, I think. It was left here for a reason.

That's when I spot another familiar face standing among the behind-the-cameras crew. Suddenly, I know who is pretending to be Rose's ghost. What I don't understand is why.

"Who are you really?" I say.

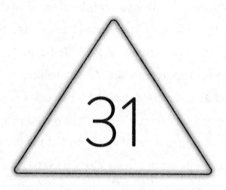

GRAYSON

While the others split up to look for Anton and Rose, I sneak outside alone. I head straight for the outbuildings next to the patio
area. Most of them are empty, but one of the doors leads into a
musty building that smells *wrong*. The hairs on the back of my neck
prickle, and my heart picks up its pace. I fumble for the light switch,
and a couple of dirty spotlights come on.

This is the pool house. This is where Rose died.

It's been left to go to ruin like the rest of the estate. The glass is
green with algae and mostly opaque. The pool still contains water
and has turned into a thick shallow swamp. That's what I smelled,
stagnant and fetid water.

Around the edge of the pool, there are several statues of women.
They remind me of the tombstones in the cemetery, except these
don't have wings. They're also not as old, although one has a missing arm and a damaged face.

I circle the edge of the pool. For nearly a year, I've done nothing but picture this place, my imagination running wild. Blood trickling between the white tiles, dripping into the water. Rose lying there dead. I try to push the thoughts away, but they always come back.

I stop by the damaged statue. I look behind it, searching for the clue that the ghost told us about. It's hard to imagine anything useful remains after all this time.

A movement makes me spin around. It's Beatrix, a startled deer in headlights. Too late, she hides her hands. But I've already seen that she's wearing disposable gloves.

"Wow, you came prepared," I say.

"It's not what it looks like; I...I didn't want to disturb anything."

She wrings her hands together behind her back. The plastic of the gloves squeaks. Dressed in bloodstained Anton merch, she looks like a deranged groupie.

Where was all the blood?

"That's what the ghost meant when she asked where all the blood was," I say, finally understanding. "You really did clean away the evidence so Rose's death would look like an accident. She didn't die in the pool, but you made it seem like she did."

She backs away from me. "She...she hit her head falling into the pool. She drowned."

"That's what the inquest said. It was the obvious conclusion. A teenager at a party rife with drugs and alcohol. Drugs in her own system. A late-night swim gone wrong. There was no evidence of foul play. You made sure of that."

She shakes her head, but it looks like it's an effort. Her eyes flick to the damaged statue, then to a crack in the tiles where a heavy object clearly landed.

"That's where she died," I say, barely able to get the words out. "The statue fell on her. Just like Emma. There would have been a lot of blood."

Her hands fall limp at her sides. "The statue couldn't have fallen by itself. It had to have been pushed. I couldn't leave it on the ground. I couldn't leave her lying there, or everyone would have known it was murder."

"Why?" I say quietly.

"I didn't kill her, I swear. I just found her body. Grayson, you have to believe me."

I don't say anything.

"I saw that the light was on in the early hours of the morning, so I came in. And she was dead. The statue was lying next to her. It had hit her on the head, and there was so much blood, but otherwise she was perfect. Even in death, she was perfect." She sits against the wall and rests her head in her hands. When she speaks, her voice is muffled. "I dragged her into the pool and cleaned up. The killer had left footprints in the blood. I made it look like Rose must have hit her head on the edge of the pool steps as she fell. Like it was an accident."

"And everyone believed it."

"Not everyone. Some of the crew who'd been close to Rose thought there was more to it, but the ones who mattered—the police, the coroner, the *press*—they accepted the story. No one questioned the damaged statue. I don't know how, but we got away with it."

"We?" I say, frowning.

At that moment, someone else appears through the door. Matthew stops abruptly when he sees the two of us. The final piece of the puzzle slots into place.

"You were protecting Matthew," I say. "He's the reason you staged the scene to look like an accident."

"What's he talking about, Bea?" Matthew says, his voice shaky. She looks up at him, tears running down her face. "There were footprints." She sobs. "A man's footprints. They would have figured it out."

"What?" Matthew says. His handsome face has gone slack and gray.

"She was covering for you," I say, a nervous laugh escaping my mouth. "She staged Rose's crime scene so you wouldn't get the blame."

"You genuinely thought that I killed Rose?" he chokes out.

"You'd been at each other's throats for weeks. Then I saw you arguing with her at the party," Beatrix says. "A few hours later, she was dead."

Matthew's mouth falls open. "And you presumed I killed her? Our friend?"

"Someone killed her! A murder investigation could have ruined Anton. As it was, Rose's death nearly destroyed everything, but he could come back from an accident."

"You tampered with a crime scene to protect the *channel*?" Matthew gapes at her, unable to do anything but ask increasingly panicked questions. I'd feel sorry for him if he weren't such a jerk.

"You and Anton were everything to me. I was trying to save *us*. All I wanted was for things to be how they were before Rose joined the Accomplices." She stands up shakily. "But it was too late. The damage was already done. Only, you're always so busy being the wonderful Matthew Bright that you don't realize we're only going through the motions of being in love."

"What?" Matthew says.

"Our relationship is over, Matthew. It has been for a long time. It just took me meeting Grayson to realize that."

Oh. Oh dear. She gazes at me with such desperate hope on her face, and all I can do is open and shut my mouth like a suffocating fish. This is not good. There's flirting, and there's breaking up someone's relationship. I don't want to be that guy.

"I'm sorry," she says, and now she's talking to me, not him. "I know that you loved Rose, and I'm so sorry I lied about her death."

"H-him?" Matthew says. For the first time in the competition, he actually looks at me. Like, really *looks* at me, instead of letting his gaze skim over me like I'm nothing. He finally finds his voice. "You son of a bitch!"

"Whoa, time out!" I duck aside as Matthew lunges at me. "This is between you and Beatrix. I'm an innocent party."

"You cowardly fuck." He grabs me by the collar and shakes me. "It's not enough that you spent months creeping on Rose after she dumped you. You had to mess with my *girlfriend*?"

"I didn't creep on anyone, I—"

"Rose hated you," he snarls. "She'd tell us stories about her *idiot ex*. That's what she called you. She played us the song you wrote her, and we all had a good laugh."

"Don't you dare!" I cry, suddenly filled with the kind of rage that makes you do incredibly stupid things without thinking.

I swing a punch with everything I have. I miss and fall against him. We both plummet into the pool. The water's less than two feet deep, so I hit the bottom hard. The filthy soup gets in my mouth and my nose, and it smells like death.

My hands tangle themselves in Matthew's clothes. I grab at wet fabric. My fingernails scrape against skin. He's trying to yell, but I drag him down, pushing him against the slippery floor of the pool.

All I can think about is Rose mocking me to her Accomplice

friends. To the people she left me to be with. The people who changed her beyond recognition, into someone who no longer needed me. I want to pin him down until he's forced to take a breath of the thick poisoned water. I want to punch him until he breaks into a thousand pieces.

Beatrix is screaming from the side of the pool, but I can't hear her over the sound of my blood rushing in my ears. Matthew manages to wriggle free of my grip. He bursts, gasping, above the surface. He lands a punch on my chin, and I skid on a thick layer of slime, going under again.

"What in the name...?" All the noise must have alerted Erin as she bursts into the building. She holds her nose with a manicured hand.

I manage to stand up, clinging to the side of the pool. I'm gasping and coughing too much to speak.

"He...he tried to drown me," Matthew says, spitting dirty water.

I scramble out of the pool, dragging myself on my belly across the tiles. I stagger to my feet and try to compose myself. Got to smile and laugh at myself because that's what I do. I'm the harmless goof without a clue. That's what people expect from me, but I can't do it anymore. I'm too broken inside.

"Can someone explain what this is all about?" Erin says.

"It's none of your business," Beatrix says.

Matthew and I glare at each other, our chests heaving. Beatrix crosses her arms and glares at Erin.

"All right," Erin says brightly. "Good chat. In other news, I found the equipment used to fake Rose's ghost. Nothing's been real. This whole game has been about getting justice for Rose. The secrets, the tricks, the pantomime. The question is, has it worked?"

She looks at me. I hold her stare. The corner of her mouth quirks in an almost smile.

"We still don't know who the killer is," Matthew says. "Because *it's not me.*"

Erin nods, then waves a photo at us all. I can't see who it's of though. "I think I know how to clear this up. Where are Amber and Charlotte?"

"I'll check in the house," Beatrix says. She pushes past us all to leave first and carefully avoids looking at either Matthew or me. Her cheeks are bright red. "You three take the gardens, maze, and outbuildings."

As we leave the pool house, Erin catches my arm. "What were you doing in here?" she says.

I shrug. "Following the clues. The ghost—" I force an embarrassed laugh. "I mean, whoever is *pretending* to be a ghost said that we'd find a clue at the scene of the crime. Something that everyone else overlooked."

"You found this building very easily," she says. "Almost like you'd been here before."

"Idiot's luck, I guess," I say.

She points at me with a long sharp nail, smiling like we're best friends. "You're not half as much of an idiot as you pretend to be, Grayson."

Only, I don't think she means it as a compliment.

32

CHARLOTTE

In my heart, I know where I'll find him.

I cross the lawn, flashlight in my hand, with the damp grass tickling my ankles. The hedge maze looms before me. I don't hesitate. It's instantly another world. The firs have become so unruly that it's hard to see the numerous paths. I try to picture the route Anton took when he led me to the summer house. But it's too dark, and within seconds, I'm lost.

"Anton?" I call. "It's me, Charlotte. Where are you?"

I hear the rustling of creatures unused to human presence. The hedge's spiky needles scratch my face and exposed roots snake out of the mud to grab at my feet. I want to conjure the remembered magic of this place, but the fairy lights that once lit the paths are nothing more than frayed wires after all this time, and the moonlight makes twisted monsters of the shadows.

I hear footsteps somewhere nearby. Light, tentative footsteps. I spin around. "Anton?"

There's no reply. I walk on, listening carefully. The footsteps come again. I speed up. Left, right, right, left. I think I'll be trapped here forever, running along these narrow passageways, searching for something that doesn't exist anymore. But then, all of a sudden, I burst out into the open area at the center of the maze.

The summer house stands surrounded by tall grass. It's bigger than the house I share with my mother and Roger, with an octagonal shape and two stories, each encased by huge panes of glass. There's a covered patio area at the front that doubles as a balcony terrace on the second floor. But where before the wood was once fresh and clean, the boards are now warped and green with algae. The windows are clouded with dirt.

There's no sign of life. I slip through the open door. "Hello?" I call.

It smells musty, of damp furniture and moldy carpets. Rain and dead leaves have blown in, and everything is coated in a layer of grime and abandonment. I sit on the red lips sofa where we slept. The fabric squelches, and my seat instantly feels wet.

This place has been at the center of my daydreams for so long. My fantasies have brought me here a million times, wrapping me up in the comforting memories of falling asleep with Anton at my side. But it's nothing like I remember. Everything's coming crashing down around me. As if my entire relationship with Anton has been built on shaky foundations. On a lie.

There's a noise upstairs. Like creaking floorboards. A muffled shuffling sound. I get up with a wet sucking noise as the sofa releases me. I tentatively creep up the stairs. The upper level of the house is empty apart from a beanbag, a large metal fridge that stands with the door open, and dozens of bottles scattered across the floor.

I'm about to go back down when suddenly there's a cry, and a person launches themself out from behind the fridge door. It's Anton, a bottle clutched in his hand like a weapon.

With a yelp, I dive aside, flattening myself on the floor. Anton stumbles and flies headfirst down the stairs. He bounces off every step, his limbs flailing like a rag doll. He lands in a disordered pile, and the bottle rolls from his hand.

"Anton, oh my goodness," I cry, racing downstairs. If I've killed him after everything, I don't know what I'll do.

He's alive. He hauls himself into a sitting position and sits slumped. God, I hope he doesn't have a head injury. I can't see any blood or obvious wounds, but his gaze is unfocused.

"Anton?" I say. "Are you all right?"

He burps loudly, and I catch the whiff of alcohol. He's not injured. He's drunk.

"Who are you?" he slurs. His purple-streaked hair sticks up in every direction, and there's a graze on his stubbled jaw.

"It's me. Charlotte," I say. He blinks at me. "Matthew's stepsister?"

"Oh right. Charlotte." He laughs, but it could also be a sob.

"What are you doing here?" I say. "I thought you'd been kidnapped."

He shushes me dramatically. "I escaped, and now I'm hiding from *the ghost* who ruined my entire life. I figured no one would find me here, but you're here, so…"

"Of course I'm here." I laugh. "This is where we had our moment."

He frowns in thought. "We did?"

My heart sinks. *He's drunk*, I tell myself. That's why he doesn't seem to remember me. He's been through a lot, but at heart, he's still my perfect, lovely Anton. Then I'm hit by an awful smell. I can't believe I'm saying this…but I think he's farted.

"I'll tell you a secret," he whispers, leaning close to my face and breathing fumes over me. "I've had *a lot* of moments in this house."

My cheeks burn hot, and my blood turns to sand. "Oh. Right." I pull myself together; the important thing is that Anton is alive. "You know, maybe we should get out of here and find the others. Everyone will be glad you're safe."

"Safe?" He makes a disgusted face. "My game's ruined, and my reputation is in pieces. All thanks to Rose. You'd think she'd be content with fucking up my life once, but she couldn't stay dead, could she?"

"I'm sure everything will work out OK," I say, brushing a strand of purple hair away from his forehead.

He gawks at me like I'm the one burping and farting noxious gases all over the place. I get to my feet and shield my nose, hoping to protect at least some of my affection for him against the stinky onslaught.

"Unless you're the one who killed Rose," I joke, forcing a laugh.

He doesn't join in. "That bitch deserved to die," he snarls. "Fuck her. You hear that, Rose? Fuck you."

I back up nervously. This isn't right. My daydreams have collided with reality, and as hard as I try to hold on to the fantasy, it doesn't fit. Anton isn't who I thought he was. I've been deluding myself. I don't know him at all.

Suddenly, I'm wondering what he's really been doing for this entire game. Was the kidnapping part even real or part of a ruse to cover up the fact that he's a murderer? "Where were you when Rose died?" I whisper.

His angry expression snaps into a smile. A nasty smile. "Wasn't I with you? Having a *moment*. Pretty sure that's what went on the police report."

"No," I say, my voice shaky and overly prim. "You were here with me until twelve at the latest."

"Are you sure about that, Charlotte?" Beneath the drunken slurring, his voice has the same viciousness as it did in that video where he threatened Rose. *I made you! And I can end you just as easily.*

I back away as he rises to his feet. He's taller than the boy in my fantasies, and his chest is broader. Not a boy. A grown man. I don't think I'd fit in his arms. I'd be smothered.

He staggers toward me. "I think I was with you all night long. Where else would I have been? Smashing Rose's brains out in the swimming pool?"

I reach the door; then I squeeze outside and run.

"I'm joking," Anton yells after me. "Probably. Come back!"

I ignore him and race into the maze. Sobs threaten to burst out of me. *What have I done?* Anton's been my everything for so long, and I don't know who I am anymore. I run and run, making no attempt to navigate the maze. I let it swallow me up with its dead ends and twisting pathways. I want to lose myself forever.

I trip on a root and fall heavily. Pain ripples through my jarred knees and shoulder. I lie on the cold ground, hiccuping so hard I can't breathe. I figure I'll stay here and let the bushes grow over me until I'm part of them. There's nothing left for me anymore. Everything is gone.

Suddenly, I can see my relationship with Anton from the outside, and I'm so, so embarrassed for myself. He never liked me. I'd see him at the parties *Matthew* invited me to, and I'd take every smile and smirk as a hint that he shared my feelings. But all along he was laughing at me. And when he took me to the summer house that night, it wasn't because he was finally ready to be with me. It was probably to annoy Matthew.

Matthew was never trying to get in the way of true love when he refused to pass my messages on to Anton. He was trying to stop me from making a fool out of myself. I'm a joke to Anton and nothing more.

Well, I was something more. I was his alibi.

All my daydreams shatter like glass. They fall around me, mocking me with glimpses of my own desperation and obsession. The Anton in my fantasies wasn't real, and I think, deep down, I knew. That's why none of my stories end with a happily ever after. I'm always gladly dying to save him because that means I never have to face up to the reality of getting to know the real him.

The tears flood out of me, and I can't stop them, so I lie there with my cheek against the dirt, salty tears and snot running into my mouth.

And it's not only Anton I'm crying over. It's my dad, leaving to start a new family and forgetting me. It's my mom, so wrapped up in planning her wedding to Roger that she has no time for me. It's Matthew, leaving to live with Anton—just when I'd started to come around to the idea of having a brother.

Everyone leaves me. No one wants me.

I don't know how long I cry for. Long enough that my stomach muscles ache from twisting themselves into knots, and my throat burns from the racking breaths.

But eventually the real world comes rushing back with a piercing scream. My tears stop. I sit up.

The scream came from somewhere nearby. A neighboring path in the maze, so close but unreachable through these thick hedges. I hear footsteps, stumbling and slow. Labored gurgles reach me from the opposite side of the bushes.

"No, please," someone gasps.

Oh no. No, no, no. I claw at the branches. I try to pull them apart to get to the person on the other side. "Stop," I yell. "Stop!"

There's another scream, short and knife sharp. The hedge shakes like someone's fallen against it. There's a heavy thud and then silence. I shine my flashlight into the bare branches at the base of the hedge. There's something there, but I can't quite see. I shift position, and that's when I see her hair.

Bright orange hair soaked with blood.

ERIN

I'm running through the maze toward the sound of screaming when the screams stop. I skid around corner after corner, so close but so far away. Then I turn and it's me.

I'm lying dead in the dirt, my hair disheveled and mud on my face, ruining my perfect makeup. My top's ripped, and my clothes are covered in twigs and leaves. There's blood everywhere.

I can't stop staring at the blood. On my face, and my throat, and my chest.

Except it's not me. It's someone who looks exactly like me, in the dark at least.

"Erin!" Charlotte races around the corner and skids to a halt when she sees my mother. She rushes over and takes me by the hands. "Don't look, Erin. Don't look."

"Is she gone?" I say.

I pull my hands free from Charlotte's and kneel next to Amber. I don't need to check for a pulse; I can see that she's dead. My flashlight illuminates her blood-splattered face. She'd hate people seeing her like this, so unposed and messy. An ugly laugh bubbles up inside me, but I stop it before it can escape.

Charlotte touches my shoulder. "The killer could still be here." Her eyes search the bushes. "Let's get to the house."

I nod. But I can't stop staring at Amber.

"Come on." Charlotte pulls me to my feet. I let her lead me, but I keep looking back at Amber. Less than an hour ago, she was taking selfies outside the cemetery. I start laughing, and this time I can't stop.

"Look at her," I say. "All that effort to be beautiful, and at the end of the day, she's just meat."

"I'm so sorry, Erin."

"Don't be," I say, my voice reedy and harsh. "It's not like I liked her, is it? So why would I be upset?"

"Because she's your mother?"

I slam a door on the conflicting emotions churning inside me and give Charlotte a businesslike smile. "She wasn't much of a mother."

"But—"

I cut her off with a raised hand. "Don't."

I don't think Charlotte knows what else to say, so she keeps quiet. Which suits me fine. I've got enough voices fighting to be heard in my head. The one that tells me I should be crying, the one that thinks I should celebrate, the one that is confused, the one that's irrationally, incandescently angry. Angry with Amber, and myself, and whoever did this to her.

The others meet us on the patio, appearing from three different directions.

"What's going on?" Grayson says breathlessly. He's dressed in a bathrobe from the pool house after his dip in the filthy water. "I heard screaming."

"It was Amber," I say. "She's dead."

"Dead?" Beatrix repeats. Her braids are stiff with dried blood, and her hoodie's stained. "Oh my god, what's happening?"

"We have to call the police," Matthew says. "This has gone too far."

"What about Anton?" Beatrix says. "My brother's missing, and if Rose—"

"Don't feel bad for Anton," says Charlotte, glancing over her shoulder. "He's fine, but I think he might be the one we have to worry about."

"Anton? You think he killed my mother?" I say.

"He wouldn't," Beatrix says.

"Let's get inside where it's safe," Matthew says. "Then we'll call for help."

We go inside the house via the patio doors, into the open-plan kitchen with its black marble floors and snow-white countertops. There are bottles lying around the place from the party. It's like Anton and his friends simply left after Rose's death and could never bring themselves to come back.

I wrinkle my nose. The air smells weird. Staleness mixed with something sulfurous, like rotting eggs. I've always been sensitive to smells.

Matthew closes the door behind him. He pats his pockets. I notice that, like Grayson, he's changed out of his wet clothes, into Anton merch he must have found in the house. "Damn. Does anyone have a phone on them?"

"No battery," I say flatly.

Beatrix and Charlotte shake their heads too. I'm about to ask Grayson what happened to the phone Lenny gave him, when there's a pounding on the door. We all jump. Beatrix tentatively peers out through the glass, into the dark garden. "Anton!"

"Anton," Grayson repeats, his jaw tightening.

Beatrix goes to unlock the door, but Charlotte stops her. "Wait. He was saying some pretty unhinged stuff earlier."

"We can't leave him out there."

Matthew hesitates. "Let him in. We can outnumber him if we have to."

Beatrix opens the door. Anton staggers inside and bounces off the units, grabbing at the shiny white surface to keep his balance. His hands leave behind smeared red prints.

"Is that blood?" Beatrix says, backing away.

Anton blinks down at his hands, both of them sticky. Then he points outside. "There's a dead person in the maze. Someone should clean that up."

Before any of us can react, his eyes roll into his head, and he slides to the ground. He immediately starts snoring.

"That's my mother he was talking about," I say.

Matthew fixes me with the saddest look. "He's really drunk. And an asshole."

"Thanks for the clarification," I say in a voice that doesn't sound like mine. I feel numb, like I'm watching a movie, not real life. My hands are shaking.

There's a sudden buzzing sound, followed by a voice. "Now that we're all together, let's finish this game, shall we?" Rose's ghost says.

We all look around. There must be speakers in the walls.

"I know who you are, and you're not Rose," Anton slurs, briefly waking from his vodka nap. He waves an arm around, pointing, then falls still again.

"That's because Rose is dead," the voice says, only it has changed. She's no longer using the voice disguiser that made her sound like an otherworldly Rose. Instead, she spits out the words like they taste bitter.

Grayson drags a hand through his wet hair, leaving tracks behind. "Shit," he says quietly.

"All of you killed her," the voice continues, full of anger and hatred. "All of you are guilty."

"Who is it?" Charlotte whispers.

"I loved her, and you killed her," the voice says, cracking with emotion. "All of you treated her like she was nothing, caring more about yourselves. But who was it who struck the final blow? Who shoved over that statue that broke her skull?"

"Who is that?" Matthew says. "I recognize her voice."

I don't answer, even though I know. I'm too tired, and the words won't come.

"A royal pain in the butt, that's who," Anton grumbles.

"Anton, all she ever was to you was a way to make money," the voice says. "You were happy to use her ideas and her image, even faking a relationship with her. But when she wanted to leave the Accomplices, you turned on her. After she died, it was the damage to your empire that mattered to you. She died at your party, and you spent a fortune on lawyers to protect yourself."

On the floor, Anton raises a fist in the air.

"And Matthew. You always went along with everything Anton wanted. You let him bully his staff and intimidate Rose, and you did nothing but protect your own interests. Rose knew that you kissed

Amber, and it put her in an impossible position. When she pleaded with you to tell Beatrix the truth, you threatened her."

"*Amber*?" Beatrix spits.

Matthew shakes his head, his eyes glistening.

"Little Beatrix," the voice snarls. "You pretended to be Rose's friend when secretly you were jealous of her and wanted her out of the Accomplices. You knew she was murdered, and you denied her justice."

"I was trying to help," Beatrix pleads.

"You gravitated toward her ex-boyfriend in this competition. Is that because you wanted something that belonged to her?"

Beatrix's tear-filled eyes flick across the room to Grayson. He's lurking in a corner, his hairy legs poking out from the bottom of his robe. He won't even meet Beatrix's stare.

"Do you have anything to say, Grayson?" the voice continues.

Grayson shakes his head and glances up. He's crying, I realize.

"All that mattered to you were your own feelings. Even when Rose told you she didn't want to be with you, you refused to respect her choice. You pestered her with letters and calls. You made her feel unsafe."

"I wanted her to listen to me," he whispers.

"It's all about you, isn't it? Even entering this competition wasn't about Rose. It was you needing to blame someone for her leaving you. Because you couldn't accept that it was her choice. It had to have been Anton, leading her astray."

"It was!" Grayson cries. "It was his fault."

"Save it," the voice says. "I have two suspects left. Let's talk to Charlotte, shall we? You hated Rose because she was everything you wanted to be. When she humiliated you at the party, you took your online trolling to a new level and posted a death threat aimed at her."

"I know," Charlotte says softly. "I'm so sorry."

The voice goes quiet for a second; then she's back. "Last but not least, Erin Love. Angry, fake, desperate Erin Love. Rose tried to help you, and you threw it all in her face. You would have done anything to protect your awful, lying mother, and look where it got you."

"My mother is dead," I say through gritted teeth. The numbness is starting to give way into anger now.

The ghost hesitates again. "A lot of people are dead."

"Because of you," I say.

"I never killed anyone," she yells. It sounds like she's crying. "But here's another secret. I don't care anymore. You're all as bad as each other. So let's play one more game, and then you can all die."

There's a loud clunking sound, followed by quieter clunks.

Matthew throws himself at the door and yanks on it. "Shit. She's activated the lockdown protocol."

"No," Beatrix gasps.

"Er, the what?" Grayson says.

"The house was built by this superparanoid prince," Beatrix explains. "He was convinced everyone wanted him dead, so he had the windows in the house glazed with bulletproof glass and installed internal deadlocks on all the doors and windows."

"Once the security lockdown is activated, the house is virtually impenetrable," Matthew says. "The only way to open it is with the remote."

"Which is where?" I say.

"She has it," Anton slurs. He laughs, then falls asleep again.

"Who is she? Why do I recognize her voice?" Matthew says. "I don't understand."

I remember the photo I took from the office. I silently pass it to Matthew. I glance at Grayson, who holds my stare without emotion.

Matthew looks between the faces in the picture, then stops. "I can't believe I didn't think of—"

He doesn't get to finish because, at that moment, the lights go out. "Here's the game," the voice says. "I have one final secret to reveal. Emma Sano's final secret. The reason both she and Jesse were murdered. She was at that party where Rose died, taking photos. And one of her photos caught Jesse talking to our killer. She sent this photo to the Anton HQ number earlier tonight, hoping that it would reach me. And it did."

"Emma was thrown out of the party hours before Rose died," Matthew says. "How's it possible that she photographed the killer?"

"Just show us already," Charlotte shouts. "Stop playing these stupid games."

The voice laughs. "I'm hiding somewhere in this house, along with the remote and the photo. Come find me and it's yours. But watch your backs—one of you is a murderer."

Thumping dance music blares out from the hidden speakers so loud that I can hardly hear myself think. Colored lights flash on and off, blindingly bright to pitch-black. I see flashes of the others, their movements made jerky by the strobing lights like something out of a horror movie.

"Game on," the voice bellows. "It's time to play."

GRAYSON

I would know Lenny's voice anywhere. But it turns out that I don't know Lenny.

The reason she never wanted to talk about her past wasn't because she's a private person. It was because our friendship's been a lie. A con. A trap. She used to work with Anton, behind the scenes, coding his games. She knew Rose. Was friends with Rose. *Loved* Rose.

She's the one who's been revealing all those secrets and playing all those games. Outing the suspects. Trying to force Rose's killer to give themselves away. And now that she has Emma's photo and claims to have discovered the truth, she's turned against the lot of us.

I should have figured it out sooner, but I was in denial. All the clues were there though. She's at college studying AI design, for god's sake. How did I not suspect her? I can't help but wonder if she sought me out on purpose, coming into the ice cream shop and striking up conversations. Was she trying to find out if I killed Rose? Did she suspect me all this time? She must have, or she wouldn't have included me tonight.

But then I think about what she said to me this morning, while I waited for Beatrix to appear with my equipment. *Just remember that I'm rooting for you.* There was something both sad and hopeful in her voice. Like she genuinely wanted me to pass these impossible tests of hers and make it out the other end.

I don't know if I am going to make it out. I need to think, but this goddamn music is so loud, turning my brain to porridge. I have to find her. I need that remote. I stumble out of the kitchen into the hall, not caring what any of the others do. I'll deal with them later.

"Where are you?" I scream, but my voice is lost to the noise.

My fingers find the polished banister, curving up the wide flight of stairs to the upper floor. I climb, tripping on the steps as I go. My spiraling thoughts question our entire friendship. All the times she encouraged me to talk about Rose. All the questions she asked me. I can't believe she'd do this. I can't fucking believe it.

"Lenny," I cry. "Come out!"

I feel my way across the landing and find a door. It opens into a big entertainment room bathed in moonlight. I can see again, and the music is quieter in here, so I can finally hear myself think. OK. I need a plan. I don't have a plan.

Where would she be? Where would she be? I need to find her. I need to get out of this house.

The room runs the length of the house with an entire wall of glass looking out over the gardens. From the outside, it's always reminded me of a rooftop restaurant. Finally seeing it from the inside, I realize it's mostly empty except for a few pinball and arcade machines and a bar in the corner, still fully stocked.

I don't usually drink, but for some reason, it feels like a good idea, to calm my panic. I pour myself a glass of clear liquid—vodka. It burns all the way down. As I lower the glass, I see a figure appear in the doorway. I think it's Amber's ghost for a second, but it's Erin. They're almost impossible to tell apart in the near dark.

"Grayson," she says, shoes tapping as she approaches. Her face is haunted, eyes hooded, skin pale, lips deep and swollen. It makes her look tragically beautiful. "Any luck finding your little friend?"

So she figured it out. Of course she did. "Nah, but I did find a bar," I say.

She pulls herself up onto a stool. She eyes me suspiciously, then pushes a photo across the bar. It's of Anton's team. Lenny is standing near the back. "When did you realize the ghost was her?" she asks.

"About ten minutes ago when I heard her voice, although I started suspecting something when I discovered she knew Jesse."

I don't like how she's looking at me, so I busy myself pouring us both a drink. She runs a finger around the rim of hers but doesn't swallow it.

"She sought me out a few weeks after Rose died, you know? Started turning up at the ice cream shop where I worked. I guess she was scoping me out." I shake my head and sigh. "It suddenly makes sense why she was helping me with the game. You were always going to be at the top of the board. As was Charlotte. But I'd have been knocked out within minutes, and that wouldn't have fit with her plans."

Erin picks up her glass and swirls it. "She must have been planning this for a while. Researching Rose's case. Compiling her suspects. Setting up this whole takeover in a last desperate attempt to discover the truth." She puts the glass down and pushes it away. "About that. I have a theory."

"Oh?" I watch her over the rim of my glass, the smell of the alcohol sharp and eye watering.

"Whoever killed Rose was seen by Jesse that night, somewhere they weren't supposed to be. Jesse didn't think anything of it until he saw them taking part in the game and began to get suspicious. Maybe he confronted the killer. Asked a few questions. Made some accusations. Whatever happened, the killer must have thought it best to get rid of him just in case."

"That's an interesting theory," I say, gulping back my drink.

"The killer bludgeoned Jesse and threw him into the river. It was a coincidence that both Jesse and Charlotte washed up in the same place," Erin continues, watching me for the smallest reaction. She's sharp, far cleverer than I am. It's disconcerting to have that ice-cold intellect directed right at me. "Of course, Beatrix thought that Matthew was behind Rose's murder, so when she found Jesse's body while she was rounding up contestants who'd fallen in the river, she covered it up like she covered up Rose's murder."

"So *was* it Matthew?" I say, pouring another drink. God knows I need one.

She laughs softly, but I think it's a trap. "Actually, I suspected Beatrix for a while. But then I thought about the photo that Emma took. The one of Jesse and our killer. How did she know they were the killer?"

I shrug. "Maybe they were wearing a little sign saying, *I'm a killer*. I don't know."

"Emma was thrown out of the party hours before Rose died. If that photo had been of anyone who was *meant* to be at the party, Emma wouldn't have been suspicious. It had to be someone who *wasn't* meant to be there. Someone who has consistently claimed that they never visited Anton's house. So Emma had to die too."

"You're very smart to figure all this out," I say, forcing a smile.

"Not just a pretty face."

"What about Amber, then?" I fold my arms. My move. "Why was she stabbed?"

A brief flash of hurt crosses Erin's face. She lifts her chin. "I don't know for sure. Perhaps she saw through the killer's lies before the rest of us?" She says it like it's a question. Same tone as Lenny. She's hoping she's wrong.

I snort under my breath. She really is clever. Way too clever for her own good.

"It's funny," I say, pouring another drink. My hand makes the bottle shake, and it's an effort to get the vodka into the glass. I screw the lid on to the bottle before downing the shot in one. "The police report into Rose's death was right in one respect."

"What was that?" she says quietly.

"Her death really was an accident."

Before she can respond, I swing the bottle. She tries to duck, but she's too slow. The heavy base strikes her on the side of the temple, and she falls from her stool, landing heavily.

I circle the bar, holding the bottle. "I didn't want it to come to this." I sigh. "You have to believe me. But you've left me no choice."

She shuffles across the floor. She keeps collapsing to one side, then pushes herself up. At least she's not pleading and begging like her mother though. That was gnarly.

"Fuck you," she spits.

"I'm sorry," I say. "I really am."

"Sorry?" Her voice is slurred, but she still manages to snarl in anger. "You murdered four people, and you're *sorry*?"

"I didn't murder Rose! I told you. It was an accident. I swear. I didn't mean to hurt her."

"Right," she says, rolling her eyes. "Of course it was."

"I came to the party to talk to her, that's all. I wanted to know why she wasn't answering my calls. I'd written her dozens of letters, but she wouldn't reply. I knew if I could talk to her, then she'd realize we were meant to be together." I'm not sure why I need her to believe me. Maybe I'm trying to convince myself.

"Guess that didn't work out for you." She scoots farther away from me. Her eyes flick to the door.

"It was an accident," I yell.

This is the truth.

———

Days became weeks became months. My friends told me losing her would get easier—that I'd move on—but the pain got worse. I'd stay up all night obsessively checking her social media for new photos, watching Anton's channel for any clue that she missed me as much as I missed her. All I saw was a girl I barely recognized.

At my lowest points, I'd alternate between tears that left me unable to get out of bed and all-consuming anger that saw me smash holes in my parents' walls and get into fights at school. My thoughts would spiral out of control as I imagined the life she was leading without me. And Anton was always there, the grinning puppet master who'd stolen her away and ruined her.

I wanted to grab her and shake her and scream at her. *This isn't you! Why are you letting him change you like this? Where has the girl I fell in love with gone?* But she wouldn't see me, or speak to me, or answer my texts and letters.

I started sneaking into Anton's garden. Rose often went for a late-night swim, and I'd stand against the glass, smothered by the darkness, watching her in the brightly lit pool house. One night she wasn't alone. She was with him, splashing around. Laughing. Just the two of them.

I sent her another letter. *I know you're sleeping with him*, it read. *I saw you together in his pool.*

After that, it got harder to break in. Anton hired better security and put up a taller fence. My only way to get to Rose was his parties when dozens of people would descend on the house. So that fateful night, I put on my best clothes and waited for the front gates to open for the first guests.

I didn't get a chance to talk to her though. I didn't even find her. Jesse found me first.

"It's G, isn't it?" he said because back then I went by that ridiculous nickname. He grabbed me by the arm and dragged me toward the gates. "Rose asked me to keep an eye out for you."

He threw me out and left me with a few choice threats of what would happen if I came back. I didn't realize it at the time, but Emma caught us on camera. Like Erin said, I've consistently denied ever visiting Anton's house. If people found out that this was a lie and I'd been there the night Rose died…well, I couldn't let that happen.

Because Rose hiring Jesse to intercept me had made me even more determined to speak to her. It had to stop. I'd had enough. I waited until the majority of the party moved into the house, and I went back. And I found Rose sitting on the edge of the pool, kicking her legs in the water.

"G!" she gasped, jumping to her feet. Then she regained her composure. "Get the hell out of here."

We argued, accusations flying. I pleaded with her. I begged. I yelled and accused. I can't even remember the things I said, just the feeling of desperation and powerlessness. I couldn't make her understand. In the months since she left me, she'd turned into this bitch who thought she was too good for me.

"I don't want you," she yelled at me. "I will never, ever want you. It's over, and if you don't stop stalking me, I'll call the police. You're pathetic. You disgust me!"

The rage was white-hot and all-encompassing. I kicked out at one of the statues, slamming my foot into it again and again. My thoughts were consumed by needing to break something. Smashing and destroying in the hope that it would rid me of all the fucked-up feelings racing through my head.

Rose was yelling at me to cut it out. She was shoving me and grabbing at me, her long nails scratching my arms. Calling me names and screaming as if *she* were the one full of pent-up rage and frustration.

The statue tipped off its pedestal. It fell. It was only after it crashed to the ground and my out-of-control fury vanished that I realized Rose was no longer yelling. The statue had struck her on the head. She'd been killed instantly.

There was so much blood, trickling along the gaps between the tiles, dripping into the pool. Rose lay there, her angry face slackening, her lips parted with the final insult she'd hurled at me. I didn't know what to do. So I ran.

I thought the police would come knocking on my door. No one ever did. I guess Beatrix made it look enough like an accident that no one asked the right questions. Jesse was the only one who could place me at the party, but he said nothing. I asked him why down on the riverbank. Turns out, Anton paid all his staff to keep their mouths shut so the investigation would conclude quickly and quietly.

My life fell apart. I got kicked out of school, and the only job I could find was at the ice cream shop. I tried to move on from her, but I couldn't. Over time, I started to forgive myself. I came to terms with the fact that it wasn't my fault or even hers. It was Anton's. When he relaunched his channel like nothing had happened, I knew I couldn't let him get away with it any longer.

I promised I would make him pay. Someone had to pay.

Nothing went to plan. For starters, Jesse recognized me at the museum, even though my hair is different these days and I entered under my given name. It wouldn't have mattered if everyone had still believed Rose's death was an accident. But the ghost—Lenny— had just revealed that Rose was murdered. Jesse was suspicious.

When I spotted him alone on the riverbank, I took the opportunity to make sure he didn't implicate me. But I was worried that Charlotte had seen me with him, so I tried to strangle her in the mannequin house. In the end, it was a blessing in disguise that Emma interrupted us. Charlotte is so clueless that she didn't suspect me after all.

Emma was less naive. I knew she was trouble the moment she mentioned she was a journalist. That's why I tried to scare her off in the building site, by pushing that scaffolding pole onto her. I should have tried harder because it was only a matter of time before she figured out the truth. She realized that she'd taken that photo of me at the party, placing me not only at the scene of Rose's death but revealing that I'd argued with Jesse, who by that point was also dead. So I shoved a statue onto her.

All the loose ends were tied up, and Lenny's plan to out Rose's killer had failed, or so I thought. I didn't realize Emma had sent that photo to Anton HQ and Lenny had intercepted it. I also didn't bank on a certain redhead sticking her nose where it doesn't belong.

———

My consciousness jumps to the here and now. Erin is still edging away from me, blood trickling down the side of her face. She blinks like she's trying to clear her head.

I grin crookedly at her. "You got everything right apart from one thing. I wasn't worried about Amber figuring out the truth. She wasn't the one who'd started to put the pieces together." I raise the bottle with a wink. "Truth is, I thought she was you."

CHARLOTTE

Anton is holding my hand as we run from room to room, banging into furniture in the dark as we race to find this ghost. Or get murdered. Whichever happens first.

"Can we stop for a snickety-snack?" Anton slurs, pulling on my arm like a drunken toddler.

I should be happy, feeling his fingers entwined with mine. This has been one of my fantasies for as long as I can remember. Only his palm is exceptionally moist, and when he talks, he sprays me with a fine mist of spittle. Some things, it would seem, are far better when they remain in your imagination.

"We have to get the remote control," I say. "It's the only way out of this house."

"But this is boring," he grumbles. "Also, why does it smell of gas in here?"

"That's *gas*?" Eyes widening, I sniff at the air. The house does smell odd, but I didn't know it was gas.

"One spark…" Anton makes the noise of an explosion, then laughs.

Great. Not only have my dreams asphyxiated in the fumes from Anton's breath, but I'm now going to be incinerated in a huge fireball.

When the lights went out, there were a few minutes of confusion and bumped heads. When we got things together, we realized both Grayson and Erin had taken off already. Matthew and Beatrix got into a big argument about whose fault it was, leaving it up to me to find a way out of this mess. But Anton appears to have attached himself to me, and I'm spending more time babysitting than I am searching.

"Come on, focus. Where would she be?" I say as I drag Anton along. "She kidnapped you. You must know something."

"Yeah, she's upstairs, in my panic room," Anton says. "She was the only other person who knew the code because I kept forgetting."

I take a slow, calming breath of gas. "Do you remember how to get to this panic room?"

He snorts. "It's in my bedroom, and I can find my bed with my eyes closed, butt naked and drunk."

"Best to leave your clothes on for now." I let him lead, even though I have misgivings.

Eventually, he finds the stairs. True to his word, he knows where he's going. He throws open the door into a bedroom. A four-poster bed and various pieces of antique furniture stand illuminated by the moonlight seeping through the windows.

He charges across the room and throws himself onto the bed.

Dust puffs up, but he doesn't notice. He stretches out on his side and pats the duvet next to him, giving me what I suspect is meant to be a sexy smile but comes off like he's trying to remove food from his teeth with his tongue.

"Care to join me?" he purrs.

I've dreamed of this so many times. But right now I'm a shaken snow globe. I wish I could curl up in the bed, the little spoon to Anton's big spoon, and have him promise me that everything's going to be OK. Only I don't think Anton has cuddling in mind, and also, he's revolting.

"I read all your stories," he says. "OK, not *all* of them, but enough. I'm totally up for humping like guinea pigs. It sounds hot."

"Ew, no," I say. "A million times, no. Just tell me where the panic room is before we all die."

"Oh, fine." Sighing, he rolls off the bed and approaches a large bookshelf on one wall. He pats at the shelves until there's a loud clicking noise, and the bookshelf swings open. Behind it, there's a reinforced metal door that looks like a person-sized safe.

I push Anton aside and yank at the handle, but it's locked. "What's the code?"

"Pfft. Like I remember. Lenny would know."

I frown. "Lenny? Never mind." I hammer on the door with both fists. "Open up. We found you; now keep your promise and let us out of this house."

The taunting voice crackles from a speaker above the keypad. "I've changed my mind," she says. "You're going to stay in here with me, and we'll meet Rose together."

"What? That is totally unacceptable!" I shout. "This house is filling up with gas."

"Because I broke the pipe to the stove," she says.

"Oh my god, that thing makes *the* best bread," Anton says. "Do you have any bread?"

"She's planning to burn us alive, you idiot," I snap.

"What?" He squeezes past me and hammers on the door. "Lenny, open up right now. I'm serious."

"Who's Lenny?"

He pauses in his hammering and turns to me. "She was one of my techies. Helped with running my servers and stuff."

"Helped you? I designed most of *Shadow City*," Lenny shouts.

"Based on my ideas." Anton rolls his eyes. "With my money."

"A lot of good that money will do you now. You'll burn the same as the rest of us."

"Don't you fucking dare," he yells. "No one burns Anton Frazer."

I put a hand on his shoulder and gesture firmly for him to sit on the bed. "Lenny?" I say gently through the door. "This is Charlotte. Can we talk? Please?"

She doesn't reply, but I figure she must be listening. I lean against the cold metal. "I didn't know Rose, not really," I say. "I never bothered to get to know the real her, but I wish I had. I was too busy being jealous of her."

"Your loss. She was funny and smart. And kind," Lenny says. "Everyone liked to think they knew her, but they saw what they wanted to see."

"I know what that's like." I glance at Anton, lounging on the bed and picking his nose. Then I think of Erin. How I presumed that I knew her when, in reality, I never even gave her a chance. If I get out of this thing, I'd like to get to know her better. If she'll let me.

"It's not fair that Rose doesn't get a chance to be who she wanted to be," I say. "But you still can. Tell me about yourself."

Lenny laughs bitterly. "There's nothing left. After Rose died, I walked away from everything. I couldn't bear to be anywhere that held memories of her. I was sick of the whole gross, shallow world. Even still, I couldn't let her go. I knew there was more to her death than everyone said, so I started investigating."

"You know a lot about us all."

"But it wasn't enough. I narrowed down the suspects. Asked questions. I even started hanging out at the shop where Rose's ex worked, trying to find out if he did it."

"Grayson?"

"He was G when Rose knew him, but she'd told me enough for me to track him down. He was so different from the boy Rose had described. According to her, he was needy and possessive—I was sure he'd be the killer at first. But when I talked to him, he was nice. He had none of the arrogance that you see working in Anton's world."

"Hey!" Anton says.

"Grayson was so cut up over Rose's death and so sweet. Being with him made me feel closer to her. I couldn't believe he'd had anything to do with it, so I focused on the other suspects. But no one would talk to me about that night. Even the people I'd once worked with wanted to leave it in the past. I had to find another way to get to the truth."

"You didn't have to hack into my damn game though," Anton snaps.

Lenny ignores him. "Grayson gave me the idea. He decided to enter the game to get his revenge on Anton. He always blamed him for Rose's death."

Anton frowns. "Er, hold on. I didn't kill Rose. Pretty sure I passed out drunk that night."

"Shush," I say. "Go on, Lenny. You set it up with a list of suspects. Me, Anton, Matthew, Beatrix, Amber, and Erin. And Grayson because you couldn't be sure. Then you revealed everything you knew, bit by bit, in the hope that the killer would make a mistake and implicate themselves?"

"I thought someone would get scared and give something away. I didn't mean for anyone to die though."

"You must have known the killer might panic and try to cover their tracks."

She goes quiet, and I worry I've lost her. "I just stopped caring," she says. "I spent enough time researching you all to know that none of you are good people. I thought that Grayson might be, but..."

"Lenny?" I say.

"Emma sent me that photo, and I couldn't ignore the truth anymore. But it's so unfair. I really thought he was different. I wanted to believe that he was one of the good guys."

"Fuck, I knew it. It's always the ex-boyfriend," Anton says, high-fiving himself.

Grayson? No way. He's the one who killed Rose? And Jesse, and Emma, and Amber...and he tried to strangle me! I don't want to believe that he's a killer; he always seemed so kind—but now that I think about it...

"I should have guessed based on his jeans," I say. "No one good ever wears jeans that tight."

Anton guffaws loudly. "You're funny," he says.

Behind the door, Lenny gives a watery laugh. "You know, out of everyone, you're the last one I thought I'd come to like," she says.

"Me?" I say. "Does that mean you're going to let us out?"

She goes quiet again. Then the door into the panic room clunks and swings open. Lenny steps out, wiping her eyes. I almost hug her in relief, but then I remember how much of a mess she's made with this game of hers.

"I'm sorry," she says. "It went too far, and I didn't think there was a way back. I was being a coward."

"It will be all right," I tell her, taking the remote from her hand.

She shakes her head. "No, it's not all right. Rose would hate what I've become in her name. I'm going to call the police and give myself up. Deal with the consequences."

"Lenny, wait." But she's already walking out of the room. I fumble with the remote. It takes me a second to find the button that will switch on the lights.

"Oh, you know what?" Anton says, sitting up on the bed, suddenly wide-eyed and sober. "The wiring in the kitchen was never all that—"

He doesn't get to finish. I've already pushed the button. The lights strobe on-off-on-off—

And the house explodes.

ERIN

A blast of heat and noise and light throws me off my feet. My ears feel like they're being stabbed with hot pokers, and I'm a tube of toothpaste being squeezed so hard that I think I'm going to burst. There's flying debris and flames, but—on the bright side—Grayson is no longer trying to kill me.

I can't believe that bastard wants to kill me!

The explosion throws me against the bar as glass bottles smash. The internal walls disintegrate into slow-motion confetti. The floor crumples and falls away. It's like when a CGI bridge collapses in a movie. I'm forced to scramble to keep up with what's left of the solid ground. I cling on to a doorframe as half the house collapses.

The sound of falling rubble and creaking metal is eventually replaced by a high-pitched ringing noise that makes my head spin.

I climb to my feet and nearly fall into a massive hole of death. Most of the room is gone.

Several yards below me, where the kitchen used to be, there's a charred hole dotted with small fires. Flames lick at the walls and creep up what's left of the hallway staircase. The ornate banister has been smashed to pieces by the falling ceiling, leaving a few sharp spindles that remind me of exposed ribs. I look for Grayson. He hasn't fallen into the hole, more's the pity. Instead, he's staggering near the pool table, clutching his ears with both hands. I snatch up a pool cue.

"Hey, asshole."

He turns in time for me to whack him right in the face. He falls onto the singed velvet.

"That's for trying to bludgeon me with a bottle."

I crack the cue against one of his knees, then hit him in the balls too for good measure. He flops off the table and onto the floor. The way he rolls around sobbing and gagging is pathetic.

I smash the pool cue on the edge of the table, and a big chunk splinters off. It leaves me with a shorter, sharper piece. I stand over Grayson, raising the broken cue like a spear. He rolls onto his back and stops whimpering. Instead, he watches me with a faint smirk on his face.

"This isn't you, Erin," he says.

"You don't know me," I reply.

"What's to know?" he says wearily.

I pull back the cue to strike.

"Stop, Erin!" Charlotte stumbles into the room, followed by Anton. They're on the opposite side of the hole, in the part of the house most badly damaged by the explosion. I'm not sure it will be standing for much longer.

"Help," Grayson squeaks. "She's really going to kill me."

"Shut up!" I press the sharp tip of my weapon against his throat, and he whimpers softly.

"You don't have to do this," Charlotte says, searching for a way to reach me.

"He's the murderer," I say.

"I know," Charlotte says. "But he's not worth wrecking your life over."

Ha. What life?

Grayson watches Charlotte with wide eyes. His knight in shining armor, coming to his rescue. She slowly skirts around the edge of the hole. There's hardly any floor left, but she clings to a light fixture to swing herself over a broken section, shielding her head as pieces of ceiling plaster drop from above.

"Charlotte," Anton cries. "Charlotte, hold my hand."

"Go away, Anton," Charlotte says. "Seriously, not the time."

The floor creaks below Charlotte, and she freezes. Her gaze is fixed on me. My hand shakes on the pool cue. All it will take is one little push, and Grayson will be dead. He deserves it. So why haven't I done it already?

"Erin, wait. Please." Charlotte whispers something to herself, and then she jumps. She lands just beyond the jagged edge of the hole, wobbles, but keeps her balance. She approaches me with her hands held out. "Put the stick down. We'll call the police and let them deal with him."

"He killed my mother," I say quietly. "Why are you trying to save him?"

"I'm not trying to save him. I'm trying to save you," she says. "Please, Erin. You're better than him."

I don't think I am, but the way Charlotte's looking at me makes me wonder if I could be. There's such concern and hope in her expression, and I'm not sure anyone's ever looked at me like that before. Like they can see a version of me that I can't, and they're waiting for me to catch up.

"You're a good person," she says. "I know I haven't been very nice to you, but I really want to be your friend. And that's going to be hard if you're in prison."

This makes me laugh. I'm suddenly struck by the thought that, even though everything feels unrelentingly shitty right now, I have this whole future ahead of me. And I can be whoever I want to be. Charlotte's right. I can't throw that opportunity away over Grayson.

I imagine using what little money is left after the sale of my mother's house to rent an apartment somewhere. I could get a normal job and save up to go back to school. I could cut my hair short and meet Charlotte for coffee in the evenings. We could talk about whatever friends talk about and even be happy.

I relax my grip on the stick the smallest bit.

"Oh my god, what the fuck happened?" Matthew skids into the room from the undamaged wing of the building. I glance at him over my shoulder. Grayson uses my distraction to yank the weapon out of my hands. He rolls to the side and is on his feet in a second. He points the stick at my stomach, forcing me to back up toward the hole.

"Grayson?" Beatrix says, appearing behind Matthew. "What are you doing?"

"Having a fucking bad day," he snaps.

"Let's recap, Accomplices," Anton shouts in his filming voice. He's halfway around the edge of the hole, following Charlotte's route to join the rest of us. Even though he's balanced dangerously above a perilous drop, he's decided that this is the right moment to start filming us on an action cam. "Basically, Lenny was pretending to be a ghost, but then she nearly killed us by filling the house with gas. She was feeling sad about her best boy being a big murdery murderer and briefly lost her sense of scale."

"Lenny?" Beatrix says. "Our Lenny? She left after Rose died."

"And now she's back!" Anton says. "Or she was. She's gone again now."

"She went to call the police, but I don't know if she was caught in the explosion," Charlotte says.

"Wait, best boy?" Beatrix looks between everyone in the room. "Do you mean *Grayson*?"

"It's not what you think," Grayson shouts. "This isn't me. This isn't who I am."

"I think this is exactly who you are," I say.

"Shut up, I'm trying to think." His voice is cracking like he's going to cry. "I need to think."

"I can't believe I liked you," Beatrix cries. "Oh my god, I have the worst taste in men."

Matthew makes a face. I can see him creeping up behind Grayson, trying to reach us before he shoves me into the hole. But the floor creaks beneath his foot.

"Get back," Grayson yells. "I'll do it. I'll push her off." To prove his point, he gives me a little poke. I teeter on the edge. Matthew stops moving.

"You sure this is what you want to do?" I say, glancing around for a way out of this mess. I can't see one.

"It's nothing personal," he says, reminding me of the first time we met. Me: chasing him into that skate park. Him: unprepared except for a sleepy smile and a flick of his hair. My first impression of someone has never been this wrong before, and that's saying a lot given the fact that I dated Jesse.

"It feels kind of personal," I say.

He smiles and wrinkles his nose. "Maybe a little bit."

The stick presses harder against my stomach. I can feel him tensing as he tries to gather the courage to murder me on film. *Think, Erin.* All right. A plan. I have a plan.

"Rose?" I say, craning my head to peer around him. "No way."

And he falls for it!

The moment Grayson turns to look, I swat the stick aside and clasp a handful of his sweater. I give him a hard tug, dragging him off-balance. He stumbles toward the edge of the hole, flailing his arms, rocking on tiptoes.

I could grab him by the collar and pull him back. I could. I don't.

With a scream, he falls. There's a sickening crunch and then nothing except for the creaking of the ruined house. The others join me, and we all stare into the firelit hole. Grayson has landed on the broken banister, and one of the upright posts has impaled him through the chest. It's disgusting and yet kind of fitting.

No one speaks. The fire crackles and the building groans. Lenny, dusty and bleeding, crawls from the downstairs wreckage and sits, staring at Grayson like the rest of us. In the distance, sirens approach.

"Um, so everyone's therapy is on me," Anton eventually says, lowering the camera. "We all have a lot to work through."

I take off my smart glasses. I've worn them for so long that I feel unexpectedly light without them. I toss them into the hole on top of Grayson's body.

"Game over," I say quietly; then I walk away.

ANTON MEETS HIS MATCH—THE FINAL INSTALLMENT!

By AntonsGirlXOXO

Fire licks at us like ten thousand fiery snake tongues. Both Anton and I are hanging on for dear life. His mansion has just exploded with the power of two planetary bodies colliding, their orbits destined to overlap, yet their union an impossible dream. Our fingers grip tightly to a twisted metal beam, but it can't hold the weight of both of us. Our hearts are just too heavy.

Together, we are doomed.

"One of us must surely let go," Anton exclaims, his dreamy blue orbs rolling wildly in their sockets. "It will have to be you. But it hurts so much to lose you, Lola. Our love has only just blossomed like a flower in the wasteland of a murderous volcanic eruption that just destroyed everything but hope."

My head dramatically whips around as I turn to stare into his impenetrable gaze with my own nondescript brown ophthalmic spheres. "Anton," I plead. "Why must I be the one to die to prove my love to you?"

His face twists in confusion because, let's just face it, I have allowed myself to be a doormat for our entire, imaginary relationship. "I don't want you to die," he ejaculates, a single tear running down his beautiful face. "But this beam cannot hold us both. One of us must let go."

"Yeah, you already said that, mate." I heave myself up into what's left of his grand, unnecessarily large entertaining space. Turns out I have more upper body strength and determination than either of us realized.

"Wait, Lola! Don't leave me. Where are you going?"

"I'm saving myself," I say. "I suggest you try doing the same."

With Anton's wails reverberating on the wind, I claw my way through the inferno and crawl out onto the dewy, poorly-maintained lawn. Matthew, Beatrix and Lenny are all there, crying because they thought I was lost forever.

Erin sees me and we run to each other, throwing our arms around each other's heaving forms. "You made it, my friend," Erin wails. "I am so proud of you."

"I am proud of you too," I vocalize. "I value the way that you both support me and believe in me without making selfish demands of my friendship, nor patronizing me with unnecessary interference."

"That's because you've got this, girl. We don't need each other, but our lives are better for having discovered the bond of female friendship."

We stand together on that lawn and watch as Anton's house—and my childish crush—burns bright against an endless night of vanquished loneliness. It wasn't Anton's fault, not really. I was the one who fell in love with the idea of him, not the real boy. Because I didn't believe that I was enough without him.

"You're enough," Erin declares. "We are both enough."

I entwine my fingers with hers. Smoldering confetti rains down from above as sirens and flashing lights mark the divide between our past and our future. And now, in that fleeting breath that is the present, I know that we're going to be all right.

In the end, I didn't win Anton's game, but I won something far more valuable.

COMMENTS (134)

Sean23

I hate you Char02. You kicked me in the chest and left me to drown. I didn't drown, by the way. Thanks.

MatthewBrightIsTheBrightest

NONE of this happened. What is wrong with you Charlotte?

AntonStanFran

Why is this tagged with Anton when the character is so unlike him that no real fan would recognize this whiny boy-child character? Stop trying to trick people into reading your self-insert fantasies.

Eatmyfeet

I lvoe your work so much!! <3 <3 <3

ErinLoveHates...

Please turn him into a guinea pig again. He deserves it. Love Erin x

ACKNOWLEDGMENTS

It's taken a team of incredible people to bring *Tag, You're Dead* to life. Chloe Seager and Lauren Fortune have been an arterial spray of invaluable ideas, insights, and jokes about murder. I couldn't pick better people to work with.

A huge thank-you also goes to everyone at Sourcebooks Fire who worked on this book, including Steve Geck, Jenny Lopez, Thea Voutiritsas, Aimee Alker, Manu Velasco, Erin Fitzsimmons, and Karen Masnica. I am endlessly humbled that so many clever, brilliant people work so hard to help turn my ideas into something to be proud of. Thanks also goes to all my writing friends and fellow YA authors. I'm lucky to be part of such a lovely community.

The biggest of the thank-yous goes to Eliza, whose love of YouTubers inspired this book. Thanks as always to Phill, who makes my writing career possible, and Max, who is the best distraction I could ever wish for.

ABOUT THE AUTHOR

Kathryn Foxfield is the bestselling author of *Good Girls Die First* and *Come Out, Come Out, Whatever You Are*. She blames her love of the creepy and weird on a childhood diet of Point Horror, Agatha Christie, and Doctor Who. She writes about characters who aren't afraid to fight back, but she wouldn't last five minutes in one of her own stories.

Kathryn is a reformed microbiologist, one-time popular science author, cat wrangler, and parent. She lives in rural Oxfordshire, England, but her heart belongs to London.

#getbooklit

Your hub for the hottest young adult books!

Visit us online and sign up for our
newsletter at FIREreads.com

 @sourcebooksfire

 sourcebooksfire

 firereads.tumblr.com